wynn
in
doubt

ALSO BY EMILY HEMMER

The Break-Up Psychic
(Dangerously Dimpled, Book One)

Plus None
(Dangerously Dimpled, Book Two)

wynn

in

doubt

emily

hemmer

LAKE UNION
PUBLISHING

Text copyright © 2014 by Emily Hemmer

Published by Lake Union Publishing, Seattle

www.apub.com

Amazon, the Amazon logo, and Lake Union Publishing are trademarks of Amazon.com, Inc., or its affiliates.

ISBN-13: 9781503948198
ISBN-10: 1503948196

Cover design by Kerri Resnick

Printed in the United States of America

*This book is for Lena and the women of
my family who inherited her legacy:*

*Wilma, Billie Jean, Rebecca, Kim,
Jamie, Carrie, Kristen, Lauren, Emily, Corrie,
Kiley, Lilly, Brynn, Margaret, Catherine,
Hailey, and Collins.*

*And it's for you. Go. Dream as big as you can.
Have the life you want.*

PREFACE

My great-great-grandmother's name was Lena Buchanan. In many ways she inspired the book you're about to read. She was a wife, mother, sister, and daughter, and by all accounts she was a lovely, kind woman. On August 29, 1917, just past eight o'clock in the morning, Lena was shot and killed by her husband on the sidewalk in front of a department store. He then turned the gun on himself and ended his own life.

She was thirty years old.

My grandmother told me about Lena's death when I was in my late twenties. She told me how her mother, aunt, and uncle were separated, each sent to live with a different relative after the tragedy of that day. A few years later I discovered the original newspaper article, which would, for me, hold great significance. What it said, and what it didn't, set me down a path of self-discovery I remain on to this day.

Lena had filed for divorce from her husband in the weeks prior to her death. Can you imagine being a woman with three small children and filing for divorce in 1917? It would've meant public scrutiny, financial hardship, and a departure from the only life she'd known for more than a decade. How much courage must it have taken to stand, alone, against so much uncertainty?

I began imagining what Lena's life could have held had she lived. Would she have gotten a job, stood on her own two feet? Would that have made her proud? Could she have been happy in a new town? Made new friends? Did she want to explore the world? Was there a chance she could've found love again? True love? Every time I looked at her picture, her story became bigger, fuller.

Although *Wynn In Doubt* is not about Lena, it is, at its heart, inspired by her life, which was cut too short. I wanted, in some way, to give her another ending. One that allowed her to be young and brave in a world that often makes it hard to be either. More than that, I wanted to honor her memory and the legacy of strong women she left behind.

Her daughter, my great-grandmother, was a fierce, intelligent woman. A force to be reckoned with. My grandmother was wild in her youth and headstrong all her life. My mother—articulate, bold, loyal, and kind—is my rock. And my sisters and I are, I hope, a mixture of them all. Now we have daughters to pass the story onto. Daughters who will grow up with the strength of five generations of amazing women standing behind them.

This is not Lena's story. It's Wynn's story. She's a young woman looking at her life and asking, is there more? How much of what I want for my life is possible?

I hope you enjoy reading this book. I hope it inspires you to not take life for granted but to go out and seek what makes you happy, no matter your age or situation. That's what Lena wanted. Regardless of what happened that day, remember that she was brave enough to try and write her own ending. She knew a hundred years ago what many of us struggle with right now: that life is what we make of it, and our greatest responsibility is not to waste it.

—Emily

WYNN IN DOUBT

ONE

Those lips touched my lips once. They were warm and soft and made my stomach drop three feet to the ground, right next to my pink polka-dot espadrilles.

I draw an invisible heart around his face with my finger. Oliver Reeves. The best and most beautiful thing to ever come out of Downers Grove North High School. And that's really saying something, because Denise Richards went to North. Her family moved away before she graduated, but there's still a picture of her in the glass case at the front entrance.

I worked night and day to maintain my 4.0 GPA. I was president of the government club, editor of the school newspaper, and chairman of the Students Against Destructive Decisions council for four years. But I guess to get your picture in the glass case, you had to have a three-way with Neve Campbell. Oh well.

Champagne bubbles tickle my tongue as I flip through the yearbook, knowing every page where his face appears. Here he is at Homecoming, crown on his head adorably lopsided as he poses for a picture with his date. And where was I that night? I was sitting at home in my Hello Kitty pajamas, eating chocolate ice cream out of a tub with a Snickers bar and reading *Angel* fan fiction.

There's Oliver in his soccer uniform. Knee-high socks clinging to muscular calves. Even in high school, the guy was tall and broad and walked with a certain swagger. A walk that said, *I know what I want to do with my life.* This made him unique among every other person at North, including the teachers. I followed him to every away game, watched every amazing play. My best friend back then, Lisa Menopolous, was disgusted with me. Not that I could blame her. I was pretty gag worthy.

Another drink, a big one. The dress I wore to my younger sister's engagement party will have to serve as my nightgown this evening. I'm too depressed for pajamas. Tabby's getting married. She's getting married, and soon she'll be living in a gorgeous new house with her gorgeous new husband and probably 2.5 gorgeous new children.

And I'll remain in this one-room apartment with no career, no money, no boyfriend, no . . . life. Forever. Because that is the fate of a brunette born into a family of blondes.

Page 124. The Torture Picture. A black-and-white candid of Oliver covers almost every inch of the glossy paper. He stands, lips parted and eyes closed, on the stage in the school auditorium, a guitar hanging casually from one shoulder. That was the last night we ever spoke. The night he kissed me. The night my fate was sealed.

Because once I kissed Oliver Reeves, I never wanted to kiss anyone else.

Not that I've been a *nun* since graduating ten years ago. I've had a handful of well-meaning, boring boyfriends who each lasted somewhere between meeting the parents and cohabitation of toothbrushes. But none of their kisses were ever as exquisite as the one Oliver gave me in the gym parking lot. I can still feel the lightness in my chest. Like I could have floated right off the asphalt and into the night sky.

I used to think there was nothing worse than being in love with him at sixteen. I was constantly on edge, waiting for him to smile at me in the hallways or acknowledge my existence in physics class, always half-terrified he would. I was wrong. Because being in love with him at twenty-eight is much, much worse.

And I have Anthony Laurito to thank for it.

Rolling Stone magazine lies open at the foot of my bed. I slide one bare leg from beneath the covers and grab the pages with my toes, pulling it toward me.

Oliver's band, Multitude, is the focus of a few short paragraphs on the third-to-last page. It seems that after touring for the past seven years, selling out midsized venues, and opening for acts like Green Day and Blink-182, the band has called it quits. Thanks in part to a rather cantankerous relationship between Oliver and the band's drummer, Anthony Laurito.

The article goes on to say that the lead singer has decided to take some time away from the spotlight and return to his hometown of Downers Grove, Illinois, for an undetermined hiatus.

I've spent ten years thinking of Oliver and his lips. When he left, just after graduation, I told myself the next time I saw him I'd be living a fabulous life. A life full of stories to tell. I'd be restoring priceless works of art at the Louvre or just returning from my second Everest expedition. I would be worthy of his attention. I would be different. I would be better.

But none of those dreams have come true. My life got stalled somehow. Like one of those watches that stops turning if you don't wind it. But it's not the time that's stopped; it's me.

I place the magazine on the pillow next to my head. Oliver's handsome face stares back at me. He's lived so much already, seen things I've only dreamed about. I actually went to one of his concerts once. It was my twenty-fourth birthday. I went alone and stood near the back. I couldn't even see his face most of the time, but his voice reminded me of being young, and that made me sad. Because Oliver had a dream and he made it come true, and I couldn't do the same with any of mine.

***

"Why does this have your name on it?" Franny, her golden bob in disarray, holds out a turquoise necklace.

Tabby and I look up from our positions on the floor. "I called it," Tabby says.

"You *called* it? When?"

"When Grams went into the hospital."

Franny narrows her eyes and places a hand on her hip. "Let me get this straight. While our ninety-three-year-old grandmother lay dying in a hospital bed, you came over to this house with a label maker to stake your claim on her costume jewelry?"

"She told me I could." Tabby holds up a pair of matching turquoise earrings, obviously confused by Franny's tone.

"No, she didn't."

"Yes, she did."

"No, she didn't."

"Yes, she d—"

"Girls," our mother interrupts, stepping into the room. "My God, it's like you two are in pigtails all over again. There's plenty of jewelry laid out in the dining room, Franny. Take something from there."

"But that's not the point, Mom." Franny gestures at Tabby, whose vacant expression is as lovely and pleasing as it was when our parents brought her home from the hospital twenty-six years ago. "She can't just come over here and label things. We're supposed to be splitting everything evenly."

"Grams told me to take whatever I wanted. She said I inherited her good taste." Tabby unfolds a mink stole from the box beside her and drapes it across her slender shoulders.

"Mom!" Franny complains.

"Stop it. Both of you. This is a somber occasion, remember? Our last week in your grandmother's house? My family home." Mom's voice cracks as she picks up a silver picture frame from atop the dresser. Her smile is frail, as though it could come apart at any moment. "After next Sunday, it'll belong to someone else."

I rise and step over Tabby's legs to wrap an arm around my mother's waist and lean against her shoulder.

"She was beautiful, wasn't she, Wynnie?" Tears slip across the smooth surface of her cheeks. She's cried so much these last few weeks, I wonder if she'll ever be able to stop.

I squeeze her. The photo is one of my favorites, my grandparents on their wedding day sixty-plus years ago. It's black and white, but I can imagine the yellow of her hair, coiffed and curled into perfection, and the electric green of her eyes. Tabby resembles her most, except for the mouth. I got her mouth. Full, pink lips, perpetually pouty, frowning too often. But on that day, the day of the photograph, hers were bent into a radiant smile as she stared at the handsome young man, dapper in a black tuxedo, beside her.

"I miss her." The words threaten to stick in my throat.

"I know you do. I do, too. But we got to have her for a long time." She lowers her voice to a whisper against my ear. "She loved you so much. She was proud of you."

I take a deep breath, trying to stop my chin from wobbling, and turn into Mom's hug. She doesn't know about the argument. It happened right before Grams had the stroke.

I'd been offered a teaching position at a small school in Guatemala. It's run by a non-profit out of Chicago, and I'd thrown my name into their applicant lottery the year before. I never thought they'd call. It was just a whim, an old dream that came floating, unexpectedly, to the surface. Things like that don't happen for me. Because I'm the rock.

The one that's always around. The one everyone depends on. Every day, something else for someone else. And I fucking hate it.

It's a terrible thing to resent your own life.

So when they called and offered me the job, I said yes. Not out of any great desire to make the world a better place. I just needed a reason to leave. To become someone else.

I gathered my courage and blew the dust off my passport. I decided to tell Grams first. She's always been . . . always *was* . . . my greatest ally. I knew she'd worry, but ultimately I thought she'd be happy for me.

I was wrong.

I told her I was leaving and she said it was selfish. That I should be ashamed. I didn't understand where it was all coming from. I still don't. Her anger felt old, and it made me flinch. She might not have understood my need to leave, to wander and explore, but she knew I wanted it. How much I've always wanted it. Maybe it was just the first time she actually believed I'd go.

I was hurt and confused by her reaction. I struck back, accusing her of living a purposeless life. One void of anything bigger than herself or what she wanted, what she knew to be right and wrong. I loved her with all my heart, but there were times when her expectations left me feeling suffocated.

She died a week later. The doctor thought she might recover at first, but she passed away in her sleep on a Sunday morning.

I held her hand and kissed her a thousand times, but I never told her I was sorry. I think in the back of my mind I worried that if I apologized, it would mean I'd finally given up, and I couldn't do it. Not yet. Not even for her.

I did turn down the job, though. How could I leave my family right after her death? They needed me. Grams had needed me. Shame and regret over our last words have followed me like a shadow. My sisters can carry on, knowing they were good granddaughters and content with how things ended. Everything ends, after all. I guess the difference between the three of us is that I'm still waiting for something to begin.

Franny, oblivious to the somberness that's settled over the room, asks, "What're we doing with all these wigs? Throwing them out?" She picks up a beehive-styled wig from the bedside table.

My mother releases me. "I don't know. Not throw them out. It'd be such a waste. They're expensive, you know?"

"But who'd buy someone else's used hair?" I ask, wiping my nose with the back of my hand.

"Maybe we could donate them to the homeless," Tabby offers.

Franny, wig in midair, looks down at our beautiful baby sister. "Why would the homeless want used wigs?"

"Maybe they could use them during winter? To keep their heads warm?"

Everyone looks at Tabby.

"You're going to be someone's *mother* one day," Franny states, her eyes wide in disbelief.

Tabby, outraged and offended, pulls the stole off her shoulders. "Mom!"

"Alright, enough. You girls finish in here, and I'll be in the kitchen with your father." She replaces the photo on the dresser, then looks at each of us in turn. "No more fighting. Understand?"

Shamed for the moment, we hang our heads.

"I said, do you understand me?"

"Yes ma'am," we say in unison, then wait until she's out of earshot to throw things at one another.

"Okay, enough!" Franny dodges a pillow. "We need to stay focused. I've got to be out of here by five. Who wants to do the closet?"

Shouts of *"Not me!"* come nearly simultaneously. As usual, my voice is last. I could claim slow reflexes, but the truth is, putting what other people want before what I want, even unconsciously, has become habit. A therapist told me it was transference. That it's easier for me to put other people first because there's no risk involved. No chance of losing out on all those dreams I keep dreaming about. But his appointments coincided with my nephew's Little League games, so I never learned how to reverse the cycle.

Franny hands me a cardboard box, and I settle into the dark, musty space of the small walk-in. All the clothes and shoes have been removed, donated to Goodwill in the week following Grams's death. Mom couldn't stand the thought of her clothes hanging in the closet, never to be worn again. But even with them gone, the familiar scent of Virginia Slims mixed with White Diamonds hangs in the air.

I miss her so much. The way she hugged me, like I was the most precious thing in the world. I miss her patting my hand while we watched TV together and kissing the crown of my head whenever she stood behind me. I should have told her I was sorry, that I wouldn't leave. Why couldn't I do that simple thing? I remove a pillow from a waist-high shelf and bury my face in it, inhaling her scent.

"Oh God, are you going to be able to handle this?" Franny's voice pulls me out of my thoughts.

The pillow muffles my words. "Leave me alone. I'm just . . ."

"Smelling a pillow. I'll tell you what, I'll peel Tabby's label off the bottle of White Diamonds in the bathroom and give it to you, if you can just focus long enough to get the closet sorted out."

"Hey!" Tabby calls from somewhere in the bedroom. "I claimed that."

I turn to Franny. Her smile is conspiratorial as she leans farther into the closet. "I've been peeling her labels off everything." She reaches into her pocket and comes out with a dozen folded white labels marked "TABBY." My smile comes unbidden, but welcome. Conspiring against our little sister is the one thing Franny and I have always been able to agree on.

I return her wink and get down to business.

Grams loved her blue glass. It's everywhere in her house, even in the closets. Blue glass figurines, blue glass jewelry boxes, blue glass paperweights. When I was little, she gave me a set of glass marbles. They were a deep royal blue. I pretended they were sapphires stolen from Buckingham Palace and entrusted to me for safekeeping. I buried them along the tree line behind her house one night—I took my duties as protector very seriously. Only, that was the summer we got a season pass to Six Flags. What were priceless jewels in the face of the Screamin' Eagle? I forgot about them.

Years later I thought it'd be fun to dig them up, but I was never able to find them again. It's funny, the things you miss. Those marbles probably cost two dollars and yet, I'd give almost anything to have them back. I carefully wrap each ornament and bauble in tissue paper and place it in the box at my feet. One by one, I wrap, store, and label all of her possessions until nothing remains but a stack of books collecting dust on the uppermost shelf.

I stand on tiptoes, batting at each one until it falls into my hands. The box at my feet is full, so I ask Tabby for another.

"There aren't any more, we're out."

"Well, what am I supposed to do with the books?" I flip through a leather-bound volume of *Anna Karenina*.

"I dunno, don't you read a lot? Isn't that, like, your thing?" she asks, her tone bored.

"My thing?"

"Yeah. Like, I have Dex and the wedding, and Franny has Ben and the boys, and you have"—she gestures at the novel in my hands—"Harry Potter."

"This is Tolstoy."

"See?" She brightens. "You even know all the characters' names."

She's going to be someone's *mother* one day.

I turn back to the closet and sit against the wall, my grandmother's books spread around me. My thing. Books are my "thing." I've never felt more like an Austen heroine than I do at this moment.

My fingers trail across the covers: Orwell, Fitzgerald, Brontë, Melville, Dumas . . . Books about rebellion, excess, passion, adventure, and dreams. Not one of which reflects the Grams I knew. She was kind and thoughtful and I loved her, but she was also hard-nosed and put duty above all else. Did she read these stories? Did she get lost in them, as I do, or did she shake her head and wonder why anyone would want to read words so full of magic?

I stack the books gently and carry them under my arm out of the closet. I've got work in three hours, and if I sneak out now, I may just have time to do my "thing" before I spend the rest of Sunday night slinging beer.

Tabby diligently re-labels a silver watch. No doubt Franny stripped off the original.

"Tell Mom and Dad I have to go to work." I head for the door.

"Alright. Tell Oliver I said hi, 'kay?"

Her words stop me like an invisible wall. "What?"

"Oliver. Tell him I said hi when you see him," she repeats, slower this time.

I stare at her blankly.

Tabby waves her hand at me. "Oh, no, you're right. I shouldn't be saying hi to other men when I'm engaged." She admires the sizeable rock on her left ring finger. "It's not fair of me to do that to them."

I feel like I've stepped out of the closet into an episode of *The Twilight Zone*. "Why would I be seeing Oliver?" I ask, my mouth dry.

"Well, you're going to work, right?"

"Yeah."

"Then you'll see him at the bar."

I step over a pile of photo albums and kneel before my sister, grabbing her arm. "Tabby, focus. Why would Oliver be at Lucky's?"

Tabby's forehead, too firm and beautiful to properly wrinkle, shows the barest sign of concentration. "Because he works there now?"

I shake my head. The words issuing from her pink lips don't make sense. "I don't understand. Why would Oliver—rock star Oliver—be working at a Downers Grove dive bar?"

My little sister pulls her arm from my grasp and returns her attention to the label maker. "Dex said he came in last week and asked Lucky for a job. I guess he's taking some time off from the road and moved back in with his parents."

I draw back and stand up, the books wedged against my side feeling disproportionately heavy. "Oliver . . . is working at Lucky's?"

Tabby applies a new label to the back of a chunky green bracelet. "Pfft. And you guys think I'm the slow one."

TWO

Freshman year, fifth period lunch: I tripped over Mandy Krasinski's backpack and fell, landing on top of my food tray. Bits of sloppy joe and macaroni and cheese dropped to the laminate floor with audible plunks when I shifted onto my knees. Oliver smiled and helped me up, pulling a piece of red ground beef from my hair as his friends behind him howled with laughter.

Sophomore year, Mr. Hill's health class: We were learning about sexually transmitted diseases, and I was chosen to hold up the chlamydia card. The entire class burst into a loud and prolonged clapping fit. Oliver winked at me over Mike Turley's head and flashed me his herpes card.

Junior year, badminton lessons in the gym: In an effort to appear athletic and graceful, I volunteered to make the first serve of the championship game. I whacked the birdie over the net with such ferocity it hit Oliver in the mouth and chipped his eyetooth. That afternoon, as I prepared to board the bus home, I caught his eye as he sauntered out the front door. He pointed to his newly altered smile and gave me a thumbs-up.

But those things were nothing compared to the four long, torturous years I endured because of alphabetical locker assignment. Because I, Wynn Jeffries, was the perpetual locker mate of Shannon Jefferson. And Shannon Jefferson was Oliver Reeves's girlfriend. And she liked to French kiss. A lot.

My own kiss with Oliver was not quite so long or wet, but it remains to this day the highlight of my academic career.

Now he's here, twenty feet away, leaning across the bar to set two beers in front of a couple of sorority sisters. Blonde, perky, and with matching purple tote bags emblazoned with the Delta Phi Epsilon symbols. I know that's what the Greek letters stand for, not because I'm a sorority sister of the magnificent order of the DPhiE's, but because I'm a nerd. A big, huge, Tolstoy-loving nerd.

And he wipes his hands on a white dishrag like a sex god.

"Hello? Earth to Wynn, come in, Wynn."

Startled, I turn toward the sound of my boss's booming Boston accent. Lucky's thick hands are steepled against his nose and mouth. "And we have liftoff," he says, his voice muffled to imitate an old radio. He drops his hands, grinning at his joke.

"Hey, Lucky."

"Hey, you." He punches me a little too forcefully in the shoulder.

I rub the spot and return his awkward smile. "What's up?"

"Oh, nothin', nothin', just making the rounds. You say hi to our new bartender yet?" He moves his bulky frame in Oliver's direction.

"Um . . . no. I haven't had the chance yet."

We glance around. There's not a patron anywhere near me, and the towel I'm fiddling with is both dry and not currently in the vicinity of a hard surface. In my defense, this position offered the least noticeable, most unhampered view of Oliver and his lips. I can't shake the feeling that once I get within three feet of him, I'm going to spontaneously combust.

"Right," he says, dragging out the vowel. "Well, go give him a welcoming hello when you find some free time. He might be here a while."

"Really? Why do you say that? Did he say he was going to be here a long time? Did he talk about the band? About his future in music? Why would he choose to come back here, of all places, when he literally could've picked anywhere in the world?"

Lucky's look conveys that he has not done any of those things. It's possible he also thinks I'm a lunatic. "I don't really know how long he's staying. But having him behind the bar will be good for business."

He shifts and rubs the back of his beefy neck.

"Right." I twist the towel over my knuckles. "Sorry."

"No, no, that's alright. You're curious. It's what I like about you. Always thinking. But, just out of curiosity, did your thoughts possibly involve a check on the ladies bathroom? Someone's complained about a backup in there." He holds his palms out before him. "I mean, if you're not too busy."

I'm not eager to give up my bird's-eye view of Oliver, but I can't exactly defend my position. "What do you mean by backup?"

"Backup. A backup. In the can."

"You want me to clean up . . . a clog in the ladies bathroom?" I don't bother hiding my disgust at the idea.

"Yeah."

"But I have a degree from Loyola . . ."

"And now you have a plunger from Ace Hardware," he says, handing me the brown rubber plunger that had been sitting unnoticed near my tennis shoes. "Congratulations."

I take it from him woodenly. He pats me on the head, then turns back toward the bar. Oliver is leaning over the glossy surface, smiling at Tweedledee and Tweedle Nose Job. Their squeals of delight carry across the dark space. I wonder how they feel about French kissing?

I push my way into the bathroom and flinch at the smell. Using my index finger to gingerly push the thin steel of the stall door inward,

I avert my eyes from whatever hell is waiting for me. I notice a heart carved into the dull gray of the left wall. Within its exaggerated curves are the words "Oliver 4-Ever."

Sunday evening at Lucky's Bar: Oliver Reeves walks back into my life and bestows his smiles on two pert, twenty-one-year-old neuroscience majors, if my luck holds. The water beneath the plunger squelches and bubbles up over the porcelain, sloshing onto my shoes.

And all is right in the world.

***

"Wynn?"

I hear my name clearly. I know who's calling me. So, naturally, I keep my head buried in the deep freezer.

"Wynn Jeffries, right?"

I straighten slowly, doing my best to convey confusion and indifference with a mask that says, *I can't quite place your name . . . Who are you, again?*

It's funny, what your mind registers when in a superheightened state. It's not his dark hair, cut shorter than I've ever seen it, or the familiar clear gray of his eyes that I notice. It's the chip in his tooth. My chip.

"Hey, I thought that was you." He moves forward to embrace me.

Suddenly his arms are wrapped around me and he's squeezing me, and all I can think is, *Shit, how do you hug?*

He releases me, unaware or unbothered by my robot arms, and smiles brightly. "Wow, so good to see you."

I don't know words or how to make my mouth work.

Oliver nods. The smile slips a bit from his face. "So how long have you worked here?"

What is work? Who works? Me?

The smile falls into a mildly polite grimace. "I just got back a few days ago. Staying with my parents until I can wrap my head around everything that's gone on the last few weeks. Maybe you've heard?"

I open my mouth and Oliver perks up, no doubt waiting for me to say something, anything. But my tongue weighs a hundred pounds, so I just swallow and continue to stare at him.

He pushes a hand against the short crop of black hair on his head. We stand across from one another in complete and utter silence. After years of imagining running into him on the streets of Paris, fresh from my triumphant lecture at the Sorbonne, the reality of meeting him while unearthing a bag of nacho cheese from the deep freezer at Lucky's Bar seems too unfair to be real.

"I should get back." He thumbs at the door over his shoulder. "Lucky's got me bartending for some insane reason. I don't know the first thing about mixing drinks. I just keep giving everyone who orders anything a beer." His laugh is exactly like I remember. Full and uninhibited.

He steps forward as though he's going to hug me again, but changes his mind halfway. Instead, his hand connects with my arm, just below the shoulder, and he slaps me lightly a few times. It is the most unbearably awkward, exhilarating moment of my life.

As he pushes open the swinging door, I finally find my voice. "It's just that the last time we talked . . ."

He turns to me. His eyes move down my face and settle on my lips. "I kissed you."

I hold my breath and nod in agreement.

Smile gone, he turns his gaze to mine. "I remember." Then Oliver Reeves disappears behind a swish of white plywood, leaving me standing beside an open freezer with my heart in my throat.

***

"He looked at her the way all women want to be looked at by a man."
Boy, you got that right, Fitzgerald. I run a finger over the imprint of letters. Mesmerized not by the beauty of the words, but by the thought that my Grams might have read them. I close the delicate cover of *The Great Gatsby* and place it beside me on the bed.

So he remembers the kiss. Does he also remember the gangly, dorky, unblossomed girl attached to those lips? No doubt I left him in a state of lustful frenzy tonight with the way I fought to pull open the door marked "Push."

Oh, yes, a Fitzgerald heroine if there ever was one—never mind the soiled shoes and the inability to open well-marked doors. And the shockingly inappropriate response to polite conversation. Save for those minor things, of course.

From my spot beneath the lilac-colored duvet, I spy the neck of last night's champagne bottle sitting in the sink. It's possible there's another swig or two. I throw the covers off and roll to the floor. My grandmother's book falls onto the scored hardwood, landing open. A yellowed scrap of paper is wedged between the pages. I pull it out and carefully unfold it. It looks like newspaper, stiff and brittle with age.

I turn on the lamp on the small desk near my bed. The article has clearly been cut out of some periodical, although I can't tell which one. I lower my face to the print and squint to read it.

BARDSTOWN, KY. 1931, August 18 (Special)—Federal Treasury authorities, working with the Nelson County Sheriff's Department, Monday, Aug. 17, arrested Michael Albert Craig and Lola Elizabeth Harrison, a single woman, east of Bardstown on Bloomfield Road just before five a.m. Mr. Craig was thought to be transporting illegal alcohol. Federal agents, acting on an anonymous tip, apprehended the suspects after the car, a 1926 Ford Model T, was disabled by a road snare set by police. No persons were reported injured.

A dozen pints of corn whiskey were discovered beneath the lining of the rear seat, which had been hollowed out for illegal transportation. It is unknown at this time what role Miss Harrison may have played in the bootlegging operation. Special Agent Samuel T. Murphy of the United States Treasury Department Bureau of Prohibition, the commanding officer on the scene, said, "Let all Kentucky moonshiners beware. You may be able to distill it, bottle it, and blind the family dog with its proof, but if you drive it across the county line, I'll be waiting for you."

The suspects have been taken to the sheriff's department in Bardstown, pending arraignment by the judge on Thursday morning. Investigators are now searching the Craig family home and lands for evidence of illicit whiskey stills. The home is located on the westernmost corner of

My heart racing, I turn the article over in my hands, hoping the rest continues on the other side. It's just an old advertisement for Ovaltine. Elizabeth McConnell Druitz was Grams's name. But Lola . . . I've seen that name before. The article has been torn; the last sentences at the bottom are missing. I search the book and shake it by the binding, but nothing falls out.

I turn it back over, then smooth out the folded lines, careful not to damage it. Lola Elizabeth Harrison. I stare at the words.

There's a grainy, sepia-colored picture to the right side of the article. It shows armed sheriff's deputies and a man, I presume Agent Murphy, leading away another man in handcuffs. The man in custody has thick black hair and a wide, careless smile, like he's in on a joke no one else gets. Behind them is an old car, its doors open, and beside it another officer guards a smaller person wearing a fitted, bell-shaped hat. I look closer; definitely a woman.

In twelve steps, I make it from my bed to the small, eccentrically decorated kitchen. My grandmother's obituary is pinned to the fridge by a sunflower magnet. I remove it with shaky hands and bring the strip of fresh newsprint back to the desk.

Elizabeth Susanna McConnell Druitz, 93, passed away peacefully in her sleep Sunday, May 25, 2014 at Saratoga Grove. She is preceded in death by her husband of 66 years, Isaac Zacharias Druitz, and her parents, William D. "Dutch" McConnell and Lola Elizabeth Harrison.

My great-grandmother. It has to be. I sit heavily on the bed, the prospect of champagne forgotten. This makes no sense whatsoever. My great-grandmother died when Grams was just a little girl in the 1920s. I know that. I've been told the story a thousand times. Her mother died and Grams stepped up, cooking meals and attending to her father's shirts and pants with an eight-pound iron on Saturday mornings. Grams almost always told the story directly before a scolding when she thought we, her granddaughters, were taking things for granted. Which we always were, which means we heard the story a thousand times.

But the name in the article . . .

I switch off the light and turn onto my side, taking the blankets with me. How is it that my great-grandmother was running whiskey in Kentucky when she was supposed to be six feet under in Illinois? Try as I might, I can't remember Grams ever saying more than a few words about her mother. But did I ever ask? I don't think so. I'm not sure I ever gave much consideration to her having a mother at all. It was like she sprung, fully formed and opinionated from the garden behind her house. She was never young to me. She was never passionate about life. She was never anything more than Grams.

Thoughts of my grandmother, Oliver, and the article keep me from sleep.

It's funny, Grams never approved of my crush on the boy with the big dreams. She wanted me to marry a nice young man, have lots of babies, and live a quiet life, as she did. But if the woman in the article was, in fact, her mother, what kind of life did *she* live? And why was Grams not a part of it?

I open my eyes and feel around behind me for the book. The paper is rough with age. I pull out the article and lay it on the pillow beside me, the same place that Oliver's face stared back at me last night. I used to fantasize about a secret family that would rescue me from my boring one and take me on noble quests and dangerous expeditions. It seems I may not have given my real family enough credit.

THREE

"Hello? Mom? Dad?" I close my parents' front door behind me and walk to the kitchen. Every square inch of white countertop has been taken over by lumps of brown clay in various shapes and sizes. I pick one up and turn it over. It looks like something a kindergartner would make. If they were really bad at crafts. And didn't have hands.

I call out again, more urgently this time. "Mom, where are you? What's with all the pottery?"

"Just a minute," she yells from down the hall, her voice stifled by a closed door.

I return the clay whatever-it's-supposed-to-be to the counter and gingerly take the article from my purse. I reread it for the twentieth time today, focusing again on the name. Lola. My mother inherited Grams's zeal for a normal life. I've debated for days whether or not to ask her about the woman in the article, but I've decided I need answers. Was she my great-grandmother? If so, why were we told she died years before then? And the question bothering me most of all: What was she doing in Kentucky? Why did she leave? What could have driven her away from her daughter?

"Hey, honey, why didn't you tell us you were stopping by?" My mother breezes in, running a hand through disheveled hair. Her shirt is buttoned crookedly and inside out.

Something's off. Something's very, very off . . . "Mom, your shirt," I say, pointing.

She looks down, her fingers skid across the mismatched closures. "Oops! I guess I was in a hurry this morning." The corners of her mouth are turned up innocently, but I'm not buying it. I shared a room with Tabby. I know the booty-call smile when I see it.

"Mom, where's Dad?"

"Right here, sweet pea." Dad's big hands squeeze my shoulders, making me jump. He's showing too many teeth.

"Eww." I step away from my father. A war between knowledge and ignorance has begun in my brain. I close my eyes and shake my head, trying to erase all thoughts of my parents' afternoon delight from my mind like an Etch A Sketch.

"What? What, eww?" My mom fans herself with her crooked shirt.

"Nothing, just—let's not talk about it." I give them both a warning glance. "What's the deal with all the pottery?"

Dad tosses a smallish piece in the air, then catches it easily behind his back. His manner is giddy and spry, and I don't want to think about what's caused it. "This"—he says, handing me the . . . what? Vase? Pot? Ashtray? I take it with my free hand—"is your mother's and my new hobby."

"You're making clay pot things?"

"Don't be too hard on us. We just started yesterday," Mom says, admiring a wonky piece.

"And what brought this on?"

"Oh, you know." She shrugs her shoulders at me. "We were watching *Ghost* on TV the other night and, well, you know that scene with Patrick Swayze and Demi Moore? When she's at the potter's wheel and he comes and sits behind her and one thing leads to another—"

"No. No, no, no, no, no. No." I set the pot my father handed me back on the ledge, then do the same with hers. "No." I've had enough surprises for one week. My father becoming Patrick Swayze is going too far.

"What?" Her level voice reveals nothing, but the upward tilt of her lips is unmistakably playful. I'm torn. She's been so sad, it's nice to see her mood lighten—but I don't want to know any more about what's brought it on.

"I'm sorry. I can't listen to a story about you and Dad making . . . pottery together."

"Oh, we made pottery." Dad plucks the largest piece from the table and raises his eyebrows at me. "We made pottery all night long."

I'm going to need a lobotomy.

"Oh my God, you guys," I whine, slumping forward.

Mom wraps an arm around my shoulder and leads me down the hallway and into the living room. "Cut it out. You can't blame your dad and me for being in love."

"Mom," I warn.

She holds her hands up in surrender. "Fine. Just remember this when you have kids of your own."

"No, just, I came—whatever. Can we talk for a minute? I've got something I want to show you."

She crosses her arms and waits for me to continue. I hold out the article and she takes it from me.

"What's this?"

"Just read it," I say.

She inclines her head toward the paper and narrows her eyes. "I can't." She hands it back to me. "I don't have my glasses."

"Fine. I'll read, you listen." I've read the words so many times in last three days, I practically have it memorized. When I get to Lola's name, I pause and look at my mother. I've known the woman for twenty-eight years. I know when she's mad. I know when she's annoyed. And

I know when she doesn't want *me* to know something. She's still and silent, too silent, and there's something wild in her look.

I finish reading and return my eyes to hers. She asks no questions, forcing me to prompt her. "Well?"

She releases a noisy breath through her nose and lowers her gaze to the ground. "Where'd you find that?"

Until she spoke I wasn't sure, but now I'm positive I'm right about Lola being my great-grandmother. The hand holding the article falls limply to my side. "In one of Grams's books. Did you know about this? About her not dying when Grams was a little girl?"

Mom faces the dining room table. It's cluttered with boxes from my grandmother's house. "Yes, I knew."

"But why lie about her mother being dead? And why didn't you tell us it wasn't true?" I lean to the side and try to read her face.

"Wynn, this is all in the past." She faces me, the good humor from earlier forgotten. "Let's not dredge it up."

I don't understand why she's being so secretive. Grams is dead. It's not like she'll care if her secret gets out now. "Mom—"

She holds up her hand, stopping me. "No. I'm not discussing it, and you shouldn't be either. It's none of our business."

"None of our business? It's our family history, *your* grandmother's history. Why won't you tell me what happened to her?"

"Because I don't really know." The words come out in a bark. She shrugs and sighs loudly. Her eyes roll up toward the ceiling. Lines mar the soft skin around her mouth as she presses her lips together. She's trying to keep the words inside. Holding onto whatever secrets she knows for as long as possible. When her eyes find mine again, they're full of pain and pity. "Your grandmother was just a little girl. She was seven years old when her mother abandoned her."

"Abandoned her?" I glance down at the article in my hand.

"Yes. Abandoned. Look, all I know is what I heard from my great-aunt Goldie, one of your great-grandfather's sisters. Goldie said Lola had run off to be a showgirl. Apparently that woman was . . . young and wild and a terrible mother for leaving her child like that."

That woman. Knowing how difficult it's been for her since Grams died, I was expecting my mother to be surprised, maybe even sad, but she sounds angry. I wasn't expecting that. Before last weekend, I'd never given my great-grandmother a moment's thought, but listening to my mom tear her down fills me with unease. "Maybe there was a reason for . . ." I let the sentence fall away. The proof of Lola's corrupt life is held gently between my fingers.

Wetness makes my mom's brown eyes sparkle in the sunny room. She steps toward me, cupping my cheek with her hand. "People are the way they are. Your grandmother lived under the cloud of her mother's desertion her entire life. I didn't know about the article," she says, looking down briefly, "but it was very painful to know that her mother preferred living as an outlaw to being with her only child."

"But haven't you ever wanted to know why she left?"

"She left because she didn't care about her family." Her eyes are eager, willing me to understand. "When your Grams told me the truth, years ago, she said the day her father told her her mother had vanished, she vowed to put the responsibility of family above all else. She was a child, but she made that promise to herself, and she kept it for more than eighty years."

"Mom, this isn't about Grams. It's about finding out what happened to Lo—"

"Don't." She raises her hand abruptly. "Don't say her name again." The force of her anger quiets me. She looks away and takes several deep breaths before shaking her head. "I just lost my mother, Wynn. I won't fantasize about what became of the woman who left her behind. She never spoke of her, and there must've been a good reason for that. Your grandmother wanted what happened kept from you girls, from everyone. I didn't even want her name in the obituary, but your dad thought it would look strange if we left it out."

There's no goodwill in the smile she gives me. "You're looking for a story with a happy ending, but you won't find one. When you think only of yourself, as my grandmother did, you hurt the people who love you. She walked out on her husband and left him to raise a child all on his own. They never got divorced, you know. It crushed him." My mother stares at me, her eyes weary. "She isn't the person you want her to be."

"I don't *want* her to be anything. I just want to know what happened to her."

"I know you too well to believe that." She steps forward and hugs me tightly. Her embrace feels pleading and urgent. When she pulls back, her arms still half around me, she finds my eyes again. "You loved your grandmother, didn't you?"

The question breaks my heart. "Yes."

"Then let this go. Please, for her." Tears cling to her lower lashes.

She wants me to trust her and drop this. I don't know that I can, but I nod slowly and watch some of the tension leave her mouth. She'll have to accept my silence as compliance. That's all I can offer her right now.

"Good. Now, why don't you follow me out back? I'll show you my new potter's wheel?"

Hearing more about my parents' rediscovered sensuality is the only thing I want to do less than give up on finding out what happened to Lola. "Actually, I've got to head over to the school. My union rep called this morning. I've got an interview at North for a position as their new social studies teacher."

The chance of me putting fifty thousand dollars in college tuition to good use lifts her spirits considerably. "Well, that's great news!" She reaches out to fluff my hair. I watch the worry drain from her shoulders, but there's still a trace of it behind her eyes. She does her best to disguise it as affection. "I'm sure you'll get it. They'd be crazy not to take you." She pinches my cheek, a familiar gesture.

I yell a good-bye to my dad, who may well be humming the chorus to "You Sexy Thing," and step into the sunshine.

I replay Mom's words in my mind. *"When you think only of yourself, as my grandmother did, you hurt the people who love you."* Was Lola the reason Grams reacted the way she did when I told her of my plans to leave? Was she worried I'd abandon my family as her mother had?

Lola's article is still in my hand. I look at it briefly, studying the elegant curve of what I now know to be her hat. *Where did you run to, Lola, and why?*

***

It's weird sitting in the hall outside the principal's office. I feel like I've been caught pulling the fire alarm. My hands are sweaty. I wipe my palms on the felt chair next to me, looking around to make sure no one's watching. No one is, which makes it feel even more like high school.

I tap the purse at my feet with the toe of a borrowed black pump. The frayed end of a red ribbon is just visible inside the bag. It was pinned to a board crowded with medals outside the school office. The words "Lifetime Achievement" are printed in black ink across a bronze button affixed to the material.

I shouldn't have taken it, but staring at the words . . . made me angry. Where is my lifetime achievement award? I've done everything I was supposed to do. I got good grades, came home at curfew, saved my virginity for college, stayed home to help Mom take care of Grams when I could have been out there somewhere, achieving a life. So I took the medal. I deserve it. The irony that I would never have done something so impulsive when I was actually a student here isn't lost on me.

The door to my right opens, and a handsome man with a touch of gray at his temples smiles down at me. "Miss Jeffries?"

I stand and take the hand he offers. "Yes, hello."

"Hi. Carl Sharland. It's great to meet you. I've heard lots of good things." He stands aside and ushers me into his office. The walls are gray and mostly covered with those inspirational posters that feature images of eagles and glaciers with words of enlightenment written in small type beneath. His desk is orderly, with only a computer, a pencil cup, and a few neat stacks of papers and folders sitting on the mahogany top. I settle into one of the blue leather chairs across from the desk and wait for him to sit. He leans back in his chair so confidently I wouldn't be surprised if the bachelor's degree framed on the wall is in self-assuredness.

"So, Wynn. May I call you Wynn?"

"Please do." My hands are sweating again.

"First, thank you for coming in on such short notice. We usually have more time to prepare for these things. And I just want to say how delighted I am to have a North graduate here to interview for the social studies position."

I raise my fist midway in the air. "Go Trojans."

He beams at me. "I love it. And I saw you were among the top in your class. Impressive."

"Thank you, it was a great achievement." There's that word again.

"And"—Mr. Sharland flips open a manila folder, reading from a piece of paper on top—"it seems you were heavily involved in a number of school activities as well."

I fold my hands together to prevent them from fidgeting. Restless hands, Grams called it. "I was, yes." He smiles, waiting for me to go on, but I've lived a decade since high school clubs, football games, and yearbook photos. Those things no longer hold the same importance for me, if they ever did. "There were—are—a lot of great activities for the students here. I was lucky to be able to take advantage of them."

His eyes scan the length of the page. "I see you went to Loyola and got an art history degree. What made you think of teaching?"

I open my mouth and take in a breath, my body preparing to respond, but nothing comes out. I lick my lips and cock my head to the side, smiling, buying time. I can't tell him the truth. That teaching became my default dream. That I'd arrived at it only after I'd given up on having a grand adventure. That it made my family happy to think I could be content with a simple life, and that I'm too much of a coward to go against them. "I just . . . wanted to share my love of knowledge with the next generation."

His smile suggests he expected more from me. "You didn't want to work for a gallery or a museum? Something more in line with your degree path?"

I pretend nonchalance, moving my head side to side. "That was . . . you know . . . the economy. The economy really limited my career choices when I graduated." I nod importantly, how I imagine the Fed chair must when sitting in front of a congressional caucus.

"And—" He stretches the word over several seconds.

"And . . . my grandmother was ill. I needed to stay close to home, to help care for her." *Okay, so it's not the truth, but who tells the truth at a job interview?*

His face perks up. "Oh, well, I hope she's on the mend?"

The words stick in my throat. I don't think I've actually spoken them aloud. Tabby told Lucky about Grams, and it seemed everyone else knew before I had an opportunity to tell them. "She died a little over a month ago." The sentence seems hollow, like a lie.

Mr. Sharland steeples his fingers together and looks at me with compassion. "I'm sorry to hear it."

I can hardly swallow. "It's fine, really. She lived a long life."

The room is quiet for a few seconds, as though we're observing a moment of silence for my loss. I've waited years for the opportunity to teach full-time. For any opportunity, really, and now I'm ruining it by laying the image of my dead grandmother across his gleaming desk.

"Wynn . . ." He says my name in a slow, considered way. "Let me ask you a question."

My fingers slide against one another. I don't stop them. What's the point? There's no way I'll get the job based on this interview.

"What do you want?"

His question catches me off guard. I stare at him. His eyes are blue and his eyelids sag a little, like a basset hound's. It makes him look both sad and endearing.

"I want a full-time position teaching here at this school."

"Do you?" He pushes himself toward the desk, one elbow taking his weight, and rests his chin against a fist. His gaze doesn't lock on mine but wanders across my face. "High school's no picnic, as you may well remember. These kids ooze hormones like jars of hot jelly. I need to know, are you up for that? Do you want that in your life, now and twenty years in the future? Because we're looking for a long-term commitment and, if you don't mind me saying so, you're still incredibly young. Are you certain that's something you want for your life?"

An irrational desire to crawl across the desk and hug Mr. Sharland consumes me. I suppress it, lest I find myself the defendant in a sexual harassment suit. But his words fill me with gratitude. No one ever asks me what I want for my life. They tell me what *they* want for my life. They shower me with opinions and forewarnings, but they never ask what I want. I'm not even sure *I* know anymore. Teaching sixteen-year-olds about the Industrial Revolution isn't exactly what I'd planned, but anything is better than standing still for one more minute. I'm so tired of not moving.

I stop fiddling with my hands and try to put all of my gratefulness into the smile I give him. "Thank you, Mr. Sharland. I appreciate the question more than you know, actually. I think what I want is to just have a meaningful life. One that allows me to do something important. Something I can be proud of."

"Teaching is a difficult career choice, Wynn, but it can be incredibly fulfilling."

I nod and listen as he moves on, telling me about the school, the staff, and the responsibilities of the position. I answer how I'm supposed to, when I'm supposed to. I try to care. Try to be engaged in the moment. He speaks passionately and gestures with his hands. I think I've fooled him, and when he stands to usher me out of the office, he closes both of his hands around one of mine and smiles warmly down at me.

By the time I make it back to my car, I'm sweating. The interior is even hotter than the air outside. I turn the key in the ignition and focus all of the vents in my direction. The hybrid engine whirs so quietly I can hardly hear it. I pull the ribbon from my purse and stare at the black inscription. *Lifetime Achievement.* Maybe this job is it, the thing that'll give my life direction. I want it to be. Not because it's convenient or even because it would get my family off my back, but because I need something, anything, to believe in. I look at the brick and concrete school with its pretty windows and manicured lawn and try to remember what it felt like to be excited about my future.

I roll the window down as I pull onto the road. The wind gains momentum, pushing hair across my face, as I accelerate. I let the ribbon slip from my fingers, watching in the side-view mirror as it falls to the ground. It seems fitting to leave it behind.

***

Oliver shakes his head, smiling at her and the rest of the girls crowded around him. "Sorry, girls. Can't do it."

"But we go back to school tomorrow," says another one.

He hands the big-lipped girl a white receipt. "Be careful driving back, alright? And stay away from those frat boys. They're all trouble."

Her breasts threaten to de-shell the peanuts scattered across the bar as she bends toward him. "I thought musicians were trouble," she coos.

"Oh, we are." He leans close to her. I strain to hear his words. "Which is why I'll be staying right where I am, and you'll be heading back to school." His tone is slow and disarming. "Education is very important to me."

"I bet your favorite class was sex ed." Her hooded eyes focus on his mouth, the corners of which have turned upward. Her smile makes me want to take a shower.

My mouth opens, and I speak before I'm conscious of doing so. "We're closing!" My voice is loud, high, and alien to me. Oliver grins curiously in my direction, but the spell is broken between him and his groupies. I set the glass in my hand on the counter, too hard. It bounces out of my grip, falls to the cement floor, and breaks.

"Oh my God." I squat to pick up the shards with shaky hands.

Oliver says something to the girls before crouching down and taking the broken glass from me. "Here, let me get that."

I lean back on my heels and watch the muscle flex beneath his short sleeve shirt.

"You okay?" He turns his head toward mine.

His closeness makes me unbalanced, and I sway slightly. "What? Yes, yeah. I'm fine. It just slipped." I rise with him, wiping my hands on my black apron. "Thank you."

He tosses the glass into the trash. "No problem. Anyway, I should be thanking you. Those girls didn't know when to give up."

"Oh. I totally didn't notice. Were you talking to them?"

He squints at me. "They've been here for, like, four hours."

I wipe the counter with my dry rag, flinging crumbs across the bar. "Are you sure you're okay?"

No, I'm not okay. I've been in love with you since ninth grade. "Me? Yeah, totally . . . totes magotes."

"You're acting a little strange."

The burst of high, giddy laughter doesn't help my case.

Oliver's hand falls over mine. "Tell you what. Why don't I lock up and grab us some beers, and you can tell me all about grown-up Wynn Jeffries?"

Well, at least it'll be a short conversation.

With the exit of his fan club, the bar is empty. Music from the old jukebox plays on as Oliver flips the dead bolt. He smiles on his way back to me. A knot of nervous energy has taken up residence in my stomach. I take a seat on one of the wooden stools and press stray crumbs into the counter with my finger.

He removes the tops of two green bottles of Mexican beer and sets one in front of me. I watch his drink take the journey from the bottle to his lips as he stands behind the bar. "So"—he clinks his glass against mine—"how pissed were your parents when you grew up to be a bar wench?"

His joke breaks the ice, and I return his wink with a sheepish smile. "Pretty pissed." I take a sip from my bottle. The alcohol weaves a warm stream of ease through me.

"Seriously, though, I thought you'd be running the country by now. What happened?"

I'll give the guy points for bluntness. *What happened?* It's the question I ask myself every day. I lift my shoulder. "I don't know. Things just haven't panned out the way I thought they would."

"Yet." He points the neck of his bottle in my direction before taking another drink. "Things haven't panned out for you *yet*."

I turn the glass bottom of my beer on the wooden bar. "I'm starting to think there isn't a yet, only a never-ending string of somedays."

"As in?"

"As in, someday I'll leave this town and see the world. Someday I'll find a career that excites and fulfills me. Someday I'll become whoever it is I'm supposed to be." I roll a wayward peanut shell back and forth, unable to keep eye contact with him. *Someday you'll kiss me again . . .*

"That doesn't sound like the girl I knew at all."

Knew? The only thing Oliver Reeves knew about me in high school was how to maneuver around my book bag when Shannon Jefferson wanted to play doctor between classes. I shake my head. "Maybe you just had the wrong idea about me back then."

"I don't think so. You were smart and interesting, not like everyone else." He rests his elbow on the counter and leans forward. "I'll be honest, when I saw you here the other night, I couldn't believe it. Weren't you valedictorian? What happened?"

My face warms uncomfortably. "Nothing happened, per se, and I wasn't valedictorian." The disappointment of being edged out of our class's top honor by Kristen Jarecki still haunts me. I wasn't even a remarkable nerd. "I applied for every museum and gallery job within a five-thousand-mile radius. I was qualified, but apparently I wasn't a"—I raise my fingers in quotation—"'good fit.' So I got my teacher's certification. You know what they say about those who can't do . . ."

"What? Give up?" His grin is almost as fast as the wink he gives me.

My hand moves to punch him playfully in the shoulder, but I stop myself. I purse my lips together and give him a wry smile instead. "Haha, very funny. No, I thought I'd try my hand at shaping young minds and contributing to the fabric of society."

"All that shit, huh?"

Why does he have to be so adorable?

"So what happened next?"

"Next?" I blink at him, unsure of the answer he's looking for. "I haven't found a permanent job yet. Budget cuts and everything. I sub regularly during the school year. I just had an interview to teach social studies at North, actually."

"And?"

Frowning, I take another sip. It seems I'm not measuring up to anyone's expectations today.

Oliver pushes back from the bar. "Come on, Wynn. Give me something else, here. Where have you been? What have you experienced? What else have you *done?*"

I resume crumb collecting, embarrassed to admit that I haven't really done anything. Certainly nothing he'd find amazing. Amazing is hard. Amazing is scary, and I'm nothing but a big, fat coward. I shrug, again unable to meet his eyes. "Like I said, someday."

"C'mon, you must've gone on a few road trips or run out on a future husband at the altar." He leans toward me across the bar. Humiliation keeps me focused on the peanut. "Spent the night in jail? Echoed into the Grand Canyon?"

He's teasing me, and every unanswered guess makes me feel more and more like a failure.

"You must've done something."

Tears blur my vision. I did plan a road trip once. I was going to drive solo in my old Volvo from Chicago to Lake Tahoe and try to match the paint on my canvas to the colors brushed across the sky there. But Grams broke her hip, and I stayed to help take care of her. My sisters couldn't do it, and I couldn't leave my mom to do it on her own. Then my ex, Tom, wanted me to move to Thailand with him. He got a job selling futures for some big-shot firm there, but that was the month Franny had Samuel. My passport was in my hand when Grams called to tell me she was in labor. She said Thailand would be there next year, but my nephew would smile and walk and talk for the first time only once.

So I put those dreams away. But "next year" never came, because there was always something else, some other reason to stay. How do I tell him I've allowed guilt and fear to keep me from having my own life?

"Hey."

I look up and into his eyes, which appear dark gray in the low light. They're full of sympathy. It's the last thing I want. Oliver Reeves pitying me. "I need to go." I say as I slide off the stool and onto my feet.

"Can you close up on your own?" I turn away and dab at the wetness collecting beneath my eyes.

"Wynn, I'm sorry." He sounds sincere, which makes it worse.

I wave him off as I walk the length of the bar toward the back office. "It's fine, I'm fine."

"Wait." He jogs along the counter, staying parallel across from me. "I just wanted to catch up. I didn't mean to make you feel—"

"What?" My heart pumps erratically in my chest. "Like a loser? Like a nobody that's done nothing with her life?" I take a shaky breath, embarrassed and angry at him, myself, and the delusion that I've been living under the past fourteen years. Hope that I could ever be interesting enough for someone like Oliver. The memory of my résumé lying limp and pathetically short on Mr. Sharland's desk comes to mind. I can't even make myself sound good on paper. "We're not all you, Oliver. We're not all cut out to have remarkable lives."

He opens his mouth, but I cut him off. "I'm the support person." I place my hands over my heart, willing my voice not to crack. "I stay behind to make sure everyone is taken care of. It may not be exciting or seem important to you, but it's my place."

He looks crestfallen and sorry. It breaks something inside of me.

"I have to go." I rush into the office and grab my things from the metal locker by Lucky's desk.

The late-July air is thick with humidity as I walk to my car. I gulp it down, glad to be away from Oliver and his sympathetic eyes.

FOUR

"I'm not saying this to hurt your feelings, but you should burn that dress." Tabby smiles and elbows me out of the way.

I turn from the reflection in my full-length mirror. "It's not that bad."

She tosses hanger after hanger of my clothes onto the bed. "It looks like you bought it at the thrift store downstairs."

I stop twirling. I did buy it at the thrift store downstairs.

"God, how do you stand that smell?" she asks, her nose wrinkled. "Everything you own smells like an estate sale."

When I leased my sweet little studio apartment three years ago, I intended it to be a transition home. I'd been dating Matt Beale for eight months, and things had taken a turn for the serious. We bought a fish and named him Major Sirna. But it turns out most betta fish live only about two years. Major Sirna lived one, which was three months longer than my relationship with Matt.

The apartment is a steal at $750 per month, but I didn't anticipate the strength of the mothball odor.

It. Is. Potent.

"Ugh. This is useless." Tabby throws another armful of clothes across the room. They land in a tangled mass on the floor. "Why don't you have any nice things?" she complains.

"I'm poor?"

"You'll just borrow something of mine. C'mon." She yanks me forward, grabbing my purse from the petite kitchen table as we go.

"Wait." I struggle out of her grip. "Why can't I just wear what I had on when you came over?" I look longingly at the jeans and white T-shirt that have become my daily uniform.

"Because Oliver's going to be there tonight, dummy, and we need you looking your best. Or . . ." She cocks her head to the side. "Maybe *my* best."

Spend the evening with old classmates and come face-to-face with Oliver after our argument? *Sign me up!* At least it's been busy at work. The place was so full yesterday, the only words I exchanged with him were "Another round, please," and "Pass the peanut bucket."

I tried coming up with an excuse not to go to tonight's party, but Tabby's my sister—she knows I don't have a life. In the end I caved.

I slide my feet into my favorite aqua-colored flip-flops.

"Uh-uh. No way."

"It's, like, ninety degrees outside." I fall dramatically against the plush cushions of the purple love seat.

Tabby grabs her hips and glares at me. "Two years I had to share a room with you and listen to 'Oliver this' and 'Oliver that.'" Her imitation of my voice is horrifying. "Now you want to just give up and die?"

"I don't want to *die*," I mumble. "I just want to wear sandals."

"You can wear sandals when you start getting pedicures." She kicks a pair of black heels at me, the ones I wore to the job interview.

I make a halfhearted attempt to shove my feet inside. I don't know why I'm bothering. I ruined my chances with Oliver when I unloaded on him at the bar. I didn't have the nerve to tell Tabby about it when she mentioned he'd be there tonight. Anyway, she'd just tell me I'm being stupid. She's never understood what it feels like to be trapped between what you have and what you want. She wants something, she gets it. End of story. I envy her for that.

The shoe refuses to give entrance to my foot. I give up and fling it across the small room. "I'm drawing the line at heels."

Tabby blows out a huff of air, probably exasperated that I'm not a life-sized doll with thin feet and no opinions. "Fine. But no tennis shoes and no sandals." She gets on her hands and knees and digs through the bottom of my closet. "Are you excited?" She resurfaces with a pair of tan ballet flats.

Am I excited? It's like there's a flock of hummingbirds in my stomach, and every person I've seen today has looked like Oliver, who probably thinks I'm the saddest sack to have ever walked the earth. "Eh."

"You'll be fine. A ton of people from both our classes will be there, so you can, you know, mingle until you've built up some confidence."

"Tell me again who's throwing this party and why?"

Tabby stands and dusts herself off. "Luke Manning. He wanted to throw a welcome-home party for Oliver."

"Luke the Puke?" Gag. Luke Manning was the class clown and a world-class jerk.

"He's not so bad anymore. He owns a real estate firm. Weren't you in chess club with his wife?"

Jenny Burton. My old friend and fellow yearbook committee member married Luke the Puke a few years ago, to my utter astonishment. We saw each other here and there for a while, but the friendship didn't survive college. I guess most don't. I wasn't even invited to their wedding. Not that I would've gone . . . "We were in band together."

"What's the difference? The dork club."

"I resent your use of the word 'dork.'"

"Okay. Nerd."

I throw a flip-flop at her head and try not to smile when she catches it.

"Alright, get up. We'll go raid my closet."

My good mood lasts five whole seconds. "I don't want to go to Luke's house. I don't like Luke. He's mean."

Tabby falls onto the love seat beside me, resigned for the moment. "He's not going to give you a wedgie, Wynn. Besides, Dex and I will be there. We'll protect you if he tries." She wraps her arm around me.

"Alright, I'll go. But I have one condition."

"I'm listening."

"If at any point in the evening Oliver tries to talk to me, you need to intervene. I sort of made an ass of myself the other night. I don't want it happening again."

She squeezes my shoulders. "Getting me to agree on the flip-flops would've been easier."

***

"Oh my God, you look like a hooker." Franny eyes me from the door-way of Tabby's bedroom. Tabby and Dex's place looks like a Restoration Hardware showroom. Everything is heavy, soft, and in various hues of cream and gray. Franny's house looks like a day care center. Watching us try on dresses for the party tonight must feel like an afternoon at the spa by comparison.

"She does not." Tabby dismisses our older sister with a wave, then smiles at me in the mirror. The black halter dress hugs every meager curve of my body. "You look hot."

"Like a hot hooker. Like you're working the streets of Miami in August," Franny insists.

"Franny, that's my dress she's got on." Tabby holds up two different earrings on either side of my face.

"I know."

Tabby huffs. "So you think I dress like a hooker?"

Franny moves into the room and lies down across the white bedspread. "Well, yeah. But a really high-class one. Like the kind that sleeps with actors."

Tabby rolls her eyes, tossing a pair of pink chandelier earrings onto the vanity. She seems momentarily pacified. She holds a pair of blue teardrop earrings over my shoulder. "These," she commands.

I recognize them. "These were Grams's." Blue glass catches the light as I place them in my palm.

"She wanted me to have them. Because of my long neck."

Franny groans. "Not this again. You just take all the good stuff and leave us with the crap."

"Hey, I resent—"

"Did you guys know Grams's mother didn't really die?"

Puzzled stares meet my interruption.

"What?" Franny pulls herself to a sitting position.

"Yeah," I say, facing them. "She didn't die like we always thought. Well, I mean, she died, obviously, because she'd be well over a hundred and ten by now, but—"

"I think your ADHD just kicked in," Franny says, picking at her nails.

I smile, embarrassed. "Sorry. Anyway, I talked to Mom, and she confirmed Grams knew her mother left her. She just didn't want us knowing."

Tabby sits atop the clothes piled on the bench at the end of her bed. "How'd you find out?"

"About Lola?" The name is familiar by now. "I found this." I reach for my purse, unearth the article, and hand it to Franny.

She reads it aloud, not pausing for dramatic effect as I did when I read it for our mother. "Wow. So she was a bootlegger?"

"Yeah, I guess. See here." I reach over the top of the paper and point to the woman in the photograph. "That must be her."

My sisters regard the picture intently for a few moments, then Franny hands it back. "What an asshole," she says.

I balk at her choice of word. "We don't know that."

"Don't we? The woman left her husband and kid and was never seen or heard from again. Sounds like an asshole to me."

"But what if . . . I don't know." Actually, I do know. I've done almost nothing but think of Lola's disappearance for nearly a week now. She's even taken precedence over Oliver in my thoughts at times. That's quite a feat. "What if she had to leave, and we just don't know why?"

Franny stands and unsettles a red scarf from the pile on the bed. I watch it fall to the carpet. "You've always been a romantic, little sister."

"Me? Tabby's the romantic one."

Tabby nods her agreement.

"Her?" Franny points at the blonde on the bed. "There's a sizeable difference between being romantic and being easy."

"Hey!"

"But what if we could find out what happened?" I ask.

"What do you mean, find out? We know already. She had a kid and a husband, and she up and vanished like a fart in the wind. Grams must've been ashamed if she felt compelled to lie about it. So, like I said, the woman must've been an asshole. We don't need to know any more than that."

"You sound like Mom." I toss the earrings onto the table, no longer in the mood to play dress-up.

"Good. At least someone's making sense." At the doorway, she turns to face me, shaking her head. "When you were four, you were obsessed with Indiana Jones. Do you remember?"

I'm really not interested in another lecture about letting go of the past.

"Dad thought it was adorable. He got you a little Indiana hat and round glasses with the lenses removed. And then he brought home that big bullwhip. It was heavier than you I think."

I remember.

"First day, first minute you got that thing, you gave me this." She rolls back the sleeve of her blouse, revealing a thin white scar on her bicep. "You wanted to outrun boulders and chase bad guys. Lola"—she spits out the name—"obviously wanted a different life, too. When you refuse to live in the real world with everyone else, you put the people you love at risk to get hurt. Don't upset Mom. This lady, whoever she was, doesn't deserve to be resurrected."

***

"Dude, you got hot!"

I clutch my purse to my stomach and try smiling at Luke as Tabby, Dex, and I pass through his front door. A large curved staircase dominates the foyer. I'm shocked to see actual artwork hanging on the walls. Jenny's doing, no doubt.

"Tabby." Luke takes my sister's hand, bends over, and places a dramatic kiss on the back of it. "You're still super hot, too."

Tabby curtsies as Dex nudges me. I roll my eyes toward Luke, and he smiles. Dex is a good one. How'd my little sister get so lucky? Six four, blond haired, blue eyed, and rich. He's like a twenty-first-century Viking, with good teeth.

"C'mon, you guys. Come see the pool. It's fucking awesome."

Luke leads us through the main level, his hand on my back. I nod at old classmates whose names I can't remember. Time has given everyone a fun house appearance. Slightly distorted but still recognizable. Luke is the same way. A little older, a little fatter around the middle, but with the same abrasive, untamed charisma he possessed in high school.

He'd see me overloaded with books in the hallway and call me "brain." And I was a brain. But I wanted people to see me as more than just the girl who studied too much.

"Jen-Bean," Luke gestures wildly at his wife.

Jenny Burton glides toward us on thin, tan legs. She's not the clarinet player with cystic acne anymore. She's a full-blown goddess, and the guy belching in my right ear is her Zeus.

"Wynn. Oh, it's so nice to see you." She smells heavenly as she wraps me in a fierce hug. She looks . . . rich. Like gold bullion dipped in rubies and covered in rose petals.

"Jenny," I squeak out. "Wow. Great house."

"It's Jen now." Her smile is perfectly symmetrical. Another new addition. "And I know, right? It's the biggest one on the street. Did you see the fountain as you walked in?"

The fountain is seven feet tall with stone swans carved into either side. You'd have to be blind *not* to see it. "Yeah, I did. It's . . . really great."

"Thanks." She flicks the hair from her shoulder and looks around, as though she's already bored with me. "Oh my God, it's been, like, forever since I've seen you." Her smile is affected, like a waitress who gets stuck with a table full of kids and old people.

"Yeah, it's been a while. I think last time was during break our junior year of college." I remember it clearly. I'd gone to the store to pick up groceries for dinner, and ran into her. She was working in the cafeteria near the salad bar. We caught up over two bowls of chocolate mousse. Some fell onto her white polo shirt, and she joked that it looked like she'd shit upward. We laughed so hard we nearly fell out of our chairs. It had been fun, nice. "It was at Dominick's, wasn't it?"

She laughs uncomfortably, pushing away the sound with her hand. "Was it? God, it was so long ago. I can't even remember."

"Yeah, we sat in the food court area, and your manager gave me free chicken wings because his sister had gone to Loyola."

She stiffens. "Oh." The word barely makes it past her lips.

I play with the strap of my purse and look for signs of Tabby and Dex. They disappeared the moment Luke's hand left my back. I grin at my old friend, confused and unhappy with the way the conversation is going. "So, do you guys have any kids?"

Jenny relaxes considerably. "No, not yet. We wanted to wait a few years. Luke's been so busy setting up the *firm.*" She puts a lot of weight on the word. "And I'm doing so much charity work right now, it's become, like, a full-time job."

The Jenny I knew wanted to earn a chair with the New York Philharmonic. I want to ask her what happened, if she got sidetracked, like I did, somewhere on the way to adulthood, but I hold back. This isn't the Jenny I knew. "Wow, that's . . . Which charities?"

"Oh, you know." Her manicured fingers flitter before her. "Homelessness, literacy campaigns, clothing drives . . . I'm on a million committees at the moment. What're you up to?"

Why? Why couldn't she return the favor and simply not ask? Why does everyone suddenly have an interest in what I've been doing with my life? For some reason, I don't think my "illustrious" career as a bar-back at Lucky's will be up to *Jen's* standards. I stretch the truth a little. "I'm going to be teaching at North soon, actually. A social studies position."

She places a hand on my arm and squeals with excitement. "Oh my God, no way! That's amazing! How cool would it be to go back to school?"

My laugh comes out in a stutter. High school isn't high on my list of do-overs, and I can't imagine it would be any different for her. If I was a nerd, Jenny Burton was sitting with scepter and crown on a velvet-covered throne atop the biggest float in the dork parade. "Really? You'd want to go back?"

She rolls her eyes. Her eyelashes are heavy and fake, the seam glued down beneath a row of shiny rhinestones. "Well, not as we were then; as we are now!"

I stare back at her, speechless.

"No, really, think about it. With all we know? We could be so popular."

Her clear desire to go back and be someone else saddens me. I loved my friend. We danced in her parents' basement to bad pop songs and made up a secret language so the cool kids wouldn't know we were making fun of them. We were outcasts, but we had each other. Her desire to erase all of that makes me feel small and alone and ashamed. Because I wish I could be someone else, too. When I smile I avoid her eyes. I don't want her to see the falseness of it.

We stand in polite silence for a few seconds, then she cranes her neck to look behind me. She squeals and grabs my shoulder with a clawlike grip. "Oh my God. Have you seen Clista and Jessica yet?" Her lips curl in excitement.

I assume she's talking about Clista Kurtz and Jessica Albini. They were North's resident mean girls when we were in school. In fact, I distinctly remember them gluing tampons to the front of Jenny's locker sophomore year. "Uh, no, I haven't."

"They just walked in. You're going to die when you see how big Jessica's gotten."

Relief washes over me. Finally, the friend I remember. "Did she get fat?" I whisper conspiratorially as I look at the guests spread around us. "You always thought she had a fat face, remember?"

Her mouth drops into a frown. "I never said that."

"Yeah, we decided that's why she never wore turtlenecks." I laugh, but it goes unanswered. Her silence unnerves me. I look up and see that her face is pinched, unhappy. "What?"

"She's pregnant. With twins."

I shake my head slowly, heat erupting from every pore.

"She was maid of honor at my wedding."

An involuntary giggle escapes. "What? Oh no." I place a sweaty hand on her arm. "I was totally kidding." Panicked, I keep talking, trying to undo the damage. "I'm so excited for her. Twins! Wouldn't it be great if they were Siamese?"

Her mouth drops open.

"Identical! I mean, identical twins. Not Siamese twins; that would be weird."

Stop talking.

"Because then they'd be attached at the forehead or something, and . . ."

Shut up now!

". . . they'd never be able to—"

Oh my God.

"Have . . . sex."

It's as though my mouth is an independent limb and I'm hitting myself in the face with it. Jenny yanks her arm from my grip.

"Oh, Jenny, I didn't mean . . . I'm so sor—"

"It's *Jen.*" She tosses glossy brown hair over her shoulder and stalks away, leaving me to remove the foot wedged firmly in my mouth.

Tabby and Dex appear beside me. He hands me a wineglass. Both are unaware of the travesty that occurred in their brief absence. I gulp down the dry red, then reach for Tabby's glass and do the same with hers.

Dex laughs. "Thirsty?"

"Uh-huh." I flap my hands and arms, trying to cool down. "Anyone else hot out here?"

They exchange worried glances. From across the stone patio, I see Jenny point in my direction. Older versions of Clista Kurtz and Jessica Albini—stomach swollen beneath a maroon dress—stand on either side of her. Their expressions are outraged. And justified. I need to get away.

"I think I'm going to go put my feet in the water." I turn quickly from my sister's questioning face.

The pool is dark, and light glitters off its surface. I walk down the long side of it, my humiliation growing with each step. This is a disaster. A nightmare. Soon everyone will know about me calling a pregnant lady fat and will think I want her children to come out attached at the head.

I kick off my shoes, unconcerned where they land, and sit on the edge of the pool. The water slips over my calves, cooling me some. I grip the rough ledge and close my eyes. It's so unfair to grow up and still be the same person. We spend years trying to remake ourselves. College, marriage, Roth IRAs, organic produce. Deep inside, we're all just playing at being adults. Because we'll never be better than the people we were at six, or worse than the ones we were at sixteen.

Well, maybe not Jen.

A loud shriek of delight jolts me. I look over my shoulder. A small commotion has begun in front of the double doors leading to Luke and Jenny's family room. Several old classmates bob and weave to get to the center of the pack.

His dark hair appears over Carrie Willoughby's head. She must've been the one screaming. Her body practically levitates when he pulls her in for a hug. Between releasing her and turning to pay the same attention to Jeananna Smith, he looks at me. One second. One blink. But that's all it ever took with Oliver.

I know it's the wrong move. I hear the long, drawn-out *No!* in the back of my mind. I visualize a slow-moving hand trying to pull me back. But my body cares about only one thing: escaping the brutal reality of just how much I'm capable of fucking up in one evening. I slide limp from the concrete edge into the cool dark blue of Jenny Burton-Manning's swimming pool.

FIVE

I open my eyes and look around. The absence of sound and the pressure on my brain are really quite soothing. Arms out to either side, I float a foot above the bottom, enjoying the weightlessness. My lungs tighten. I should've brought a hollow reed down here with me. I could stay all night.

I scan the surface. The chlorine makes my eyes sting. No one appears to be on the ledge and no life rafts have been thrown frantically after me. It seems I dropped in unnoticed. Kicking my feet, I pull my arms down and propel myself upward. Noise. Partygoers laugh and shout, reminiscing behind me. The shallow end is only a few yards away. I begin to swim as quietly as possible, staying close to the edge to avoid detection.

"Getting out so soon? I was just about to jump in and save you."

I swirl around in the water and look up. Oliver, one hand in his jeans pocket, grins as he walks the ledge beside me.

"I, uh, I was . . ." I rack my brain for a plausible excuse. Practicing scuba diving? Training for the Olympics? Trying to drown myself? ". . . hot."

He's not buying it. "Well, I'm relieved. I thought maybe you jumped fully clothed into the pool to avoid talking to me."

Water droplets fall with soft plops next to me as I shake my head. My God, I must look like a crazy person. Hair sopping, makeup probably running in streaks down my face. Tabby's dress floats around my legs. Treading water, I shove one hand under the surface and hold the skirt against my thighs. I laugh because I don't know what to say.

Oliver reaches the shallow end of the zero-entry pool, removes his shoes and socks, and steps forward. The bottoms of his pants disappear as he wades into the water.

"What're you doing?"

"Swimming."

"But your clothes—"

"You're right. It's hot out here." A few broad strokes bring him closer. "Besides, I can't let you swim alone at night. You have any idea how dangerous that is?"

Waves lap against his shirt. He dips beneath the water once, then circles me. "I take it coming here tonight wasn't your idea." He wipes the water from his eyes and looks toward the party on the other side of the pool. "In a million years, I never thought Luke Manning would be successful."

I release the dress to better paddle in place, too stunned to look at anything other than the man bobbing beside me. "It's kind of weird, seeing everyone again."

"You didn't go to the reunion?" He turns light-gray eyes on me.

I shake my head.

"Why not?"

That question has a lot of answers. I lower my chin, letting the water slide over my lips. It smells like childhood. "I guess because it sort of feels like high school never ended."

He's quiet, contemplative. "I've always liked that about you."

Despite the refreshing temperature in the pool, my body heats up. "What?"

"You give real answers. No empty pleasantries or superficial responses. You say what you're thinking. I've found that to be a rare thing."

I'm increasingly speechless around him, so I just smile at the compliment.

"Sorry about the other night." The good humor on his face disappears. "I didn't mean to make you feel bad. I just meant, I don't know. You always looked like you had everything figured out back then."

"Me?" I ask, stunned. "I'm the least figured-out person on the planet."

"Well, you're not alone there." He juts his chin toward the people behind us. "Perception is nine-tenths of everything. People believe what you want them to. Most of these guys are just as lost as you or me."

He's trying so hard to make things right. The least I can do is give him a bit more honesty. "Lost would be an understatement. To get lost, you'd need to be going somewhere, and I never even got behind the wheel."

"And why is that?"

I tread away from him. "I don't know."

"You don't know?"

I churn against the water, lifting my eyes to meet his.

Oliver swims over and places a hand on the ledge. I copy the movement, facing him. "Let me ask you a question," he says.

I hold my breath, watching him watch me.

"Who did you want to be when we were in high school?"

Water slaps against the cement wall. When I was seventeen, I would have given anything for him to look at me the way he is now, focused and interested in whatever it is I have to say. But now that it's happening, I'm unsure of myself. "I guess I wanted to get into a good school so I could find a good job—"

"No. Those are things you wanted to do. I'm asking who you wanted to *be*."

"I don't understand."

He pulls himself closer and rests his bicep on the ledge. "That night, in the parking lot . . ."

The night you kissed me.

". . . I came out after you because I was . . ." He looks down, shy. "I was so taken by what you said to me in the auditorium."

It was the night of the senior talent show, two days before graduation. The night eternalized in the Torture Picture. He captivated the entire school with his talent. Singing not like the eighteen-year-old boy that he was, but the talented musician he was destined to become. I can still picture the look of pure intensity on his face. I couldn't take my eyes off him. No one could. I sat in my seat long after everyone else had wandered off. Replayed his song over and over in my mind. He came to sit beside me.

"I asked what you were thinking about, and you said, 'An adventure.' Just like that. I think it took me a couple of seconds to recover. I'd never heard anyone say something so . . . honest before. It shocked me. And then you got embarrassed and ran, and I had to follow you because"—his fingers brush damp hair from my cheek—"I needed to know more."

"Ran" is an understatement. I practically trampled the vice principal and the history sub in my effort to leave the embarrassment of my words behind. When he'd sat next to me, I'd thought I was still daydreaming, still seeing the Oliver I saw whenever I closed my eyes. I can't remember what I'd been thinking, exactly, but I know it must have been about being away from the dullness of my life. So I opened my mouth and said the words, and then he touched my hand. That's when I realized it wasn't a dream. And it terrified me.

I got all the way to my car before he caught up, out of breath and shaking his head.

"Wait," he said. "Wait."

The keys dug into my palm, and I began to tremble. He ran his hands down my arms, drawing me to him. I closed my eyes, afraid that if I opened them, I'd find I really was lost in a dream. But his breath was warm on my cheek. I raised my head out of instinct, shaking in his embrace. And he kissed me. Just once and for no more than three or four seconds. Every cell in my body shook from the joy of it. Oliver Reeves kissed me.

Ten years later and I'm still trembling. I take a shaky breath. "Are you disappointed? Now that you've seen how my life's worked out?"

The corners of his lips rise, teasing me. "You planning on drowning yourself tonight?"

"The thought had crossed my mind." I want to laugh, but I'm too nervous.

"Then I guess it's a good thing I got here when I did." Oliver's hand is cool and wet beneath my chin. I raise my eyes slowly, more scared than I've been in years. "There's still time for your adventure, Wynn."

The water in my eyes has nothing to do with the pool. "It's not that easy anymore."

"What's not that easy?"

"Just taking off. We're not kids anymore."

His thumb runs along my jaw. "No, we're not. And you're no longer held back by age or inexperience." He moves closer. My dress and his T-shirt float toward each other, then touch. "So I'll ask again. Who do you want to *be*?"

His lips are close to mine. "I don't know."

"Try."

"I . . ." His eyes are so clear. Can he see through me? "I want to be someone who's not afraid."

His mouth moves almost imperceptibly toward mine. "There's nothing to be afraid of."

The wooden click-clack of shoes on travertine jolts me. Oliver pushes back just in time.

"Wynn? What the hell are you doing?" Tabby squats, ladylike, before us, her eyes traveling at light speed between Oliver and me. "Why's my dress in the pool?"

I open my mouth, but nothing comes immediately forward.

"I thought it might be fun to crash Manning's pool. Your sister spared me from looking like too much of an eccentric musician by jumping in with me."

He turns a megawatt smile on Tabby, and luckily, she buys it. "Oh, okay. Well, Dex needs to head out. The hospital just paged him, so we need to leave really soon." Her look indicates that transporting her sopping-wet sister in her fiancé's new Range Rover is not something she's looking forward to.

"I'll give her a ride home."

Both Tabby and I turn our attention to Oliver, floating a few feet behind me.

"I borrowed my Dad's Olds, so we'll be riding in style tonight," he jokes.

I look at Tabby and plead with her not to abandon me, to remember her promise. But she smiles prettily and nods over my shoulder at him. "Great! Then I'll just talk to you tomorrow, sister."

Am I crazy, or does she wink as she walks away?

I paddle myself around, facing my crush, my own personal heartthrob.

"So it's just you and me tonight," he says.

"Seems like it." I look over at the party. "How are we going to get out of here without everyone seeing our wet clothes?"

Oliver swims backward. "Just come with me. I know a thing or two about avoiding detection when I want."

I follow him to the shallow end, crouching as he does. We make our way out of the pool.

"Where're you taking me?" I whisper, a little giddy over our clandestine exit.

He smiles, a note of mischief in his eyes. "On an adventure."

***

If pressed to define what separates wealthy people from the rest of us, I think I'd go with landscaping.

I wait on the other side of Luke Manning's hedgerows, cowering in the dark of his neighbor's yard. I've never been good at dealing with stress, so sometimes, like now, I label everything I feel. I guess giving these feelings names makes them seem less threatening. Fear seems the first logical emotion. Followed by terror, doubt, excitement, and, buried deep beneath them all, joy. For the first time in a really long time, I'm happy to be right where I am.

The greenery quivers and Oliver appears between two thick bushes, wet, smiling, and clutching my purse and shoes in one hand. "You really know how to fling a shoe. Took me forever to find one of them."

He hands them to me, and I stick my pruney feet inside the shoes. "Thanks. Do you think anyone saw us?"

"Not a chance." He wrings out the bottom of his shirt. "Luke and Joe Avila were attempting a kegstand. I predict a hospital ride in their future." He grins, then gestures for me to follow. We arrive on a quiet residential street, the lights and sounds of the party behind us.

I look for a car, but see none on this side of the road. "Where's your car?"

Oliver looks sheepish. "I don't actually have one."

"But you—"

"How else was I going to get you to come with me?" There's something wicked in his smile.

"I thought you were taking me on an adventure?"

"I am." He spreads his arms wide. "The best kind. The kind with no plan and no rules."

I look away, a little afraid of his effect on me. Spontaneity and I have never been close friends.

My dress sticks uncomfortably to every inch of skin it covers. He notices. "I don't suppose you've got an extra stash of clothes hidden somewhere nearby?"

I laugh and say no.

"Then we'll just go somewhere we can dry off." He stops. "How do you feel about breaking into the old school?"

"We can't break into school," I squeak, gaping at him.

"Sure we can."

"But, but . . ." I dig for a suitable excuse. "What if we get in trouble?"

"Get in trouble?" The chip in his tooth has never been more noticeable than it is right now. "I'm a famous rock star, remember? If we get caught, I'll just give them an autograph."

"I don't think that'll work if we're caught breaking into government property."

"Why? You don't think cops like music?"

"I just don't think you're that famous." I slap my hand over my mouth.

Oliver turns, pretend hurt on his face. "You wound me, Wynn Jeffries." His hand covers his heart and he staggers back in an exaggerated motion.

"Oh my, I'm so sorry. I can't believe I just said that. It was so . . ."

"Sassy?"

I try to suppress my laughter but fail, hiding it behind my hands.

"For that, you will pay. Last one to the school has to streak naked down the hallway." And he takes off, running ahead of me.

I pause only a moment. Then I call on muscles I haven't used in years. When's the last time I ran for anything other than exercise? Arms pumping, shoes smacking against the road, heart hammering in my chest . . . I feel young and free and reckless. Good feelings. I want to chase them, so I do.

Oliver slows and waits for me to catch up. Out of breath and exhilarated, we walk in companionable silence for a while. When he speaks, his voice is soft and almost wistful. "I love walking around at night. It's so quiet. No one to bother you, no one expecting anything from you."

I know what he means. Before Grams got too old, she had the most amazing garden in her backyard. Rose and lilac bushes, a big white pergola covered in morning glory vines. We'd all get together for brunch on Sunday afternoons, and while everyone else perched on couches and chairs in the family room, I'd go and sit in the iron chair she kept in the center of the garden. It was the only place I could truly escape from my family or my job, even from my thoughts. I loved sitting in that garden. And in a matter of days it will belong to someone else.

Oliver walks beside me, quiet. I can't imagine his life. His job requires him to be something different for everyone. Rock star, celebrity, sex symbol . . . And now that he's home, we want the boy we knew—the one who had us spellbound by his talent and passion to live a big life. He's probably met a million strangers, each wanting their piece of him. I look over, wanting to ask how that feels, but don't. I don't want to be another person needing something from him.

We arrive at the school and jog past the curved stone entrance.

"C'mon." He takes my hand, and we run faster along the front of the building.

There's no one around, but we hunch over, doing our best to be sneaky and quiet. We cross the parking lot. The slightly cracked version I stood on when Oliver kissed me is now cobbled and pretty. He releases my hand and asks me to wait, then skims the side of the brick wall and disappears around the corner.

Crickets and cicadas chirp noisily in the lawn. My heart races a thousand miles a minute. Are we really doing this? Breaking into the school? If we get caught, I'll never teach in this district again. I scan the parking lot for signs of security. All is quiet, save for the bugs.

I jump at the sound of a lock turning. It scares me half to death, and I nearly drop my purse as Oliver sticks his head out of the door to my left.

"Alright, let's go," he whispers.

I squeeze through the half-open door. The corridor is dark. It smells like rubber erasers and clean white paper. Or maybe nostalgia is messing with my senses. "How'd you get in?"

He holds a finger to his lips, then takes my hand again. "While you were busy acing the SATs, I was mastering the art of skipping class. I have my secrets." He leads us to the entrance of the girls' locker room. I hold back.

"You're not allowed to go in there," I mouth.

He leans close, his mouth inches from my ear. "What makes you think this is my first time?" It's dark in the hallway, but the look in his eye is unmistakable. You can take the boy out of the high school, but you can't take the high school out of the boy. His smile reflects my own.

We creep into the unlit room. He flips on the light. Rows of gym lockers and benches stand across from us.

"I'll be right back." Oliver holds up his hand to signal for me to wait and again disappears.

I walk between the rows, dragging my fingers against the slotted cubicles. Locker 1091. This spot, this very place, is where I experienced some of my worst teenage moments. Undressing in a room full of girls was nothing new. I shared a bedroom with each of my sisters at one time or another. But having to disrobe in front of girls who'd developed beyond my meager A cups was a daily lesson in agony.

"Here."

The loudness of his voice startles me. He hands me a pair of deep-purple gym shorts and a gray T-shirt with a white Trojan emblazoned across the front.

He shrugs. "Best I could find on short notice."

"Are you sure there's no one else around?" I'm suddenly very aware of our aloneness.

"It's seems totally empty." His gaze skims my wet dress. "I'll change in the shower room." His voice is rough.

I wait until he's out of sight, listening as his footsteps move from cement to tile before removing my shoes and peeling off the dress. The bra and undies beneath are equally wet, so I strip those off as well and roll everything into a neat ball. The T-shirt is a little baggy and the shorts are a little snug, but I'm dry.

I sit down on one of the wooden benches. If someone had told me yesterday I'd be breaking and entering my potential place of employment with Oliver Reeves as my wet accomplice, I'd have thought they were crazy. But here I am. And I have no idea how.

"You decent?" He pokes his head through the doorway. Dressed in a nearly identical outfit. Gone is the boy I fantasized about in health class. A man, broad and solid, stands in his place. I look down at my own too-big shirt and see the same old Wynn. Unchanged, untethered, and uncoordinated. I wonder what he sees as he looks at me. Does he see a woman, or the girl who silently worshipped him?

Oliver sits beside me on the bench, his expression playful. "How do you feel about time travel?"

"Time travel?"

"It's a little something I've been working on while touring. Follow me." He nods toward the door and stands up, not offering me his hand this time as we leave our wet things behind in the girls' locker room.

I haven't been in this part of the school since graduating. The hallways look lonely without the usual bright bits of poster paper littering the walls. My bare feet pad noiselessly next to Oliver's. We turn into the English corridor, one of my favorite places in the school.

"Don't tell me you've got a time machine hidden in Mrs. Warnerbaker's class."

"Ah-ha. That's a common misconception. See, you don't need a physical vessel to bend space and time. You only need this." He taps a finger against his temple. "I met a yogi once who told me that everything in life is limitless if you just believe in it enough."

"Are you sure your yogi master wasn't just reading you *The Secret*?"

He turns the handle of the door to our eleventh-grade English classroom and pushes inside. "I don't know what secret you're talking about, but I promise you, I'm about to blow your mind."

Oliver finds the light. The desks and chairs have been neatly stacked against the walls, all but Mrs. Warnerbaker's desk, which is clean and void of the little knickknacks she always kept there. A miniature Henry VIII, a plastic bust of Mark Twain, the paperweight in the shape of a red rose, all stored away until sometime in September when she'll no doubt open the year with her famous performance of *The Raven*.

I watch out of the corner of my eye as he examines the walls and touches the desktops.

"It's kind of creepy with no one here," I say.

He smiles at me. "I like it. No one here to quiz me or ask me to read anything out loud."

"You're joking, right? You always wrote the best stories."

"No way. You were the star in every class we had together."

I flush at the compliment. "I didn't know you remembered me from school."

Oliver moves to the center of the room, closer to me. His eyes lock on my face. "Why wouldn't I remember you?"

I pull my wet hair to one side, twisting it into a rope. "You were popular, you had a million friends. Everyone worshipped you." The last sentence I utter quietly, almost to myself.

He steps forward and moves a wayward strand of hair from my cheek. "Not everyone. There was this one girl who wouldn't give me the time of day. I'd make eye contact with her, and she'd look away. It drove me crazy."

My breathing is rapid and scratchy against my throat. He couldn't mean me. I was a nobody. A clumsy, nerdy, self-conscious dork with eyes too big for my face and boobs too small for my body. I was invisible compared to his light.

Oliver's eyes focus on my parted lips. My arms and legs feel tingly, panicked, undecided on whether they should wrap themselves around him, or spirit me away. I try swallowing, but my mouth is dry.

"So where's this time machine, anyway?" I turn and walk to the wall behind me.

He sighs softly. "I told you, it's in your mind. You just need to access it."

"Okay, and how do we do that?"

"First, I need you on your back."

My head turns so fast a twinge of pain runs down my neck. He smiles and sweeps his hand across the brown Berber carpet below our feet. "After you."

I lower myself to the ground. I'm so nervous, I worry I'll levitate off the floor. He kneels beside me and stretches out. We lie side by side on the scratchy carpet, and I wait for him to speak.

"Relax your arms, hands, legs, and feet, and close your eyes."

It's impossible to relax when everything from the hairs on my arms to the atoms in my cells are violently trying to collide with his, but I do my best.

"Now take a deep breath."

I do as instructed, listening as he exhales slowly.

"Are you relaxed?"

No. "Yes."

"Good. Now I want you to imagine where you'll be exactly one year from this moment."

I open my eyes and turn to face him, confused. "I thought we were going back in time?"

I see his smile in profile; he shakes his head. "I never said we were going back."

"But . . ."

Oliver turns his face to mine. "Let me ask you a question. Is there anything worth going back for? Anything you'd really want to repeat?"

I think of Jenny and the expression on her face when she talked of going back. I felt sorry for her. I felt sorry for myself. There's nothing in my past but disappointment. I shake my head.

"So close your eyes, and focus on your future."

I do as he asks. One year from today—365 days from this moment, 8,760 hours from right now. And . . . nothing. The blankness of a clear mind and closed eyes are all that greet me. Panic jabs my sides.

Where is my future?

I force thoughts of my possible teaching job forward but can't hold the image for more than a second. I think of my family, but they swirl away from me, out of reach. Every conjured image slips past my eyelids. Nothing but blackness remains.

Then I see the subtle curve of a cream-colored hat. I trace it with my mind, following it from side to side until all of the nothingness falls away, and it shines bright in the darkness.

"What do you see?" His voice is deep and calm.

"Lola."

"Who's Lola?"

An old car, its doors pulled open, on the side of the road . . . "My great-grandmother."

"I thought we decided we weren't going back in time?"

"I'm not—I didn't know her."

"Alright. Then how does she fit into your future?"

The short answer is, I don't know. But I can't help but feel that my discovery of her past is somehow connected to my present and, therefore, to what's in front of me. "We all thought she was dead, that she'd died when Grams, my grandmother, was a little girl, but I found an article. It fell out of a book my Grams had. She didn't die. Lola, I mean. She left. She left her husband and my Grams, and all I know is that within four years, she ended up running whiskey in Kentucky. I know it's a ridiculous thing to think about. It happened so long ago."

"But not for you."

I look at him. Our eyes meet in the still classroom. "What do you mean?"

"I mean, this all happened a lifetime ago for your grandmother, but it's all new to you." He pauses, his eyes searching my face. "Why is it that when I asked you to think about your future, you couldn't come up with anything besides something that happened to someone else, ages ago?"

I watch him carefully. He knows something I don't. Something about me.

"Is it because her story is more interesting than anything you can imagine for yourself?"

His words wound me. They make me sad and uncomfortable because they're true.

"Wynn . . ." He rolls onto his side, cradling his head in the crook of his arm. "If you could find out what happened to Lola, would you?"

I look away and lick my lips. I've thought of almost nothing else—well, nothing else besides Oliver—since that newspaper clipping fell out of Grams's book. "Of course. I want to know. But where would I even start?"

"Kentucky seems a likely place."

"Kentucky?"

"Yes, Kentucky. It's the last place you know her to be, right?"

"Right . . . but wouldn't it be easier to just do some research online?"

Emily Hemmer

"What happened to the girl who wanted to go out and see the world?"

"Oliver, I can't just up and go to Kentucky."

"Why not?"

I smile at him, caught off guard by the simplicity of his argument. "Because I have a job and I just had an interview and . . . I've got a family! A family that relies on me to . . . help." The words sound lame and whiny.

He returns my smile, though his is easy and confident. "You hate your job." He holds up a finger to stop my protest. "I've worked with you for one week, and I already know you hate it. Don't bother denying it."

I close my mouth.

"And if they want you for that teaching position, they'll call and give you plenty of notice. And you don't have any kids, right?" He rushes the last word. I shake my head. "Right, so your family can do without you for a couple of days." He doesn't blink, and the steadiness of his gaze is like a challenge.

The energy coming off him is palpable. It makes me feel wild and happy. "I guess, but . . ."

"But nothing. Look. Maybe you'll get there and find nothing, but maybe you'll find something."

"Maybe all I'll find is moonshine."

"Then at least we'll have a good time while we're searching for answers."

"You"—the question is on my lips before my brain fully registers his words—"want to come with me?"

"Why not?"

"You literally just started a new job."

"I don't know if you've heard, but I'm kind of a rock star." His words are full of amusement. "I don't need to work in a crappy dive bar to get by."

"Then why'd you ask Lucky if you could work there?"

He rolls over onto his back. His words are quiet and measured. "At some point, I lost my desire to play. I thought maybe if I came home and started over, I'd remember what I loved about music in the first place."

"And have you?"

His fingers find mine on the floor. I clench my other hand. "Not yet."

We lie still and silent, but I know something loud and restless stirs in us both.

"Maybe I'll find my inspiration in Kentucky."

I bite my lip. Fear, terror, doubt, excitement, and joy. But now there's something else. A new emotion to label and catalog. Is it hope?

"I think you finding that article was meant to be. Maybe she's been waiting for you to find out what happened to her."

His words bring back the conversation with my mother. I know she's sad. I know she thinks finding out what happened to Lola was not what Grams wanted. But Mom didn't know about the article. She didn't know that her mother had kept it tucked away somewhere secret. I've thought about it a lot, and I think she must've read it a hundred times. Knowing her hands folded it so neatly makes me want to cry. Something hard like a stone sits heavy in my throat. I can barely speak around it.

"My mom wants me to let it rest. She said it isn't what my grandmother would've wanted. She asked me to let it go."

"And what do you think?"

I close my eyes and look into the darkness. This time it's not Lola that comes to mind, but the man with the black hair and the careless smile. "I think there's more to her story than a woman who abandoned her child."

I hear the sureness in his voice. "Then what have you got to lose?"

The answer is nothing. I do hate my job. The thing that's kept me there so long is complacency. It's the same with my family. I need them as much as or more than they need me. It's just easier to claim duty than admit I'm scared. That after so much inaction, I'm terrified to face the possibility that I'm not the person I so desperately wanted to be.

I slip my fingers between Oliver's and hold his hand. The pace of my heart quickens. He's asking me to leap, to jump and risk the fall. And fall I might, but at least I'll land somewhere new.

"When do we leave?" I ask.

SIX

The bag on my bed is in chaos. Shirts, shorts, a dress, shoes, toiletries are all crammed into a small wheeled suitcase that's been masquerading as a craft trunk for three years. I can't think about which shoes go with which outfit. I just need to fill the bag and get downstairs to wait for Oliver. Because every minute I wait is another in which I'm scared I'll change my mind. This is new territory for me. I'm not . . . impulsive. I'm basically a high-functioning agoraphobic. I don't call in sick to work. I pick up the slack for everyone else. I don't *do* things. What was I thinking?

Am I even capable of this? Am I, Wynnifred Michelle Jeffries, prepared to be locked in a car with Oliver Daniel Reeves—*mental note: don't reveal knowledge of middle name, as that will make you sound like a stalker*—for the next five hours? I packed my toothbrush before realizing it was a Q-tip and my black bandana before recognizing it as a black lace thong.

I collapse atop a pile of cast-off clothes. I can't do this. Years of suppressing my base desires have turned me into a rational, albeit poorly adjusted, person. The most reckless thing I've done in the last twelve months was file my tax return on April 15.

The sound of the buzzer sends me reeling. I run toward the call box and step on the pointed heel of a hot-pink stiletto Tabby tried to force me to wear. I hop toward the door, the sole of my left foot screaming in protest, and hold down the worn-out answer button. "Hello?"

"Hey, sweetie, it's your mom."

My mom always announces herself as though I have many surrogate mothers who I see and correspond with daily. She's helping me distinguish between them. I look over my shoulder to the open suitcase on my bed. "Uh, I'll be right down."

Her voice crackles. "I brought you groceries, buzz me in."

Shit. Shit, shit, shit. "Um, okay. Door's open!" I hold down the admittance button a few seconds, then hobble to the bed. The half-packed suitcase is too bulky to hide under the duvet. I try shoving it under the bed, but it gets stuck, refusing to budge. The floor in the hall outside my door squeaks. She's seconds away. I grab the bedding and throw it on top of the bloated case as she opens the apartment door.

"Come help with these."

I run over and take a heavy paper bag, peeking inside. Oh good. Perishables.

"You didn't need to bring me groceries, Mom."

She sets the other bag down on my little kitchen table and removes a carton of milk. "I know. I just wanted to do something nice for my baby."

Oh no . . .

"And"—she removes two grapefruit; one rolls across the kitchen counter and into the sink—"I wanted to apologize for the other day. You caught me off guard with your questions about that woman."

That woman again. "Your grandmother?"

Her chin drops. "Now, don't start with me. I came over here to make up. Don't spoil it."

"Sorry." I take more groceries and place them in the fridge, avoiding her eyes. I've got to get her out of here before Oliver turns up. I've never been good at lying, especially to my parents. My sisters had no problem asking for forgiveness instead of permission, but not me. As much as I envied the popular kids their parties and ability to simply be young and carefree, I could never risk disappointing my parents or my grandmother. I worked hard to prove myself in other ways, believing—or maybe dreaming—that my turn would come later.

She wraps me in a tight hug. She looks lovely in her long white skirt and green blouse, which deepens the gold of her hair. These days there's plenty of gray too, but the natural blonde hangs on stubbornly.

"Alright. Now"—she pulls back to look at me, her hands on my shoulders—"why don't you and I go grab some breakfast?"

I look at the clock on the stove. Seven forty-six. Oliver will be here in less than fifteen minutes. He insisted we leave first thing this morning. I think he was wary of giving me too much time to think. It's a little scary how well he seems to know me. "I . . . can't."

"Oh. Do you have plans?"

"Sort of."

"Sort of? What're you doing?" She narrows her eyes at me.

"No, nothing. It's just, I've got plans with someone."

"Who?"

My attempt at a casual *tsk* quickly spirals into a weird, strangled *yelp*.

"What's going on with you?" She bears strong hands down on my shoulders. "Why are you acting so strange? Is it that boy your sisters were telling me about?"

My surprise at least masks my stammering. "Who?"

"That Oliver. The rock 'n' roll guy. Is he—" She drops her hands and turns to scan the room. Her mom senses are keen and intent. "Did he spend the night?"

"What? No!"

She faces me. "Well, I hope you're using protection, young lady."

"Mom, stop. Oliver and I are not . . ." I'm twenty-eight years old. I live on my own. I'm six years into a twenty-year repayment on my student loan. But I cannot talk to my mother about sex.

"Oh my God. I should've bought you some condoms." She places her fingers to her lips, shakes her head, and looks up.

I toy with the lid on a jar of peanut butter. "Mom, Oliver and I are not together."

"Good." Her relief is instantaneous. "You can't trust musicians, you know. They move from town to town, picking up a new girl at every stop. My great-aunt Goldie dated one. Oh yeah"—she nods, raising both eyebrows—"a jazz player. Found out he had six children in six different states. She only listened to classical after that."

I sit down heavily on a kitchen chair. My journey hasn't even started, and I'm already exhausted. Worse, she's not going to leave until she gets the truth from me.

Seven fifty.

"Mom, I'm going to Kentucky. To find out what happened to Lola."

"What?"

I stand, walk to the bed, and toss the duvet off the suitcase, then lift it back onto my mattress. A yellow sleeveless blouse is crumpled on top. I take it out and fold it, then do the same with a pair of khaki shorts. "I know you don't approve or understand," I say, not looking up, "but I need to know what happened to her."

I refold one item after the other and place everything neatly inside the suitcase. My mother remains standing quietly on the other side of the apartment. I pull the zipper around each edge. The teeth whistle as they close in on themselves. Finally I look up.

She stares at me with an unfamiliar look on her face. I lift the bag and place its wheels down on the hardwood, slipping my feet into an old pair of faded navy Keds. I wheel the bag to the door and return to stand in front of her, gathering my courage.

"I don't want to hurt you or Grams. I just need to go." Her eyes move back and forth over mine. I brace myself with some of the courage I found last night with Oliver. "I'm not a kid, Mom."

"I know you're not a kid." Her voice is steady. "And I know I can't stop you from doing this, but I don't think you've thought it through."

"I have to go."

"You *want* to go. It's not the same thing."

"Fine. I want to go. I want to *do* something. I want to find out what happened to Lola and why she never came back for Grams."

"You know why, Wynn. We went over this. She was a self-centered woman. She thought nothing of the daughter and husband she left behind. And it nearly killed your grandmother. I mean, can you imagine? Losing your mother at such a young age? What if I hadn't been there for you or your sisters or your dad? What if I'd just up and walked out on you one day? How would you feel? Not to mention that your grandmother never wanted you to know any of this."

Something raw, like guilt, crawls up my neck, forcing me to drop my eyes. "I know, but—"

"No. No buts. You have responsibilities, Wynn. You have a job. You can't just up and leave with no notice."

"I called Lucky last night and—"

She shakes her head. The smile on her face is full of pity and disdain. "You know how I feel. I've asked you to drop this. You're being irresponsible and selfish. This is not the daughter I raised."

I swallow the cry trapped in my chest. Her words hit a wound buried within me, the one left by my last conversation with Grams. I'm not trying to be selfish or irresponsible or reckless. I'm just trying to wake myself up. "I'm sorry you feel that way."

Seven fifty-six.

"What're you hoping to get out of this?"

I bite down on my lip and shrug. "I just want to know."

That smile again. As painful as it is for me to see it, it takes nothing away from her. Even in her sixties, my mother's a stunning woman. Just like her mother before her. It makes me wonder what the woman in the hat looked like. Lola. Did she have my mother's wide brown eyes, my Grams's straight nose, or my full lips? Will I be able to find each of us in her?

I turn the doorknob and pull it toward me.

"You're going to be disappointed. It'll hurt you."

I push the suitcase into the hall and look back. "That's the problem, Mom. I hardly ever feel anything anymore."

***

We've been on the road for four hours and twelve minutes, and I've hardly said a word. Oliver sits beside me, his eyes trained on the trees moving beyond the window. After an awkward greeting and a mortifying moment when he pulled out the black lace thong that had gotten stuck in one of the suitcase wheels, he seemed content to leave me to my thoughts. He brought a few CDs for the trip. The happy tempo of the Black Keys keeps me alert and focused on the highway.

Oliver reaches for the volume control and turns the music low. "Tell me more about Lola."

I've had a persistent lump in my throat since leaving Mom standing in the kitchen, and I clear it before speaking. "There's not much to tell, really. I don't *know* much, is probably the more apt answer."

"Then just tell me what you know. We'll be there soon. We need to figure out where to start our search."

I stare sideways at him. He's so calm all the time. His stillness makes me feel safe. I reach behind his seat and into my purse, unearthing my grandmother's book. I hand it to him. "It's in the middle."

Oliver lets the pages skate across his thumb until the book lies open in his lap; the article is wedged between pages 134 and 135 as though it's always been there. I keep my eyes on the road but remain aware of his every action.

"Wow." He brings the paper closer to his face, as I did. "This is your great-grandma?" He looks at me, and I catch his smile. "Who knew you were related to such a rebel?"

I return the playfulness he's directing at me, allowing my body to relax against the seat. "I know. She was running whiskey around Kentucky when most women were churning butter in their kitchens."

"Barefoot and pregnant, no doubt."

"No doubt." We exchange grins.

"Who's the guy? What's he got to be so happy about?"

"I don't know. I've been wondering the same thing."

"Maybe he was her employer?"

Since I first read Lola's article, it's felt like a piece of thread has been attached to a patch of skin on my stomach. And whenever I think of Lola and wonder where she went, someone pulls on it from the other end. Only, I don't know who's pulling. "I think he was more than that."

Oliver waves the article before him. "Her husband?"

Something tells me that one husband was enough for Lola Harrison. It makes me blush a little. "Her lover, I think."

Oliver re-examines the photo, taking his time, going over every inch. "I think you're right."

"Anyway, I doubt she could've gotten remarried without a divorce certificate."

"She never divorced her husband?"

I shake my head. "Not that I know of. I think she pretty much left one day and never came back."

He stares out the windshield, watching Indiana pass us by. "Why do you think she left?"

"I don't know. I only recently found out she hadn't died. Remember?"

"Yeah, but I know you well enough to know that you never quit thinking."

He's got me there.

"C'mon. Tell me."

Since learning that Lola's death was fictitious, I've imagined a hundred different scenarios. Some paint her in a positive light: she left behind an abusive husband to become a traveling nurse; maybe she was thrown out of her home by cruel in-laws. Others show a darker, more desperate side: she was pregnant with another man's baby or robbed a bank. I've even considered murder and fleeing the law. But none of those stories have felt true. None of them yank on the thread at my waist, none but the same story that lives inside me.

"It's silly."

He waits for me to continue.

"I don't know." My heart thuds against my ribs. "Maybe she was just looking for something . . . more."

"More?"

"Something that made her feel alive." The words tremble against my lips. Fear, doubt, uncertainty . . . "I think she felt trapped, and so she ran. As far and as fast as she could."

"Why do you think that?"

Because that need to leave is what I feel. What I wanted before guilt and weakness turned me into a coward. I rest my elbow against the car door and rub my forehead with my free hand. I'm uncomfortable and hot, and I want to change the subject. "Just a feeling."

Oliver says nothing. After a few minutes, he turns the volume back up, and the Vaccines flood the car. I can't hear the lyrics or focus on the changing tracks. Finding out why Lola left and what happened to her is quickly becoming an obsession. In a way I feel like I'll never be able to move forward in my own life if I don't uncover her secrets. Her legacy, Grams's resentments, my family's expectations, my own doubts . . . these things are heavy. Sometimes it feels like the weight of them will bury me alive.

His calloused fingers gently scrape the skin just above my knee as he places his hand there. Taking my eyes off the road, I stare at them for a moment, not knowing if this is really happening or if I've fallen asleep at the wheel. His voice is real, though, too real to be a dream. "We'll find her."

The highway blurs. I focus on the lane and on the answers I hope we'll find in Kentucky. I don't look at Oliver again. I'm not strong; I just don't want him to see me cry.

SEVEN

"You look familiar."

Oliver shoves his hands in his pockets. The receptionist's eyes are big and blue behind red Coke-bottle glasses. Long blonde hair falls in waves down her back, and her skin is as perfectly porcelain as her lips are perfectly pink. But something about that stare makes me think she'd be more at home behind padded walls than the front desk of the Kentucky Historical Society.

"He gets that all the time." I step up to save Oliver's anonymity. "My name's Wynn, and this is"—why can't I think of a single male name?—"Marcus. Dennam. Like the jeans, only spelled different."

He rewards me with a grateful smile.

"Oh, that must be how I know you. I wear jeans all the time." Her glasses slide down the bridge of her nose as she nods. "I'm Kathleen Rice," she says, pointing to a green plastic nametag over her ample bosom.

"Nice to meet you. We're hoping you can help us." I dig the book out of my bag, remove the article, and unfold it. "We're looking for more information about these people."

Kathleen takes it from me and reads. Her lips move silently over each word. "Oh, Michael Craig."

Oliver leans against the counter. "You know of him?"

She smiles brightly and tilts her head to the side. "No."

"But then how'd you—" I begin.

"Oh"—she brightens—"it says his name, right here." She taps the article with her finger. "Is there anything else I can help you with?"

Oliver and I share a quick look. This might take a while. "Um, do you by chance know anything about the woman in the photo?" I point to Lola's bowed head.

Kathleen removes a magnifying glass from her desk drawer. The glass is as thick as the lenses over each of her eyes. "Sorry. I don't recognize that name. She's lovely, though." She straightens and hands the paper back to me.

I look at the picture. Lola's face and most of her body are obscured. Only her hat is clearly identifiable. "You can't really see her face."

The receptionist inclines her head toward me, adopting a more serious expression. "I was talking about her aura."

Oliver coughs, and I suspect it's to cover a laugh.

"Right. Okay. So where *can* we begin our search for more information?"

She places a finger against her chin and shifts from side to side. "I suppose you could begin with the microfilm of the original article."

"We'd love to, but we don't know which paper it came from, only the date."

She looks relieved. "Oh, that's an easy one. The only paper with circulation in Nelson County that would have printed photographs at that time was the *Kentucky Standard.*"

Oliver and I exchange glances again, this time surprised. Maybe there's more going on behind those big eyes than I previously thought.

"Where are the microfilm files located?" Oliver asks.

"Oh, we wouldn't have them for 1931." She smiles serenely.

We wait for her to continue, but she seems content to do nothing more than sit before us.

"Okay." Oliver draws the word out. "Then where *could* we find the original article?"

"The University of Kentucky libraries would probably have it."

I nod encouragingly at her. "Super. Could you direct us to one of the branches?"

"Sure. But you won't be able to get in this week. The closest libraries are closed for remodeling and inventory before the fall session begins next month."

I'd assumed getting information on Prohibition moonshiners would be like finding a needle in a haystack, especially in Kentucky, but we've got to find somewhere to start. "Kathleen." I say her name slowly, doing my best to guide her toward coherency. "Is there any way for us to find out about the people in this photograph? Here, in Frankfort . . . now?"

Again she smiles and nods but offers no further information. It makes me want to scream.

Oliver places a hand on my arm, then turns full rock star on the pretty receptionist. It's my first experience with Famous Oliver. "If you could give us any clues on where to start our search," he says, his eyes falling across her face, "I'd be forever in your debt."

His voice is deep and lyrical, and it lulls Kathleen into a state of renewed focus. "Hmm . . . wait." I can almost see the light bulb flashing above her head. "I've got the perfect place for you guys to begin your search."

We inch forward. Waiting for her to speak is almost physically painful.

"The Internet."

***

Oliver places a can of Coke on the gray desk at the Kentucky Historical Society where we've been stationed for several hours. I thank him by yawning in his face. My shoulders are full of kinks from pouring over online records. I thought the Internet was supposed to make everything easier, but so far we've come up almost empty-handed. Oliver discovered a few old census records, the most recent from 1920, listing Lola, her husband, William, and their daughter, Elizabeth, my Grams, who was only an infant when it was taken. After that, there's nothing.

"It's like she disappeared off the face of the earth." The can releases a hiss as I puncture the aluminum.

"Such a defeatist." He steals the Coke from my hand and takes a drink before handing it back. I stare at the top, mesmerized by the intimacy of what he's done. "We need to start thinking like her."

"Like a 1920s housewife who became a renegade bootlegger in the span of a decade?"

He raises a finger to me. "Exactly."

I push out a loud sigh. This is pointless. Lola didn't want to be found and made damn sure she wouldn't be, apparently. We've searched under her married name, her maiden name; we've tried interchanging her first and middle names, and searching only by first name and county of birth. We looked for the original article and through a series of local essays on the county during the years she may have lived there. Oliver thought we might find her by association, so we tried looking up Michael Craig. We found similar information on him as we did on her. Nothing more than census records that told us no more than who he was living with—they appeared to be his brothers and a sister-in-law—the birthplace of his parents, and his chosen occupation, which was listed as farmer.

"Yeah, he was growing whiskey in his backyard," Oliver had said.

Without online access to death certificates—and that's if they even still exist; Kathleen dropped by to twist the knife in my side, telling us many old records had been lost to fires—finding out what happened to

Lola is starting to look impossible. I thought we'd be doing things the hard way, coming out here to search for answers on foot. But it turns out there isn't an easy way to find someone who wanted to be lost. It's as though she never existed beyond being Grams's mother. Save for the article. I pull it toward me and reread every line. There's got to be something that will lead us to her.

"Here"—Oliver's hand comes close to mine—"let me see that." He pulls the paper across the desk. I take the moment to look at him, unobserved. His black hair is thick and slightly longer on the top. It curls a little at the ends. His lashes are the same, just as black and thick. I love his eyes. They've always reminded me of a lake in the winter, the way they can change from light to dark in a matter of moments.

He looks up. They're a light, clear gray right now. I should probably look away, but I don't want to.

"Hi," he says.

"Hi."

Our closeness has nothing to do with the small desk. I feel like we're connected in a way that goes beyond a shared experience. His fingers touch the back of my hand. "I've got an idea."

"Okay."

"The house."

I blink, not following his thought. "The house?" His finger moves light and slow down one of mine. My heart races.

"What if"—he taps the article in front of him—"the house is still standing?"

Of course. The article said the Craig house and grounds were searched following Lola and Michael's arrest. If he really was her lover, she might have lived there, too. I reluctantly pull my hand from beneath his and shuffle through the small stack of printouts to my right. Most of the documents look the same, but I know the one we need, the 1930 census. The one closest to the date of the article and the last time Lola left a trace.

"Got it." I set the paper down between us and drag my finger down a dozen rows before landing on the one I want. I turn the paper vertical to read the swirling script running along the edge of the page. It says "Fairview Road," and beside Michael's name, there's a house number.

***

Driving through rural Kentucky in July is like driving through a tunnel of green. Trees stretch to embrace one another over the top of my car. I wish I could enjoy it, but all I can think about is the house at the end of this road. The house Lola may have once called home, if it's still there. *Please let it be there.*

"You okay? You seem a little wound up."

"I'm fine."

"That bad, huh?"

How does he do that?

"I'm just excited. If it's still standing . . . she might've lived there. There could be a picture of her. I'd finally get to see her face." The thought makes me giddy. "I just have this feeling that I'm going to sense her presence or something." I sneak a look in his direction. "Stupid?" He stretches his arm out, and his hand rests on the back of my seat. For a minute I thought he was going to touch me. I blush.

"Not stupid. But let's try and go in with no expectations. That way, we can't be disappointed."

His reluctance to play along dulls my excitement but can't stamp it out. "I can't believe we drove all this way and ended up finding what we needed online," I say, leaning into the steering wheel.

"Not everything, just the first clue, and we would've found the house anyway."

"How's that, Columbo?"

He rubs his hands together. "Good old-fashioned detective work."

"Ah. So you're a traitor to our generation. Eschewing technology in order to do things the hard way."

"The proper way," he corrects me.

I take my foot off the gas, allowing the car to turn into the winding road naturally. Oliver's good mood is infectious, and I can't help but tease him. "I bet the only thing you use the Internet for is to search for the closest Chinese takeout place."

"Don't be ridiculous." He looks over, grinning. "That's way too complicated."

"Come on. You must at least be adept at social media. How else did you get a following for the band?"

He looks out the window, his fingers drumming on the back of my headrest. "Tony took care of setting all that stuff up. My job was to write songs and play music. I don't care for this brave new world. I think I prefer things as they were."

"Before Twitter and Instagram?"

"You've never known frustration like singing your heart out to a crowd of people looking at you through their cell phones. It takes them right out of the moment." I look sideways and watch a frown cross his face.

"It really bothers you, huh?"

"It doesn't bother you?"

"Technology keeps us connected."

"I disagree. Technology gives us the illusion of being connected. You can't connect with someone by poking them on Facebook. That's not friendship. That's staving off boredom."

"So if I hop on my timeline later to check in, I shouldn't poke you?"

A whisper of a dimple appears on his left cheek. "You can poke me any time you want."

Flustered and a little heated, I return my attention to finding our destination. The road Oliver instructed me to take bends and winds like the ones in Candy Land. My sisters and I loved that game, though Tabby almost always cheated by using Gumdrop Pass when she wasn't supposed to. Franny would run off to tell Mom, Tabby chasing after her, and I'd stay to clean up the mess.

We come out of a low and winding bend, and a flat valley opens on either side of the road. Oliver tells me to take the next exit and turn onto an outer road, paved only by packed dirt. The trees and brush are thick on this side of the parkway. The area has a wild, untamed look.

"There." Oliver points to a driveway. A green-and-white sign marked "KHS" has been driven into the ground at one corner. "What do you think that means?"

"I don't know." I pull into the drive. A log cabin with a slanted roof and wide porch sits a few hundred feet from the road. My heart jumps into my throat at the sight of it. As we approach, I stop the car to read another, larger sign at the mouth of the driveway.

CRAIG HOUSE
CIRCA 1878
THIS HOME HAS BEEN LOVINGLY RESTORED BY
THE KENTUCKY HISTORICAL SOCIETY.
VISITORS WELCOME.
PLEASE STAY OFF THE GRASS.

"I don't know about you, but I did not see that coming." Oliver leans over in his seat to get a better look at the house.

I park in an area on the right marked for visitors. It feels like I'll break into a million pieces as my feet touch the earth. Not only is Michael Craig's home still standing, it's a freaking museum.

"Don't let me forget to send that receptionist a thank-you note for all her help." My words drip with sarcasm.

"Go easy on her. It's got to be hard remembering historical landmarks with everyone's auras getting in the way all the time."

We walk up the steps to the front door. I pull the handle, but it remains closed. Locked. Oliver bends to read a sign taped to a large front window.

"Closed weekends," he says. His worried gaze darts to mine.

I keep hold of the knob. The excitement I felt in the car falls away. "Shit. Wynn . . ."

"No." I shake my head. "It's fine, really. I wasn't sure we'd find anything down here, let alone the house she may've lived in."

"Still . . ."

He doesn't need to say it. I know what he's thinking. This was meant to be a weekend trip. I told Lucky I'd be back for my shift on Monday. I can't leave him scrambling to cover for me. It's not fair. It's not what a *responsible* person would do. It's not what *I* do.

"I'll just come down another weekend. No big deal." The voice inside, the one that whispers excuses, says the words are a lie. A front. A way to prevent me from feeling hurt or disappointment.

He reaches out, and I let him pull me against his chest. I put my arms around his back and hold him. We haven't been this close since the night he kissed me. I'm very aware of him. Of the sound of his heart beneath my ear. Of the way his shirt smells, like fabric sheets. It's warm and soft against my cheek. I snuggle as close as I can get. Oliver's thumb finds a patch of skin above my shorts, and he rubs the spot tenderly. I close my fingers around his shirt, crumpling the material in my hand. His mouth moves against the top of my head as he presses a kiss against my hair.

"There's nothing to worry about, you know."

Only, I don't know that. The thread that keeps tugging at my stomach is pulled so tight, it feels frayed, close to breaking. Finding out what happened to Lola and what drove her away from my grandmother feels urgent in a way I don't fully understand. It's on the tip of my tongue, but I can't explain it. I just know that somehow our paths are crossed, that her past and my future share a connection. But right now all I have are questions. And I need answers.

I lift my head, angling away from his body so I can see his eyes. Now they remind me of the sky just before the rain, a dark, swirling gray. I part my lips to draw in breath. I want him. I need him.

He raises a hand to my cheek and drags his calloused thumb across it. "The freckles on your nose are the same color as your eyes." I watch his mouth form each word. "Did you know that?" His lips move closer to mine. I make a fist with the shirt in my hand, drawing the material tight across his back.

A buzzing feeling begins against my upper thigh. I ignore it. My eyelids get heavier the closer his lips come, but the vibration is persistent.

"What is that?" he says, his voice gruff.

I let my head fall forward against his chest, the moment gone. "My phone," I mumble against his shirt as I reach into my pocket. Franny's face lights up the screen. "It's my sister."

Oliver squeezes my shoulders. "Better get it."

I tap the answer button with my thumb. "Hi, Franny."

"Mom told me everything. She's been crying, Wynn. What's gotten into you?"

I sigh heavily and turn away from Oliver. "I don't want to do this with you right now."

"Too bad. Mom said she asked you not to go."

"She did."

"And you went anyway." It's not a question. It's a statement of my poor judgment in her eyes. "The woman you're chasing abandoned her child, *your* grandmother. Doesn't that mean anything to you?"

"Of course it does, but . . . I just think there's got to be a reason."

"Yes, and here it is. She was an asshole."

Her voice is loud. I pull the phone away from my ear. Oliver raises his dark eyebrows and smirks. Whatever else this journey is, it's brought me something I didn't know was possible. It's brought me him. And it's made me look at my life. I can't turn back. I won't.

"I'm sorry, Franny. I know the timing isn't right, and I don't want to hurt Mom or disrespect Grams's wishes, but I know that there's more to this story. I want to know what it is."

My sister is quiet. I imagine her face pinched in irritation, a look she usually reserves for Tabby. "She asked you not to go, Wynn. You have to do the right thing here. Drop this and come home."

The porch creaks beneath my Keds. I'm so tired of have-tos. "I don't know how long I'll be gone. Tell Mom . . . tell her I love her." I press "End" and look at the man across from me.

His lips are tilted up in approval. "So what now?"

I wave the phone in front of me. "Now I get to text my boss that I'm not coming back on time and hope he doesn't fire me."

"He won't fire you."

"Oh yeah?" I fire off a quick text to Lucky.

```
Trip delayed, don't know how long. Will
text when I'm back. Sorry.
```

My eyes return to Oliver. "Well, maybe you can put in a good word for me."

He lifts his arms and runs both hands over the top of his hair, making it slightly disheveled. "Hey, if anyone's getting fired, it's the new guy," he says, jabbing a thumb into his chest. "Anyway, what makes you think he'll listen to a word I've got to say?"

"Since you came back, business has tripled."

"I do know how to make a mean bottle of beer."

I laugh. What else am I going to do? "Well, I guess this means we're staying through the weekend, and that we'll soon be unemployed."

"I guess it does."

"Alright." I try to keep the exhilaration from overtaking my face. This moment. Right here. This is me falling. "Let's get out of here." He extends his arm and bows. "After you."

I walk to the car and he follows. I'm spending the weekend with Oliver Reeves. I don't know if I'll have a job when I get back. I told my sister to shove it (sort of). I smile, big and stupid, and head for the car.

The interior is hot and muggy. I turn the ignition and run the AC at full power. Oliver sits contented as ever, watching as I melt in the dense Kentucky heat.

"Well? Thoughts? Ideas?" I ask.

He cranes his neck to look out the back window. "Get a hotel?"

I busy myself with getting back to the main road as a heat wave that has nothing to do with the temperature outside spreads across my chest. I stop just ahead of the entrance ramp. "Okay. We're in Kentucky for the weekend. What're we going to do until Monday?"

He shrugs. "I think we're pretty close to Bardstown. Why don't we check it out? Just see where the road takes us?"

"Which one? The open road, the road to perdition, the one less traveled?"

He barely suppresses a grin and points left. "Just drive, nerd."

***

The sheets are stretched to a military standard beneath the coverlet. I get out of bed and pull until every inch of starched white cotton hangs loose over the mattress. I can't sleep confined. I need room to flail and toss. I flip the switch on the lamp beside the bed and close my eyes.

It's impossible. When Oliver Reeves is sleeping on the other side of a wall from you, sleep is impossible. He booked two rooms in a show of polite chivalry, and I cursed him for it. When he left me at my door after dinner, I thought, for a moment, that he might ask to come inside. But he just told me good night and opened the door adjacent to my own. I'm embarrassed to admit I allowed my hand to linger on the wall between us for a moment.

I hold my breath and listen. A faint rustle, a cough, definitely the sound of the faucet running. I don't know what I'm hoping to hear. A groan, a laugh, possibly my name on his lips? Lips that have almost touched mine twice in as many days.

The phone on the nightstand rings loudly. "Shit." I place one hand over my racing heart and pick up the receiver with the other. "Hello?"

"Hi." His voice is deep and playful.

"Hi."

"What're you doing in there?"

"I just got in bed."

"Really? I think I'd like to hear more about that," he mutters in a deep, gravelly voice. "What're you wearing?"

I smile. His soft chuckle makes my toes curl.

"It's kind of fun talking on the phone from a few feet away."

"You'd probably prefer a tin can and string," I tease.

"And what's so wrong with that? There's something romantic about doing things the old-fashioned way."

I hide my head and the stupid grin on my face beneath the blankets. In case he can see through walls.

"I was just thinking about that night in the auditorium," he continues seriously. "Actually, I've thought about that night a lot over the years."

The phone in my hand has become precious.

"I even wrote a song about it."

"You did?"

"I did. Never played it for the band. It was too . . . personal. I wanted to keep it for myself."

The room is dark and quiet, but it feels as though a lit fuse is burning toward a quick explosion inside my body. "Will you play it for me?"

He sighs. "I haven't played anything in a while now."

"Why not?"

"It just wasn't fun anymore. It began to feel like a job. Something I had to do, rather than something I was passionate about doing."

I know exactly how he feels.

"I was afraid if I kept going, it would be ruined for me forever."

"The music?"

"The pureness of doing something I loved."

I bring my knees up and curl into a ball. "I'm jealous. I've never loved anything as much as you love music."

"You'll find something. Just keep looking."

"I don't know. I look at my friends and my family, and sometimes it feels like the best we can do is . . . survive. It makes me wonder how many of us are capable of being more than only what we have to be."

Oliver's voice is softer now. "Is that what scares you? Living, but not really being alive?"

I hold myself tight.

"Can I tell you something honest? And then you tell *me* something honest?"

I wait, silent.

"I think I came back for you," he says.

I close my eyes. His quiet admission echoes loudly in my ear. "I always wanted you to."

EIGHT

"Apparently this place is famous." Oliver picks up his fork as a wait-ress places two plates of biscuits covered in thick, white sausage gravy on our table. The small café is packed with Sunday-morning custom-ers, locals by the looks of them. Women in pajama pants on their cell phones and men wrangling rambunctious toddlers at the front door. All for Mammy's famous breakfasts.

Oliver moans obscenely. "So good." He motions for me to take a bite.

What do they say? When in Kentucky? I bring the fork to my mouth. It's the kind of food that makes you close your eyes because you want to divert as many senses as you can to your taste buds. The gravy is a savory contrast to the light, fluffy biscuit. It may well be the best thing I've ever had in my mouth.

"So good," I agree, taking a too-large bite. There's a lot of nodding and chewing as we devour the meal. Neither of us spares a moment's concern for Southern decorum as we lick our plates clean. Oliver sits back and pats his stomach, though it remains flat as ever. We haven't spoken about last night. After our mutual confession, the conversa-tion turned toward our lives post–high school. I learned that he traded college for Nashville and a job busing tables while auditioning for bands.

"No one wanted me," he laughed into the phone. "But I was persistent. Eventually a guy named Decker hired me to lay down a track on a studio recording. That's how I met Tony. He's a genius on the drums, but he can't write a song to save his life. We met Pete and Dan at a festival, and everything just sort of evolved from there."

Oliver credits their success to luck, but I know better. He's magnetic. People see it. That's why they follow him. Why they root for him. While I was busy putting my dreams aside, he was headlining shows and playing stadium arenas. He was a star. And then he walked away from everything.

I had a million questions, but he didn't seem ready to talk more. So I told him my story instead. It began with Loyola, my first taste of freedom, and my unfortunate-looking roommate with her vast collection of unicorn figurines. I was less than three minutes into my story when I ran out of things to say.

The truth is, just as with my life post-Loyola, I shut college out, choosing to study night and day and only occasionally remembering to be young.

My parents had big ideas for my future. *"You have so much promise,"* they'd say. It was meant to be a compliment, inspirational, but it made me feel pressured to become someone else. I didn't know who I wanted to be.

When I dreamed of my future, the career, the lifestyle, those were secondary to what I was really chasing. Experience. Freedom. Courage. Intangible dreams that lived as secrets in my heart. And the problem with dreams is that, in reality, they're often little more than sacrifices turned upside down. They require all of you, and much of others.

So I devised a plan. I'd study hard, join all the right clubs, intern at any firm or museum with international branches, and wait. Making the grades, pleasing people, being a good daughter, those things were easy. Safe. Admitting I had no real desires beyond leaving, traveling the world like a gypsy? I knew no one would understand, least of all my family.

How many times have I dreamed aloud, only to be dissuaded by their reality? *"Where will you live? What will you live on? You'll be lonely. You'll be miserable. It's not feasible. It's not responsible. You're not thinking this through. You're not a child anymore, Wynn. "It's time to grow up."*

I told myself I wasn't missing anything. That if I just put in the time, it would pay off in the long run. I'd leave with a degree, and it would open doors. I could work in New York or London or Paris. Somewhere new and exciting. My family would support me because it would be for a job, and not simply because I *needed* to go.

So I buried those bohemian dreams deep within and tried to be clever. And I was. I made all the right decisions. But I was never honest about what I wanted, who I really was, inside, and my applications post-Loyola were met with rejection.

At first I made excuses. The other applicants had more gallery experience than me, they were better artists, had the right connections. It took me a long time to admit those weren't the reasons I failed to get one job after the other. It was because I didn't really want them, and people saw through me.

I took the position at Lucky's the winter following graduation. It was supposed to be for only three months. Time enough to come up with a new plan. But when twenty-two became twenty-four, I began to worry. I was running out of youth and excuses.

One day I woke up and found that somewhere along the way, I'd lost what little courage I'd had. And I felt stupid and useless and afraid. Because life was passing me by, and I lacked the strength to even care. That's when I went back to school and got my teacher's certification. Not because it was doing something, but because it wasn't doing nothing.

Oliver sets a Styrofoam cup in front of me. Black coffee swirls inside. "You're looking a little lost there. Maybe I kept you up too late last night?"

I pull myself away from my thoughts and try to reassure him with a smile I hope seems genuine.

"Alright." He pulls a map from his back pocket and spreads it across the table. "The hour is early and the day is long. What do you want to do?"

Colorful icons of parks, historical sites, and distilleries dot the green background. "I don't know. Let me check Yelp." I take the iPhone from my purse.

He snatches it from my hand. "No way. We're on a research trip of historic proportions. We're doing this old school."

"What does that mean, exactly?"

"It means we're leaving this"—he waves the phone at me—"in the room."

I worry my bottom lip with my teeth. "But what if we get lost and need directions?"

"We'll hail someone down and ask."

"What if we get lost, and the car runs out of gas?"

"We'll walk to the nearest station."

"What if we fall into a ravine and break our legs and can't get out?"

He relaxes against his chair, clearly enjoying our back and forth. "Then we'll get eaten by a pack of wild dogs, and it'll be *your* great-granddaughter who comes searching next time."

"Ah, but if we die, I'll never have any children, and therefore no great-granddaughter to come and find me."

He lowers his voice and leans across the table. "Who knows. Maybe we can work on that, too."

His innuendo, paired with the fitted cut of his blue jeans, renders me incapable of doing anything more than watch as he stands.

"Are you ready?" he asks, holding out his hand.

***

Oliver's idea of a good time is less erotic and more morose than I would've imagined. Cracked granite headstones lean against one another like old drinking buddies. My fingers touch a faded imprint. A name I can't make out, the word "Father" carved deeply beneath it. A designation that outlasts both name and time. I squint into the midday sun. "Nineteen oh-one," I read aloud, calling the date over my shoulder.

"Not good enough." He waves me off. "I've got 1824 over here."

Back before YouTube and Xbox, my sisters and I relied on our imaginations for entertainment. One-up was our favorite game. It could be played anywhere, anytime, and with anything. The object was to continuously one-up each other until a single victor could be declared. I would find a daisy with ten petals, and Franny would scour the field for one with eleven. Tabby would drink an entire can of cherry pop in thirty-three seconds. I'd do it in twenty-nine.

The look on his face should have warned me. I can equate Oliver's competitiveness only to a man seeking water in the desert. I'm not a very competitive person, and even less so when my opponent is so distractingly handsome. I watch him jog between rows of headstones, determined to find the oldest one in the overgrown cemetery. Every time he bends over to check a date, I get an unobstructed view of his perfect ass. It makes me feel like I've won already. I asked if he wouldn't be too hot out here in long pants, but he only shrugged, grunted, and moved on to find the largest rock in the path we took to get here.

My green cotton tank dress is sensible, cool, and short. I've been waiting for him to notice. I perch on a bulky granite headstone. Is it sacrilegious to sit on a grave marker? I look up. No lightning in sight. A horsefly intent on making a meal of my shin buzzes around me. The headstone in front of me reads "Beloved Mother. Eleanor Anne Fredrickson. 1799."

"Seventeen ninety-nine!" I call out.

Oliver pauses between tombstones, his forehead creasing as he frowns. "I'm not giving up!" He jogs to a new row, his navy shirt stretching nicely over his back. So far he's one-upped me three times. He blew the biggest bubble, whistled the loudest, and found the largest rock. If he finds the oldest headstone, it'll be a shutout.

He bends over to read an inscription, and I know I've lost again. His face practically shines with victory. "Seventeen ninety-two." He crosses his arms, smug.

I'm having serious regrets about teaching him this game. The man never loses.

I walk between gray and white stones in various shapes, sizes, and states of decay. The tall grass tickles the backs of my legs. Oliver bows and extends his arm toward the grave marker of one Eugene Early, who died 1792. Son of a bitch.

"Alright, fine, you win. Again!" I throw my hands in the air, happy to tease him, and stalk away. He follows hot on my heels.

"Oh, no you don't. We're just getting started." He rubs his hands together. "What next? Who can climb highest? Yell loudest?"

"How about who can hold their breath longest?" I suggest.

"You"—he points at me—"are a sore loser."

"No. You are an annoying winner. And I'm done." I toss my hair over my shoulder and walk faster.

Oliver skips beside me, mock outrage on his face. "You're going to quit just because you didn't find the oldest headstone?"

I stop and face him, crossing my arms. "Yep."

He mirrors me. "I don't accept your surrender."

"I didn't surrender. I'm merely refusing to encourage you further."

"Tell me, have you always been a quitter?"

The way he grins, as though he's the cat and I'm the mouse, thrills me. "I'm not a quitter." *Liar.* "I just know when I've been beat."

"Because you're a quitter." He takes a step toward me.

I match his step with one of my own. "I. Am. Not." *Liar.*

Another step and he's within two feet of me. "Prove it."

I cast my eyes around us. The air is thick with heat. Tiny bugs leap from tall grass and hover, as though they've gotten stuck in the humidity. I wipe my brow. Oliver stands, patiently waiting for me to make a move.

The desire to run as we did the night of Luke's party bubbles inside me. Something about this man makes me feel . . . free. Like I'm a kid again. Someone who hasn't quit yet. I can't stifle my smile. He returns it readily, moving to touch me. And I run. I sprint away from him before he knows what's happening, weaving between the headstones and laughing loudly for no reason other than that it feels good to be happy.

He catches me quickly, wrapping strong arms around my waist and hoisting me into the air. "Where do you think you're going?" His lips graze my neck.

The feel of him pressed against my back makes my stomach jump. I laugh, asking him to put me down, but he swings me around until I'm gasping for air. We fall together to the soft earth. He lands half on top of me, his arms still wrapped around my waist. It takes a few moments to catch my breath and grasp the situation. Oliver's smile fades. He's trapped me beneath him.

I lick my lips and draw a heavy breath through my nose. A bead of sweat clings to his temple, and I wipe it away, then run my fingers through his hair. His mouth is open, his breathing shallow. He moves one arm out from under me, and his fingertips trail from my shoulder down to the back of my hand. I move mine from his cheek to the coarse stubble of his jaw. Oliver Reeves is going to kiss me again, this time on a summer afternoon, and I wonder how life will ever be the same.

I trace his lips with my thumb. They're full and soft. We meet in the air between, his lips fitting around mine in a light, sweet kiss. I hold his head close. His lips move in lazy indulgence, unhurried in their pursuit to pluck every drop of pleasure from mine.

I open my mouth a fraction and run the tip of my tongue across his bottom lip. I don't know what possesses me to do it. I don't know anything right now. Oliver presses me into the grass and dirt and fits his hand around the curve of my hip. He slants his mouth across mine, and I let him taste me. His breathing isn't shallow anymore. It's labored and noisy against my cheek.

My hand runs down his back. He always looks so calm, so cool, but I can feel the perspiration beneath his shirt. There's a satisfaction knowing it wasn't the heat that finally got to him, but me. My lips. My hips and short dress and the bare leg he's stroking with strong fingers.

Our kisses become faster, needier. I hold his face in both hands as he touches every exposed part of me. His fingers skim the cotton over my ribs, and I move against him, desperate for the feel of his hand on my breast. He cups me there, groaning quietly against my mouth.

He drags his lips from mine; his forehead drops against my neck. But he doesn't remove his hand or take his weight from me. I arch back, glimpsing dust in a ray of yellow sunlight behind us. His shoulders move beneath my hands as he breathes in deeply. I bring my eyes back to his and see that they're full of need.

He doesn't ask, and I don't say a word. We stand and walk hand in hand, out of the cemetery and back on the gravel path, the one that leads to my car. I reach for the driver's-side door when we get there, but he pulls me away, back to him, and kisses me slowly. When we part, and the air conditioning is again crisp and cool on our skin, we drive to the hotel in silence. There are no words for this, for what each of us needs.

The truth is, our paths parted a long time ago. Now he's looking behind for something he's lost, and I'm running ahead, trying to find something I've never had. It feels like we've collided—run into each other at the place between what could've been and what can be. I don't know how it will affect what we're each searching for, but I've always loved him, and he came back for me. It's enough for now.

***

I rest my chin on my hand, which lies just below his heart. His skin is damp, and my hair clings to it. The bed in my hotel room is somehow infinitely more comfortable now, with Oliver in it. His fingers play a melody on the small of my back. "What song is that?"

He grins, possibly unaware that he's been strumming me like a guitar for the last five minutes. "I don't know. Something new, maybe."

"Something about me?"

He lets a wavy lock of my hair fall between his fingers. "I could write an anthology about *you*."

I smile and turn my cheek against him. Is this real? It feels real. "I guess I must be your muse now."

"You've always been my muse."

I pull myself up until I can look down on him. I let my hair fall to one side so half of the dimly lit room is hidden. "I can't tell if you mean that, or if you're just trying to get me to sleep with you again."

His smile is playful, but I can't return it. I'm not proud of this, but there's an insecure part of me that needs to know if he meant it when he said he came back for me. "Oliver . . ."

He plays with my hair and teases my side with his other hand, waiting for me to continue.

"Last night, you said you came back for me. What did you mean, exactly?"

His eyes reveal nothing but his usual contentedness.

"Why would you come back for me? We hardly knew each other."

His hand follows the curve of my spine right up to the base of my neck. "You have no idea, do you?" He shakes his head. "Wynn, you were my what-if." He must read the question on my lips, because he goes on without prodding. "I know you don't believe me, but I did notice you back then. You were an enigma to me. Every time I tried to help you or make you laugh, you'd turn and run away. Do you have any idea what that can do to a young man's ego?" He laughs easily.

"I was scared to death of you," I admit. "You were so cool, everyone loved you. I wasn't even cool enough to be in the drama club." The sting of my drama club rejection remains fresh to this day. They were the quintessence of geekery during my tenure at North, and *they* wouldn't have me. "I was a dork."

"You were not."

"Massive nerd."

"Says who?"

"Says every single person who knew me. Ask my sisters, they'll tell you."

Entertainment crinkles the corners of his eyes. "Your sisters did not think you were a loser."

"Hey." I slap at his chest. "I didn't say loser. But yes, they most certainly did. Tabby wouldn't even acknowledge me in the hallway, and I was two grades ahead of her. Imagine being a junior and having your freshman sister ashamed to be seen with you."

"Alright, fine. You were a little socially challenged. But I didn't care about that."

Oliver Reeves is not a good liar. I poke him in the ticklish spot I discovered a few hours ago. I can't even process how cute it is. He laughs loudly before pinning my arms to my sides and rolling us over. He kisses me three times.

"You're very persistent." He says the words between more kisses on my neck. He rubs the tip of his nose against me before raising his head.

I want so badly to believe him. His eyes travel over my face. Not for the first time, I wonder what he sees when he looks at me. "Tell me."

He sighs. "Come here." We roll over, and I curl against his side, my thigh over his leg, my hand resting just below his heart again. Oliver plays with my fingers. "Have you ever been in a situation where something you tried didn't quite work out, and you thought, what if I'd done it differently?"

He's just described every moment of my life.

"That was you, for me. I'm not saying I was waiting around for you in high school—"

"My locker was next to Shannon Jefferson's. I remember how much you were *not* waiting around for me."

"But," he says loudly, pausing for effect, "I was taken with you. While everyone else was competing to get noticed, you closed in on yourself."

"My therapist calls it crippling self-doubt."

"You can joke all you want, but—I don't know, it just seemed like you knew something the rest of us didn't. Like you were keeping some great secret to yourself. It drew me in, and I spent a lot of time regretting our missed opportunity."

I smile against him and hope he can't feel the size of it.

"And then you went and kissed me in the parking lot."

I look up. "*I* kissed *you*?"

"Hey, that's how I remember it." He squeezes me tighter.

"Fine, have it your way." I reclaim the spot between his shoulder and chest. "Before your blatant lie, it was getting pretty good."

He makes a delicious rumbly sound when he laughs. "Stop interrupting me."

I nip his skin with my teeth.

"Ow. God, you're meaner than I thought you'd be." He rubs at the spot, though I can tell he liked it. "So *you* kissed *me*, and a couple of days later, I packed my bag and left. And then you just sort of followed me everywhere. You and your *adventure*." He's quiet for a minute. The only sound in the room is his soft breathing. "When you said that . . . I recognized that need to want things. I have it, too."

I keep silent. I don't want to interrupt him. His words seem almost cathartic, like they're cleansing something that's been buried inside of him for a long time.

"I think having a dream makes you lonely. No one understands the way it invades you. The way it prevents you from having a normal life. A dream isolates you from everyone, even the people that love you, because they can't understand why you need to chase it."

He shifts beneath me, and I have to let go of him. We lie face-to-face, our hands pressed together beneath our heads.

"Do you think I'm crazy?"

I shake my head. I know he's not crazy.

He looks at me in the thin light falling through a gap in the curtains. His eyes are dark now, too dark to tell their true color. "I never wanted to be famous. I just wanted to feel connected to people, the way I felt connected to you in that parking lot. I chased it for a long time."

He closes his eyes, and I watch him rest. I've read every magazine article about him and watched every interview he's given, and I've been jealous of him. I saw a man who followed his heart and lived, truly lived, while I stayed and worried and made excuses. Listening to him makes me wonder if that jealousy was undeserved. He got away, but did he find any solace in the dream he chased? Or does he regret his choices, like I do?

I listen as his breath evens out, then roll onto my back. The light outside has faded, and the room is mostly dark. I close my eyes and think of Lola and of what we might find tomorrow. I imagine her face, what it might've looked like when she was young. Did she smile? Did she have dreams? Did something terrible drive her from Grams, or was it that she simply couldn't stay? A thought pushes its way in and as much as I want to, I can't clear it from my mind. Was Lola like me? Did she give in to the desire struggling inside her, even though it meant hurting the people she loved? Am I capable of the same?

NINE

"Are you ready for this?" Oliver reaches for my hand. The sun is heating the car quickly. Today will be another hot one.

I nod, drumming up courage. Behind the door of the Craig House might be the answers I need. Maybe even answers to questions I don't know yet. I squeeze his fingers and step onto the dirt drive of the Craig family home. There's one other car in the lot, probably the curator's. It's an old GMC with faded green paint. Oliver's hand skims my back and settles low on my hip. We take the steps up to the door together.

There was no room for breakfast in my stomach this morning. Oliver did what he could to settle my nerves, but the pull of the string at my waist was strong and persistent. I'll find her here, I'm sure of it.

Oliver turns the knob and steps back, waiting for me to go ahead. The house is cool and smells of wood. An old gas stove, a few ladder-back chairs, and a distressed rug are all the furnishings in the first room.

A man of about sixty with thinning white hair greets us through a hallway on our left. "How you doin', folks?" His accent is thick and pleasant.

I return his smile. "Great, thank you."

"Y'all are welcome to come and have a look around." He removes a folded brochure from a plastic folder on the wall and hands it to Oliver. "That'll give you information on the house and the previous owners. My name's Carlan. Let me know if you have any questions."

"This home was owned by the Craig brothers, right? The ones around during the twenties and thirties?" I ask.

He sticks out his lower lip and nods solemnly. "S'right. The Craig family owned this house from 1878 to 1994, when the last of their kin died and bequeathed it to the state. I can give y'all a tour if you're interested, though I don't know much. The regular gal is out on medical leave. Got a nasty case of gout."

My sympathy for the gout-ridden curator aside, I'm eager to find out how much this man can tell us about the Craigs and, hopefully, Lola. I look to Oliver and he nods toward Carlan, encouraging me to do what we came here for.

My hands shake as I remove the article from the back pocket of my shorts. I hand it to the older man. "This is an article about Michael Craig and a woman named Lola Harrison, my great-grandmother."

"Is that right?" Carlan removes a pair of reading glasses from his shirt pocket and holds the article out before him. "Well, look at that, you got a piece of history on you. Yeah, them Craig brothers were a rowdy bunch. Everyone from around here grew up hearin' stories about their various illegal enterprises."

"They were moonshiners, right?" Oliver's question is more of a statement.

Carlan hands the article back to me. "Among other things. 'Course, that's probably what they was best known for."

"And the woman? Have you ever heard of her?" I ask.

He grabs his chin with a hand spotted by age. "Lola, was it?"

"That's right."

He makes a thoughtful noise and squints toward the ceiling before shaking his head. "Can't rightly recall, but they had a lot of help running whiskey back then and, as I said, I'm not the expert."

My chest falls in disappointment. Oliver moves around me to look at a picture hanging on the wall. "Do you know who's in this picture?"

I stand beside him. The photograph is black and white. There are five people, one woman and four men, all in overalls, standing before a row of wooden barrels connected by pipe. I scan each face but focus on the smiling woman in the center. Her hair is short, and her arms are looped through the arms of the men on either side of her. Carlan comes to stand between Oliver and me.

"Now this I know." He points at each face. "That there is Michael Craig. The one in your newspaper article."

Michael is standing on the far end. Even without Carlan, I would've known it was him. His lively smile is wholly unique.

The substitute curator continues, pointing to another face. "That's Jimmy, his youngest brother, standing on the other side. Jimmy was the prankster of the bunch. If you look real close, you can see he's got a scar on his cheek."

Oliver and I edge forward. A very light line extends from Jimmy's left eye all the way toward his chin. I look at Carlan, beside me. "What happened to him?"

"From what we've been told, he was cheating some other boys at cards. They caught him with an ace up his sleeve or some such, and gave him a helluva beating."

"Jesus." Oliver cringes away from the photo. "Rough town."

"Rough family," Carlan says, again sticking out his lower lip. "Legend is, Daniell there gave it to him." He points to the man on the right of the pretty woman. "Spelled with two *l*s."

My eyes examine the man identified as Daniell. He has unruly hair and a scowl on his face. So unlike the others in the photo.

"Daniell was another brother?" I ask.

"The oldest. And a mean son of a gun, apparently. There beside him is Cecelia Craig, his wife."

My heart sinks as he names the woman in the photograph. For a minute, I was sure it would be Lola.

"And the fella on the other side of her is Patrick, the third-youngest brother. They called him Patty Cake." Carlan chuckles, nodding toward the photograph. "Yep, they were a right squirrely bunch, them Craig boys. This is the only picture we have of the whole family together."

"Were any of the other brothers married?" Oliver asks.

"Michael Craig was married. I'm not clear on her name. She died giving birth, I believe, along with their only child. I don't think the younger brothers ever married, far as I know."

I can't keep my eyes from Michael. Just as in the newspaper image, he looks like he's having the time of his life. I point this out to Carlan, who snickers into his fist.

"He was a handful. Tried to rob the bank when he was no more'n fifteen."

Oliver laughs. "You're kidding?"

"No sir." Carlan shakes his head. "He was a wild thing. My uncle Ty was a kid when the Craig brothers were running moonshine to Louisville. They paid him to leave signals on the railroad tracks if the police was out patrolling. I remember him comparing Michael Craig to the sun. Said people were drawn to him. I reckon that's how he managed to find his way out of trouble. Everyone wanted to be his friend, even the law. Yeah, he became quite the legend in his time." Carlan leans back on his heels.

The pull begins just beneath my belly button. "What happened to him?"

The old man nods to my article. "You've got the answer to that there in your hand. He was captured selling his moonshine. He went to federal prison in Atlanta after that."

An uneasy feeling overtakes me. If Michael was sent to prison, where did Lola go?

Oliver tells Carlan that we'll look through the other rooms on our own. Carlan takes a seat on one of the old wooden chairs and unearths a crossword puzzle and pencil from his back pocket. Oliver takes my hand and leads me to the next room, which must have been the study. Leather-bound books line two handmade shelves over a rolltop desk. Most have no titles on the spines. One is covered in a pretty floral pattern. Almost out of place in such a hard, rustic environment. We examine every surface, every photograph, afghan, and carved piece of wood in the house. But there's no sign Lola was ever here.

"What do you want to do?" He runs his hands down my arms.

I let him pull me into a hug. "I guess go back to Frankfort and talk to that crazy receptionist again. Maybe she can point us in a new direction."

He bends to kiss me. It's thrilling to feel his mouth pressed to mine. Even in this shabby house that holds no answers, it makes me feel hopeful.

We move back the way we came. Carlan stands and offers his hand as we say good-bye, a thoughtful look on his face.

"Now, if y'all are lookin' for more information about the Craigs running moonshine, there's an old-timer you might consider talking to."

"Who?" Oliver asks.

"Name's Eby White. He lives with his great-grandson out in the woods about twenty or so minutes from here. I can give you directions if you like. He's a bit long in the tooth, but he's 'bout the only one left who can give a firsthand account of what went on around here during Prohibition."

"That'd be great, thank you," I say. Carlan writes out a name and directions on the back of our brochure, then hands it to me. "So this man was alive during Prohibition?"

"Yes ma'am. I'm pretty sure he ran with them Craig brothers, too."

Oliver looks skeptical. "Wouldn't that make him close to a hundred?"

The substitute curator nods, rocking on his heels. "A hundred an' four last spring."

***

"Do you hear banjos?"

I punch him in the arm, and he grins at me.

"God, you're mean." Oliver turns the car down a shady country lane. He volunteered to drive us to Eby White's home, citing my nerves as the reason, but I suspect he misses driving, having never had the opportunity to do so on tour.

We pass a rusted piece of metal on the side of the road that's been left burned and twisted. A license plate dangles from what must've been the driver's-side door of an old car. A piece of cardboard with the message "Trespassers Will Be Exploded" is taped to the hood. Oliver can barely contain his excitement.

"Let's hope there aren't any IEDs in rural central Kentucky," I say, scanning the lane ahead.

"Don't tell me you're not having a good time."

Well, maybe I'm having a *little bit* of fun. I point to a spot on the left, about two hundred feet up the road. A white trailer rests, lopsided, in a small clearing. Massive piles of junk on three sides threaten its existence there. "That must be it."

Oliver pulls to the right and cuts the engine. Whether he's excited or not, I know the fear of getting "exploded" makes him reluctant to leave the car.

"Ready?" he asks.

"I don't know." I place a hand against my stomach. I'm as nervous about what we may find as I am about finding nothing at all.

His hand slides against my neck and he brings my lips to his. The first kiss is slow and gentle. He tugs on my bottom lip, encouraging me to open wider. Soon, I'm lost in the fog of him, his scent, his taste, the feel of his hands on me. When he pulls back, I'm disoriented and stupid with happiness, but no longer nervous.

"Ready?" He opens his door. He's tricky, this one.

We walk hand in hand toward the trailer. Birds call to one another high in the trees. Branches sway and creak like rusty hinges on a door. The wind blows up dust but offers no respite from the heat. A circle of chairs sits to the right of the front door around a patch of scorched earth. A half-dozen wind chimes, all partially broken with missing pieces, tinkle softly as Oliver raises his hand to knock. The sound of a shotgun being cocked behind us stops his fist from connecting with the metal screen door.

"What the hell you want?"

Oliver and I slowly turn toward the man's voice. He's at least six feet tall, with disorderly brown hair, a scraggly beard, and small, squinty eyes. He holds a black sawed-off shotgun.

"Don't shoot." Oliver raises his hands and I do the same. "We were told Eby White lives here."

The man is wearing cutoff jean shorts. A smiling red pig adorns the front of his blue T-shirt. "What 'choo want with Eby?"

"We were at the Craig house, and a man named Carlan told us we might be able to ask Mr. White some questions." My voice sounds calm, even though my heart pounds in my ears.

He considers us for a moment, then points the weapon toward the ground. "Y'all aren't cops? You got to tell me if you are, you know. Otherwise it's entrapperment."

Oliver and I lower our hands and shake our heads. I let him do the talking. "No sir. We're looking for information on her great-grandmother. She worked with the Craigs at one time. We were hoping Mr.

White might know something about her." It's cute how Oliver's manners improve under duress.

The man in the pig shirt spits near his feet. "You might've wasted a trip. The old man's crazier than a loon most days." He rears back and yells Eby's name. "You got some folks here to see ya!"

Oliver places a protective arm around me and eyes the shotgun. It's no longer pointed at us but remains a viable threat.

The storm door opens with a long, drawn-out squeak. The arm holding it is thin, the skin around it sagging and covered in dark-brown spots. Oliver and I step forward as the old man lowers his foot to the first of the concrete blocks that serve as the trailer's front steps. He carries a cane in one hand. I move quickly, offering him assistance. He's hunched over and has fluffy white hair coming out in tufts over each ear. His smile is happy and void of teeth. He sets me immediately at ease.

"These folks got questions about them Craig brothers," the man says.

Eby nods to one of the plastic chairs behind me. Together, Oliver and I help him to his seat, then sit down on either side of him.

"You got to talk kinda loud." The man with the pig shirt sits at the other end, laying the shotgun across his knees. "He don't hear so good no more."

Oliver nods and focuses his attention on Eby. "Hello, sir." His voice booms. "My name's Oliver, and this is Wynn." Oliver gestures, possibly thinking the man is blind and dumb as well as deaf. "We were told we could ask you some questions about the Craig family."

Eby's eyes are small and drawn, like the man's behind us, but they're a clear, vibrant blue. "You ain't got to talk so loud, son. I can hear you just fine." His voice is wheezy and gnarled by age.

Oliver looks over his shoulder at the other man, who grins and chews on a piece of straw. Eby waves him off.

"Don't you mind him. Mason likes to have his fun with strange folk."

I lean toward the old man. "We were told you may've worked with the Craig brothers during the twenties and thirties?"

He nods and rocks against the back of his seat. "Oh yes, I worked on the stills out in the woods just over yonder." He nods to the forest behind the trash heap. "'Bout fourteen when they gave me my first job. I was skinny, see, so I could fit inside the stills to clean 'em up and fix the holes the animals would make when they was trying to get at the mash."

"Did you know all of them?" I remove the article from my pocket, anticipating his answer.

"Oh yes. There was four brothers and a bunch of local boys they brought on as their business took off."

"What about women? Did you know any of the women in their operation?"

Eby nods in a slow, exaggerated fashion. "Sure did. There weren't many of them that hung around long. Them boys was too wild to make good husbands."

I unfold the article and offer it to him. "The woman in this article, did you know her?"

Mason, who I presume is the great-grandson Carlan mentioned, speaks up. "He can't read so good anymore 'cuz of the cathterax."

Oliver cuts across us, leaning forward to speak directly to Eby. "Her name was Lola Harrison. She was arrested with Michael in 1931, in a sting operation by federal agents."

Eby rocks in his seat and closes his eyes.

And I wait.

Mason grunts or laughs, I can't tell which. "Told you. His mind comes and goes."

I reach over and take Eby's arthritic hand. His skin is warm and papery. I rub my thumb across his knuckles. "Please. Anything you can remember would be so helpful."

He shakes his head, and my shoulders sag in disappointment, but he opens his eyes. "That weren't her name. Her name was Lola LaBelle. She was a showgirl from Louisville, the prettiest woman I ever saw."

Oliver straightens and smiles at me. I squeeze Eby's hand tighter. "Are you sure? Are you sure it was the same woman?"

"Oh yes. She was Michael's girl. He brought her to town in his brother's green Duesenberg convertible. She wore a sequin dress and a feathered hat. Every man in town stopped what he was doin' to have a look at her. I recall thinkin' she must've been prettier than Helen of Troy."

I hang on every word, edging forward in my seat. "What else can you tell me about her?"

Eby bounces our joined hands on his knee. His blue polyester pants ride high on his waist as though the man, rather than the pants, has shrunk. "Well, let's see. He brought her to town 'round about 1928. I was eighteen and distillin' by that time. The Craigs had the biggest moonshine operation for more than a hundred miles. Michael and Jimmy handled the sales. The rest of us brewed the corn whiskey."

I don't know why, but my eyes sting. I bite my lip and try to keep from making a fool of myself.

"She was a showgirl from some dance hall or club up in Louisville. Michael did some business there and his brother Patrick, we called him Patty Cake, told me the instant Michael set eyes on her, he was in love."

I let my eyes close as a sigh passes through my lips. I hadn't realized until now how desperately I wanted, or needed, her story to be a happy one. "Mr. White, do you know how long she'd been a showgirl?" I ask.

Eby mashes his gums together. "Don't know 'bout that. Just know one day Michael showed up with her, and they was inseparable ever since."

Oliver rests his elbows on his knees. "The man at the Craig house didn't know about Lola. Do you know why? If she and Michael were in love, it seems odd she wouldn't have factored into the Craig story somehow."

Eby smiles at Oliver, and I can see the affection he had for these people on his face. "Only us in the operation knew anything about Michael and Lola. He was a widower, see, and at that time folks around town wouldn't have taken kindly to a newly widowed man shackin' up with a dancer from the big city."

Some of my excitement ebbs away. Lola had to keep hiding. "But he loved her?"

"Oh yes. He loved her more than any man loved a woman before or after. That much I can tell you."

"What did she do for them, as far as the business was concerned?" Oliver asks.

Eby absently squeezes my fingers and continues to rock back and forth. "She worked the books some and kept house with Cecelia."

"Daniell's wife?" I ask.

"S'right. Cecelia was the town beauty. I remember Jimmy and I worryin' that she'd be jealous over Lola. Lola made any woman standing beside her look dumpy in comparison. But they became the best of friends. They used to sing when they was stringing up the laundry. We'd hide in the trees and listen. It was the closest to a lullaby most of us ever got."

"So Lola wasn't running whiskey?"

Eby's gums show as he smiles, his eyes focused on some point in the woods, though I don't think he's seeing so much as remembering. "Michael wouldn't hear of it. He liked to keep her out of the business. He wanted her safe."

Oliver eyes the article in my hands. "But, Mr. White, if Lola wasn't helping them move the alcohol, why was she with Michael the night he was arrested?"

Eby turns his head to look at me. His eyes are so blue, it's as if they've refused to grow old with the rest of his body.

"Eby?" I encourage him, patting his hand.

"You know, I never did get to say good-bye."

I wait, knowing he'll get there on his own.

"She left the keys in the ignition. The car still smelled like her perfume when I got in hours later."

"What car?" I ask.

"The one she stole from me when she went to warn Michael about Daniell."

TEN

Oliver perches on the very edge of his chair. "Daniell? The oldest brother?"

"Yes sir." Eby bounces his knee up and down. "It was Cecelia told Lola 'bout Daniell and the law. I reckon he shouldn't have hit her as hard as he did when he took to the drink. At some point her loyalties shifted from her husband to her friend."

I place my other hand atop the one Eby grips tightly. "Mr. White, are you saying Daniell somehow betrayed his brothers?"

"Oh yes. See, Daniell, being the oldest, felt his place was at the head of the table. But Michael was the smart one. He figured out how to hide the stills, which roads to take to avoid detection, how to keep the money flowin' in. Daniell resented Michael for them things. I don't know if it was the 'shine or the jealousy that finally got to him, but Daniell gave up his brothers to the lawman. He led him to the stills hidden so deep in camouflage you wouldn't have known they was there until you fell inside."

I rub my thumb across the newsprint and stare down at Lola's bowed head, then Michael's effervescent smile. He looks like the cat that caught the canary, and I know, instinctively, the next piece of the story. "Michael already knew. Didn't he? About what Daniell had done."

Eby rocks my hand back and forth. "Michael was a smart man. He knew his brother's nature and that it was only a matter of time before Daniell betrayed him. But Lola was terrified somethin' would happen and Michael'd be killed. I begged her not to go. She kissed me on the cheek and I was so flustered, I didn't notice my keys was missin' until I heard the engine turn. By then, it was too late to do anything more than watch her drive away."

Oliver pushes a hand through his hair. "Wow, that's quite a story."

Eby hums in agreement, incapable of sitting still for more than two seconds.

"Do you know what happened to Michael's brothers?"

He slides his jaw back and forth a few times. "Well, let's see. Patty Cake was caught at the still site. Michael had warned him something might happen and sent him out there to get rid of any remaining liquor and mash. Patty was sent down to Atlanta for six months or so. There wasn't any 'shine by the time the sheriff's deputies showed up, so they couldn't get him on more than a few charges, the worst being ownership of the stills themselves."

"Why were the stills empty?" Oliver asks.

Eby raises his hand to point at Oliver, the fingers too stiff to point on their own. "The gangster from Chicago."

My eyes meet Oliver's. Eby's story is so fantastical, it's hard to process. "A gangster?"

"S'right." He nods his head. There's a rhythm to this story, as though he's told it many times. "Michael made a deal to sell near all the alcohol we had. About twenty or so barrels parceled out in bottles and crates. I reckon after he met Lola, the outlaw life didn't suit him so well. He wanted to get married and start over somewhere new. Least, that was always my opinion of it."

"But"—I don't need to look down. I know the words held between my fingers nearly verbatim—"Michael was caught with only a dozen bottles of alcohol."

Eby's face lights up. He smiles and laughs, remembering. "I would've paid ten dollars to see the looks on their faces when they run him down. All those men, and they never found more than a few bottles of dusty moonshine."

His happiness is infectious. It warms me. "So where did the whiskey go?"

Eby closes his eyes again. I wonder if it helps him remember. "It was Jimmy, the youngest of the brothers. When Michael took the Model T in one direction, Jimmy set off with a flatbed truck in another. And that's when Michael, in a fit of genius"—he stops to look at me, and I see the awe in his eyes, all these years later—"had him switch to the milk truck."

"A milk truck?" Oliver interjects, his tone full of wonder over Eby's story.

The old man's toothless grin reveals only darkness behind thin lips. "That boy drove more than three hundred miles without so much as a fly hitting the windshield to stop him."

So that's what Michael Craig was so happy about in the newspaper photograph. He'd just pulled the rug out from under his brother Daniell's betrayal. I don't know if it's out of solidarity with my great-grandmother, but knowing Michael got the better of his brother and the police fills me with a sense of victory.

"It's an amazing story. Was Jimmy ever caught?"

Eby shrugs his thin shoulders. "Don't know, don't think so. But he was never around after that. Folks said he stayed in Chicago. Maybe even went to work for that gangster they was involved with. I missed him, though. No one could make you laugh like Jimmy Craig."

"We heard he was a bit of a prankster," Oliver says.

Eby chuckles and nods but doesn't respond.

We sit quietly a few moments, each lost in our own thoughts. I go over the story in my mind. Michael Craig was in love with my great-grandmother. So much, he was possibly considering leaving behind the business he'd built to start over with her. She got caught up in things when she tried protecting him from Daniell's disloyalty.

"Mr. White, do you know where Lola went? What happened to her?"

He squeezes my fingers. "The sheriff's deputy held her a little less than a day. They weren't interested in a woman that knew nothing 'bout the business. It was the brothers they were after, and without the liquor, well, they had a hard enough time making the charges stick to the boys. Lola must've walked back to where she'd left the car to warn Michael, then driven home. I found it there the next morning. But she was gone. That's all I know."

I try to be grateful for all he's given me, but I wish there was more. Oliver breaks the silence. "What happened to Daniell?"

Since the moment he stepped from the trailer, Eby's tone and expressions have been light, almost playful. At the mention of Daniell, his mood turns. "He died, 'bout a year after it all happened. Got drunk and shot himself. They ruled it an accident, but I'm not sure. It's a big thing, giving up your family."

His hand no longer pulls jauntily against mine, but lies limp on the armrest of his chair. I wish Oliver hadn't asked. "What about his wife?"

The youth I saw in Eby's eyes fades. "He beat her awful. She hadn't had time to take the girls and run before he was back at the house, drinkin', cussin', screamin', lookin' for someone to blame. He'd made a deal, see? Him and that son-of-a-bitch Fed. Daniell would turn against his brothers, no jail time, and he'd get a cut of the money."

"Not this again." Oliver and I both jump. It's a testament to the power of Eby's storytelling that we forgot about the man with the shotgun behind us. "Go on and tell 'em 'bout the money. That's what they came here for."

I look between Mason and Eby, confused. "What money?"

Mason swats at the air in our direction, seemingly bored with the story he's probably heard a thousand times.

When Eby speaks again, his voice is quiet, lulled away by memory. "Daniell told 'em where to look for Michael, and then he went to collect the money hisself. Only, when he showed up for the handoff, no one was there. And he took it out on that poor woman because he thought, somehow, she'd taken it. Next day, Cece and the girls run off. She couldn't stay after that. He would've killed her eventually. She knew it. We all did."

Eby squeezes my fingers and leans forward. His eyes are round and bright. "It weren't Cece. It was Lola. Lola stole that money. I'm sure of it."

"Lola? But why . . ." I let the sentence fall and look to Oliver. He's just as lost as I am.

Eby relaxes into the chair and closes his eyes. His hand is slack in my grip, though he continues to move his head back and forth in slow, short movements. Birds and bugs carry on around us. I let my hand slide out from under the old man's and sit back in my own chair. Oliver taps a finger against his mouth. His eyes stay trained on me. I'm trying to process everything we've learned, but it's confusing. I feel like I know more and less about Lola's story, all at the same time. She ran away and became a showgirl before ending up here, the mistress of a moonshiner. And now Eby's saying she stole something. Her story's turning out to be bigger than I could've imagined.

"Mr. White?" Oliver lays a hand on the old man's knee.

"He gets like this." Mason scratches at his neck beard. "You had him going pretty good there. Most I've heard him talk in months."

"Do you know more about this stolen money?" Oliver asks.

"Can't grow up 'round this place and not hear the legend."

I look at Eby, but his eyes remain closed, so I turn and face Mason. "Can you tell us?"

"Aww, it ain't nothin' more than a fairy story." He slaps one knee, then stands, the shotgun hanging loosely in his grip. "Y'all want somethin' to drink?"

Oliver and I exchange unsure glances.

"Don't worry yourselves. It ain't rotgut, it's apple pie. Just had a new batch ready last week."

We stand and follow him cautiously around the back of the trailer. Oliver keeps his hand on my hip. "Mason, is it?" he asks.

"S'right." He sets the shotgun against a tree stump. He doesn't verify our names. "Here." He holds out a jar full of orange-colored liquid. "Drink this."

Oliver pulls a face as he sniffs the jar. "Stuff's pretty potent. What's the proof?"

"'Bout a hundred an' ninety." Mason unscrews the lid on his own jar and takes a drink, then wipes his mouth with the back of a dirty hand. "Go on," he says, motioning to us. "It ain't going to take the white off ya teeth."

Oliver sips slowly and swallows hard. "Whoa." He raises his eyebrows in my direction. His voice is strained. "Weren't you saying something about us finding moonshine on this trip?" He offers me a drink, throwing down the gauntlet. Or, in this case, apple-flavored white lightning.

I take it. For me, holding illicit alcohol behind a junky old trailer is doing something. The liquor tastes of apple and cinnamon, but as I swallow, the burn of grain alcohol sends hot vapor through my chest. I breathe it out, blinking back tears. Oliver kisses the top of my head, and Mason nods his approval.

"It's good, ain't it? My daddy's recipe."

As the initial shock wanes, the aftertaste is sweet and pleasant. I take another sip. "It's strong, but yeah, good."

"You be careful with that now." Alcohol sloshes up the sides of Mason's jar. "It'll sneak up on ya."

Oliver takes another drink before trying to hand the moonshine back. Mason waves him away.

"Nah, that's a gift. I figure you deserve that much for visitin' with the old man. We don't get much company no more." He hands a lid to Oliver, who screws it tightly to the jar.

"He's your great-grandfather, right?" I ask.

"Yeah."

"Have you heard that story before? About the Craig brothers?"

Mason nods. "Heard it a million times." His smile ages him. He has two missing teeth, and lines are already forming around his eyes, though he can't be more than five years older than Oliver and me. "There's always people searchin' these woods for the money."

Oliver rotates his wrist, and the alcohol in the glass jar swirls. "Where'd it come from?"

"Their final score, the one he was tellin' you 'bout. Eby says the plan was for Daniell to go and meet the money men, and once the alcohol was delivered safe in Chicago, they was to pay him for the score, here in Kentucky. They was doin' it to confuse the lawmen workin' the case in both states. Only, Michael knew about his brother and changed the plan. Daniell was left waitin' while Michael and Patrick was hauled off to jail. He figured he'd been set up, and somebody else had gotten there first, taken the money and hid it. That's when he went home and beat on his wife. Only, no one seemed to know where that missin' money got off to. Not then, not now. Hell, it might never have existed at all."

"Then why does your grandfather think Lola took it?" I ask.

Mason spits on the ground and lifts one shoulder. "Don't know for sure. Somethin' 'bout protecting Cecelia."

Oliver cuts in. "Daniell's wife."

He nods and looks toward the trees. I can tell he's tired of the story and that we won't get much more out of him.

"One more question," Oliver says. I look at him. He squints at Mason, an undeniable energy in his eyes. "Why do people think the money is in the woods?" he asks.

This puts a smile on Mason's face. "'Cause that's where the stills is at."

"The ones owned by the Craigs?" I ask. "They're still standing?"

Mason takes another drink. "Not so much standing as fallen over, but yeah, they're still out there."

Oliver squeezes my shoulder. I look at him, but his eyes are on Mason. "Can you take us there?"

Mason laughs and points at Oliver's chest. "See, I knew you two was out here lookin' for that money." He turns and we follow.

I take Oliver's hand, my body thrumming with excitement. Mason steps through a small space between two trees on the other side of the driveway, and disappears.

"Are you sure you want to do this?" Oliver asks.

I look over at Eby. He may be sleeping. I'm not sure, but there's a smile on his face. I wonder if it's for Lola. I nod and follow Mason's path. I have serious reservations about going into the backwoods of Kentucky with a man who would wear cutoff jean shorts in 2014, but we've come this far . . .

***

Oliver pulls me up a steep incline, using tree roots as stairs. The forest is dense and the floor is littered with branches, vines, and plants that threaten to overwhelm us. My pretty floral top, chosen specifically for its sweet-to-sexy ratio, is matted down with dirt and sweat. Oliver's doing no better. The back of his gray T-shirt has turned dark. He holds my hand as we struggle to keep up with our guide.

Mason stops at the top of a hill. He takes a drink from his nearly empty jar and howls loudly, the echo bouncing off the ravine below. "How y'all doin'?" He looks no worse for wear. As far as I can tell, he hasn't even broken a sweat. But maybe he sweats moonshine and it reabsorbs into his skin.

"Here—" Oliver helps me jump from one jagged stone to another. "This the high-octane life you always imagined?"

I'm too busy blinking sweat out of my eyes to return the wink he gives me. We reach Mason and look over the side of the hill. The land beyond slopes away dangerously.

"We're going down that?" I say. There are dozens of smaller trees and rocks beneath us.

"No point buildin' an illegal still if it's easy to find."

The man may have serious orthodontic problems, but he has a point. Oliver releases me so I can walk between them. His hand rests against my lower back. He keeps finding ways to touch me and every time he does, a flutter of excitement travels in a circuit through my body. I still can't believe he's here. Holding my hand. Smiling against the skin of my neck. Kissing me. Making love to me.

Mason sings disjointedly as we walk down to the valley below. His spirits lifted considerably when he found out Oliver was a musician. "You know those guys from Primus?" he asks, twisting like an Olympic skier down a tricky patch of mud and grass.

"No." Oliver grabs me around the waist as my foot twists out from under me.

"Megadeth?"

"No."

Mason's disappointment is evident. "Well, who do you know?"

"We opened for Young the Giant a few times."

"Young the *who*?" His small eyes get impossibly round.

I pull up to avoid running into Mason, who's stopped to stare at the rock star behind me. Oliver collides with my back. His hands wind around my waist and cover my stomach. It makes my breath hitch. I can feel the vibration of his voice.

"How much farther?"

Mason shakes his head, disappointed, and continues walking. "We almost there."

I'm hesitant to move, wanting to feel Oliver's body against mine as long as possible. But it's either follow Mason or risk getting lost out here. There are probably scarier things than moonshiners in these woods, so I step forward.

We have to bend over to maneuver through a particularly short clump of trees. It's the most overgrown of any area we've passed through. I step out of the thicket and onto spongy grass. Bright sunlight filters through tree branches. At first all I see are more trees, more hills, and rocks and bumpy ground. Then my eyes pick apart the mirage in front of me.

The soft hills aren't hills at all, but wooden walls draped in vines and moss. They extend forty feet in front of us. Some are caved in and completely overgrown, others still intact, camouflaged by time.

Mason motions for us to follow. "C'mon, I know the best place to get inside."

Oliver reaches out and touches a piece of wooden wall, hidden behind lime-green moss. "You can get inside this?"

"'Course. We used to play out here as kids. I still come out, time to time." He points to a section that's caved in. A piece of rusted pipe is visible beneath the debris. "That there was where they kept the copper stills. Those were all blown up when the area was raided. All the copper's gone now, but some of the old caps and cylinders are still lyin' around." He kicks at a woodpile with his boot, unearthing something. It slithers away.

I grab Oliver's hand.

Mason stands aside and motions us through a gap in the boards. Oliver goes first. The air inside is cool. It's dark, but fingers of light poke through the patchy roof that sags dangerously, preventing Oliver from standing upright.

"Don't freak out."

When someone says "don't freak out," what they're really saying is that there's a reason for you to freak out. I stop moving. "What?"

His hand brushes my cheek. As he pulls back, I see that it's cupped around something with a long black leg. He turns his hand and opens it. A fat black spider falls to the ground. He squishes it beneath his boot, and I sway a little.

"Oh my God." I grab him, barely stopping myself from climbing up the length of his body.

Mason pokes his head inside. "Cool, huh?" He juts his chin to the left. My eyes follow Mason's to a long row of wooden barrels. Pipe, split open and rusted through, reaches to connect one to the other. They extend as far back as the section of caved-in roof over the now-discarded stills.

Oliver steps toward the first barrel, taking hold of my hand. His fingers touch the place where an ax must've busted through the tough wood, spilling its contents to the floor. "This is where they stored the whiskey?"

"S'right." Mason crouches beside him and beckons us to his level. "See, the mash was made at the far end"—he points to the destroyed area—"'cuz it was nearest to the creek. Then they'd heat it up to get the steam going. It'd travel through the cap arm and into copper coils in the cold water box. Coolin' the vapor makes it liquid again, see? The whiskey'd come out through them pipes straight into these barrels here. And *wah-la*"—his smile reminds me of a jack-o'-lantern's—"white lightnin'."

For someone with so much hillbilly, the man knows a thing or two about chemistry.

Oliver nods, taking in everything around us. "Pretty amazing that they were able to run an operation so big without electricity. You could even call it"—he looks squarely at me—"old-fashioned."

I roll my eyes and stand up. As fascinating as the science lesson has been, I want to search for clues. Eby made it sound like the still operation was destroyed after Michael's arrest, which means something may have been left behind. It's a long shot, I know, but I need to look. I leave Oliver and Mason and move to the back of the building.

A three-legged table stands precariously in a corner, its only salvation the roof above it, which must've shielded it from wind and rain over the years. The wood is thick with grime. My fingers hardly remove the top layer as I trail them lightly across. Under the table is a broken chair and a glass jar, foggy with mildew.

I move against the wall, looking for a forgotten piece of paper or a torn photograph. Anything that might fill the gaps in Lola's story. But there's nothing. Oliver moves toward me, hunched over.

"Find anything?" He kisses the damp hair of my temple.

"No. There's nothing here anymore." I step through the makeshift doorway and into the sweltering heat. Oliver hugs me from behind. I know I shouldn't be discouraged. I've learned so much about Lola's life. And it's brought me closer to Oliver, which is something I never thought possible.

We walk back to the thicket of trees. Oliver asks Mason where the stolen money is said to be. He spins around, his hand before him.

"You lookin' at it. This whole area has been combed over by treasure hunters. Ain't none of them found a goddamn thing."

Oliver catches my eye. "Want to have a look around?" I know exactly what he's thinking. The man loves a competition.

The answer is no, not really. I'm hot, sweaty, and persistently fearful of being eaten by wildlife. But there's not a lot I wouldn't do to keep him grinning at me like this.

He calls to Mason over his shoulder. "We're going to have a look around."

Eby's great-grandson sits with his back against a tree trunk and unscrews his jar. "Take ya time." He gulps down moonshine like it's bottled water.

Oliver rubs his hands together. "One-up?"

Oh God. "I knew it. I never should have taught you that game."

"First one to find anything wins."

"What's my prize going to be?"

"My prize," he says, coming close to nuzzle my neck, "will be collected back at the hotel."

Best. Game. Ever.

We break apart to scavenge the area within sight of the ruined still. We call to each other every few minutes. It's unbearably hot out here. I pull my shirt away from my skin and try fanning myself. Who thought it was a good idea to hike in hundred-degree heat? Oh yeah . . . it was me.

I head for shade under a group of trees at the far end of the field. Oliver's whistle carries across the open space. I respond, then sit with my back to a wide tree trunk. The leaves above me are dappled by sunlight. It's peaceful. Quiet. I can see what Lola saw in the place. I let my head fall against the wood and look around. Oliver's black hair is just visible. Then I see something. Something that pushes the breath from my lungs.

I stand and walk slowly, then faster, until my hand falls across the bark of a tall oak. The wood has been scored by a knife. I trace the lines with my finger. Two letters joined by a plus sign.

M+L

ELEVEN

My fingers follow the lines cut into the wood. New bark has tried
growing around it in places, but the cuts were deep, and they've withstood the time that's passed. My chest is crowded with wonder at what
I'm seeing. M+L. Michael and Lola. I know it. A piece of their life has
been carved out and left here for us to find. I let my fingers fall from
the markings but keep them against the tree.

I sense Oliver's presence even before I hear the twigs break under
his boots.

"Jesus." His hand comes forward and he touches the initials. "Do
you think—"

"Yeah. I think so," I cut in, knowing what he's going to ask. I look
over my shoulder. Oliver's gray eyes are almost blue.

"It's amazing. I can't believe you found it."

Blood pounds in my ears. I part my lips, inviting him to kiss me. I
need him to. His mouth touches mine without hesitation, and he turns
me toward him. One of his hands cups the back of my head while the
other holds my waist. The sensation he brings is dizzying and volatile.
It scares me, and I relish it.

He releases my lips. "You're shaking."

Tremors move beneath my skin. "I know."

"Why?" His thumb runs across my cheekbone.

I wait until his eyes are on mine. "I don't know," I admit, laughing. And I don't. Eventually I turn away and focus again on the tree. My great-grandmother's hands touched this place once. Was she happy here? Did she find what she was looking for?

"You want to take a picture of it?"

I shake my head. "No." I feel the letters beneath my fingers one more time. "This was something special, between them." There are things about Lola I want to know, things I need to know, but this . . . this was meant to belong only to her. To them.

The arm he drapes across my shoulders is heavy. "Are you sure?"

"I'm sure." I turn into him, and we step toward the clearing.

Oliver drops his arm and takes my hand instead. We walk to where Mason sits, slumped, beneath a tree. He's passed out, an open jar lying just beyond his fingertips.

"Mason," Oliver says loudly.

The moonshiner grunts but stays asleep.

I get closer and call louder, with no luck. The man is dead to the world. Oliver bends and shakes him until his eyes flutter open.

"What 'choo all doin' here?" He pulls himself up clumsily. He's bleary-eyed and drunk.

"We're ready to head back now." Oliver reaches out and firmly shakes his shoulder. "Mason. You okay to lead us back? Mason." His eyelids sink closed. Oliver grabs his jaw and shakes his head side to side.

Mason fights to gain coherency. His words are less articulate than they were before. "You's red head back?" he mumbles, struggling to his feet. He defies all laws of physics by managing to stay vertical. "Hol' on a min."

He staggers toward the crumbling building and drops to his hands and knees, rooting beneath leaves and debris, unsettling more unseen creatures. Oliver and I exchange worried glances as he pushes himself up, standing bent over, with his back to us.

"What is that?" Oliver leans forward, his head bent to one side, listening.

It almost sounds like he's . . .

Eby's great-grandson turns to face us, a jar of clear liquid tilted against his mouth. The man has found more moonshine. He guzzles it greedily. The shine runs from the corners of his mouth and onto the smiling red pig on his T-shirt. He wipes at his soppy beard, then rears back and crows so loudly, it scares the birds from the trees.

"Goddamn!" He leaps off the ground, a capacious smile on his face. "What y'all waitin' for? We got to get out of here before the rain comes."

***

The windshield wipers work furiously, but the narrow back road remains a blurry mass of brown mud. Oliver leans over the steering wheel. "I can hardly see a thing. I think we should pull over."

But there's no place to pull over to. A thick line of trees butts up to either side of the lane. If another car were to come from the opposite direction, we'd have no way to avoid getting hit. After another minute of driving, the tree line on the right breaks away. I squint through the foggy glass. There's a metal gate a few yards ahead of us. It's hanging open. I can make out the shape of a barn a short distance behind it. The faded red roof calls out like a beacon in this bad weather.

"What about that?" I point to the smudge of wood in the distance. "Maybe we can pull into the barn until the rain lets up."

Oliver turns the car onto a gravel drive and stops. "Do you see a house anywhere?"

I turn in my seat, looking as far as I can see in every direction. The land surrounding the barn is vacant. "No, nothing."

He pulls the car as close to the front of the building as he can get. It's clear from its weathered wood and unhinged doors that the place was abandoned a while ago. Oliver places his hand on the door release. "Ready to run for it?"

I nod, and we climb out of the car and run. The rain pelts my face and arms. Thunder rumbles so loud and close, it makes me jump. Oliver pulls one door back, just wide enough for us to pass through. The noisy hammering of rain barely subsides as we step inside.

Oliver runs a hand over his hair, sending water droplets to the dirt floor. He looks around, assessing the building. "I really hope this thing doesn't collapse on us."

The walls of the barn are full of holes and gaps. Water streams down in several places through cracks in the roof, but otherwise it's dry, and a lot safer than the road we were stuck on.

"I think it'll be okay." The last owners left nothing behind but a few wooden crates, an old boot, and a half-dozen moldy hay bales. I test one of the upturned crates. It seems solid, so I turn it over and have a seat. I'm shivering again, but now it's from the chill of wet clothes. I wrap my arms around myself.

"Cold?" He squats in front of me, running his hands up and down my arms.

"A little. I'm soaking wet."

I watch his Adam's apple bob as he looks at my shirt. His hands stop moving. Every place his gaze lands warms the skin beneath it. I find myself breathing heavily, even though I remain seated.

His eyes linger on my collarbone, and gooseflesh breaks out across my skin. "Do you have a jacket or something in the car?"

My voice is low when I finally find it. "There's a blanket in the trunk."

He stands slowly, almost unwillingly, then turns and disappears through the crooked doorway.

Within seconds he's back, a red wool blanket tucked beneath his shirt to protect it from the rain raging outside.

"Come over here." He picks a dry area and sits with his back against the barn wall. I move over to him and sit between his legs, my back to his chest. He drapes the blanket across me.

I relax, enjoying the comforting way his body rises and falls as he breathes. His fingers brush away the hair stuck to my neck.

"What're you thinking about?"

I don't know where to begin. I'm thinking: How is any of this real? Has he really thought of me, all these years? Why did Lola come out here? Was she running from something, or had she come for Michael? I wonder how Grams would feel about me doing this. She kept the secret of her mother for so long. Was she ever able to let it go? Why did she keep the article?

And beneath all of the unanswered questions about Oliver, Lola, Grams, even my mom and how it'll be between us when I get home, I'm thinking about myself. My life. Can I change it? Do I have the courage to walk away from my family, my friends, the expectations of the life I should be living, and become something . . . more?

I turn my body against him and search his eyes. How much should I tell him? How much does he really want to know?

"I don't want to think anymore right now."

He leans forward and presses his mouth to mine. I'm shaky and scared. I need something tangible, something I can hold in my hands to prove this is all actually happening.

My tongue moves impatiently against his. He guides me to his lap, and my knees fall to the ground on either side of his waist. He peels my shirt away from the damp skin beneath. I grab the hem and pull it over my head. My hair falls in wet waves between us. He unhooks my bra and pulls it down my arms, then grabs the waistband of my shorts. When he slides them down my legs, his eyes grow very dark.

Our movements are hurried, anxious, the need to touch over-whelming. I lean forward to taste the sweat and rain clinging to him. He kisses my shoulder. I unbutton his jeans.

Once it's just us, and nothing else, his fingers move lightly against me. His explorations are met with sharp intakes of breath. I run my tongue across his lips. I feel wanton, blinded by my need to be with him. To feel anchored to him. I move my hand between us, but he pulls it back and tells me to wait. He reaches into the back pocket of his jeans, removing his wallet. His actions are fast and jerky, his body hard with impatience. He takes a condom from the leather billfold and quickly rolls it on.

In my need, I forgot about protection. Maybe I'm becoming care-less, because the more we're together, the more I want to let go, be reck-less and young and not worry about what I'm *supposed* to do. I close my eyes and let my head fall back, giving in to the pleasure of the moment. Being connected to him feels surreal, dreamlike. But I don't want it to be a dream. I want him to love me. I want him to stay for me. Would he, if I asked? He holds me close and I rock back and forth, forgetting where we are or why we came. All I know is the sound of my name on his lips. I close my eyes and let go of everything but this moment.

***

I run my fingers across Oliver's chest. Wool fibers prick and scratch my skin as I move closer to him. The last time I used this blanket was during a field trip to the pumpkin patch last fall, when I subbed for a fourth-grade class. Good thing I never clean out my car.

Oliver runs his hand across my shoulders. "I will never be able to drive past a barn again without smiling."

I laugh against him. The rain has let up some. Every once in a while, thunder rolls slow in the distance. His steel-gray eyes are focused on the wooden shingles of the roof. I drop my gaze to his chest and the waistband of the jeans he put back on. We're both a little sticky from the lingering humidity the storm didn't wash away.

"Let me ask you a question. If you could go anywhere in the world, where would it be?"

It seems like such an Oliver thing to say. "I don't know." I draw circles over his skin. "Australia? Africa?"

"You want to go on safari?"

"Maybe."

"Where else?"

My lips graze the skin just below his nipple. "Um . . . New York, Paris, London, Berlin, Rio—"

"You've *really* never been to any of those places?"

I burrow into the crook of his arm. "Nope."

"I'll take you to all of them." His fingers tickle the dip of my back. "You would?"

"Would you go with me?" His voice is soft, pensive.

I close my eyes. "Yes."

"Promise?"

I rub my lips against him so he can feel my smile. It's one of those things that makes you want to cry for no good reason. A happy thing that makes you sad at the same time. "Promise."

He shifts, dislodging me from my resting place. He places an arm under his head, facing me, and uses the other to pull me against him. I wish I could read his thoughts. I loved him from afar for so long, I convinced myself I knew him. But I don't, really.

"Are you glad we came?" he asks.

"Yes."

"Me, too." His breath feels like a whisper against my cheek. "Do you think we'll find anything else?"

"Yes."

"Why are you so sure, all of a sudden?"

I concentrate on the tugging sensation against my abdomen. "I just know."

His gaze won't release me. "Are you worried?"

"Yes."

He waits for me to tell him.

"Everything up to now has been about her life after she left. I think what I really want to know, what I need to know, is *why* she left."

"Why does that matter?"

I look down. "I'm afraid maybe she was a bad person." My throat constricts, forcing me to swallow. "It scares me. Because I think I might be like her."

Oliver's fingers move back and forth across my hip. "You're not a bad person, and chances are, she wasn't either."

I wish he would kiss me now, so I wouldn't need to say any more. "She hurt her family."

"She did."

"She ran away."

"Yes." He places a light kiss on my mouth. "Is that what you think you're doing? Running away?"

His words unsettle me. "Yes."

He leans forward, and I close my eyes. His lips press gently against my forehead, then the bridge of my nose, then the apple of both cheeks. "You're not running from anything. You're running toward something."

"How do you know?"

"Because you're looking for answers. People who run away don't look back." He raises an eyebrow. His smile is tender, gentle. He has experience leaving. Moving on. "Whatever your family believes, you know there's more to her story."

"But what if—"

He quiets me with a kiss. "No more what-ifs."

I pull my arm away and touch his face. "Sometimes I can't believe you're really here." I rub my thumb across his lips, tracing his smile as I did the letters carved in the tree. "Would you do something for me?"

"Anything." I know he means it.

"Sing to me."

His laugh is quiet. He shakes his head. "You had to ask for that, didn't you?"

I run my fingers through his hair. "I wasn't trying to trick you."

"I know. I want to, and I will, just not yet."

"This from the man who doesn't believe in putting things off?" I tease.

Oliver places his hand over mine on the blanket. There's something tired in the way he looks at me. As though he's exhausted. "I feel like I've been trying so hard to make something fit, I've damaged it."

I know what he's saying. Every day I force myself to live a life that doesn't feel right. I want it to, and I try my best to make things work, but you can't be something you're not—at least, not forever. But he and I are not the same. He's bold, fearless in what he wants.

I lean forward and place a kiss on his cheek. "You're going to be okay."

The rain has died away. We'll need to leave soon. For now I let the weight of his hand press against mine. He's quiet so long that when he answers me, I have to think back to what I said.

"Thank you," he says, pulling me close. "Thank you."

TWELVE

"You all packed?" Oliver grabs the handle of my suitcase and pulls it toward him across the bed.

"Yeah. Hey, have you seen my phone?"

"On the nightstand." He opens the door, and early morning sun bathes the room.

I spot the black phone beneath our map. The weatherproof pages are bulky from an improper fold. I spread it out on the red-and-gold comforter and refold it carefully. A green-and-white placard is printed across the top, declaring it property of the Kentucky Historical Society. Oliver returns to the room, and I hold the map up so he can see.

"Did you steal this?"

"What?" The word is overly exaggerated. "Of course not. What kind of rock star do you think I am, stealing government property?" He busies himself throwing the remnants of our breakfast, which consisted of dry cereal, yogurt, and coffee, in the trash can.

"Oliver." I cringe. I sound just like my mother.

"Wynn," he imitates. He can't hold the innocent look on his face. "Okay, I took it, but I didn't steal it."

I wait.

"Honestly. That receptionist told me I could borrow it."

"Huh." I slap the pages against my side. Enjoying the way he squirms when put on the spot. "Borrowing usually implies that you intend to return it."

"It does." He crosses his arms and nods in agreement.

"But we're not going back to Frankfort. Are we?"

He raises a finger in the air. "A technicality for which I cannot be held responsible."

I throw the map at him. A mistake. He bounds around the bed, picks me up, throws me on the mattress, and tickles my sides. My body aches from laughter after only seconds. I really should learn to pick my battles with him.

"Uncle!" I scream, and he withdraws his fingers, only to wind them around my wrists, which he holds over my head.

"I love it when you use your strict teacher voice," he murmurs against my throat.

"Oh yeah?" I move my hips beneath him.

"Yeah. Say something else." He drags his lips up my neck, sending a thrill through me.

I can barely think with the length of his body pressed against mine. "Mr. Reeves, I think you need detention."

His groan, mixed with a deep laugh, vibrates through me. "More," he begs.

I tease his earlobe with my tongue. "I think you need to be punished for stealing. Come and stand at my desk."

He moves his hips, trying to part my thighs. A loud bang, like a car backfiring, makes us both jump. The door to the hotel room is still open, and I hear voices outside. They're close.

Oliver hangs his head momentarily, then rolls off me, pulling on the front of his pants. He bends his knees and throws an arm over his face. "I'm going to need a minute."

I kiss his cheek and get up. As I approach the door, a young woman passes by with a little girl and boy in tow. They're arguing loudly, and the boy is trying to take something from the girl. Her hair is dark brown, like mine, and she's wearing it in pigtails. The object of their fight is a small pink book. The woman turns and snatches it out of their dueling hands.

"I told you both to stop fighting. Now no one gets the book." She looks up and notices me in the doorway.

I smile, not wanting her to think I'm eavesdropping.

"Sorry," she says, putting the book in an orange canvas bag, the kind you take to the beach.

"Oh, no problem." I look down at the small faces staring up at me. "I like your pigtails," I say, bending to place my hands on my knees.

"Fanks," she says, her mouth wobbling dangerously in a frown. She points a chubby finger at the boy. "He tried to take my dairy."

"Your dairy?" I look up at the woman, who I presume to be their mother.

She rolls her eyes. "Her *diary*," she explains.

"Oh," I say. The girl's eyes are a light brown, ringed in green and swimming with unshed tears. "I understand. Diaries are very personal."

"Yeah," she says, shoving her brother in the shoulder. He sticks his tongue out at her and then at me.

I wave good-bye to both as their mother ushers them forward, warning them to behave or they won't get to play in the pool. I straighten, and an idea takes hold of me so firmly, I nearly lose my balance. Oliver, who must've seen this, jumps up and comes to stand beside me, placing his hand beneath my elbow.

"Are you okay?"

I nod, walking slowly to the bed.

"What happened? You look pale."

I touch the polyester of the bedspread, not even realizing I sat down. I look at my hand. I didn't notice the pattern on the bedspread before. The dots connect slowly in my mind. Red roses lined in gold. Red flowers . . . I saw a similar pattern yesterday, one with red, pink, and blue flowers sewn on the binding of a book.

Oliver's face is lined with worry. "What is it?"

I can't stop tracing the flower beneath my hand. "We need to go back to the house."

***

The green car is parked in the same spot as yesterday. Oliver pulls in beside it, removes the key from the ignition, and hands it to me. I was too nervous to drive. *What if I'm wrong?*

My hands are shaking and he covers them with one of his. "You ready?"

No. Yes. I've got so many thoughts running through my mind, I can hardly think. My stomach is in knots, but the pulling sensation is stronger. I look past Oliver, out the window, and take a deep breath before nodding. He squeezes my hands and releases me, then steps out of the car. I pull myself from the passenger's seat slowly, almost high with excitement. My heart is beating a thousand beats a minute, like I've run a marathon.

He waits for me to come around and places his hand on my back. I'm grateful to him. Not only for the strength he's lent me during this trip, but also because when I told him about the idea that had struck me in the hotel room, he didn't laugh. In fact, the look he gave me said he believed I might be right.

The porch creaks beneath us. Oliver pulls open the door, and I step again into the Craigs's home. Lola's home. Footsteps click across the floor from the hallway. Carlan appears and smiles, clearly remembering us. I don't suppose the house gets too many visitors. Especially ones that show up twice in less than two days.

"Well, hello again." He offers each of us his hand. "What brings you two back so soon?"

"We were hoping to have another look around," Oliver says, dropping his handshake. He's using the same voice on Carlan he used on Kathleen from the Historical Society.

"Of course, of course." The curator moves around us. I see a new crossword puzzle folded in his back pocket. "Say, did you two make it out to Eby's place?"

I'm too full of energy to adopt Oliver's casual tone, so I let him continue to do the talking. "We did, and thank you for the information."

Carlan tilts his head to one side, looking keenly at us. "Was he able to give you the information you were looking for?"

"He did. It was pretty amazing, actually," Oliver says.

"Good. Yep, there's still an old-timer or two in this town that can weave a story. I'm glad he was up and around. That grandson of his is a rascal, ain't he?"

Oliver and I look at each other and share a small laugh. His presence steadies me, and my intuition makes me feel strong and sure of myself. "He was quite interesting," I say.

Carlan chuckles into his fist. "I'll tell you. That boy is crazier than a cat in love with a dog. But I'm glad you got some questions answered. Go on and have another look around. I'll be on the porch with my puzzle." He pulls the paper from his back pocket, waving it at us as he leaves through the front door.

We remain standing, half-facing each other, both waiting for the other to make the first move. Excitement, fear, anticipation, hope . . . I try to tame my smile, try to reel it in, in case I'm wrong. Only, I don't think I am.

We move quickly to the room that looks like a study and stand before the two slightly crooked bookshelves. I reach out, and my fingers land on the spine of a book that's different from the others. The faded floral pattern is feminine, and the book itself is smaller and thinner than the ones beside it. I pull it out, holding it with both hands. Shaking hands.

Oliver says nothing, just waits beside me, ready to let me take my time. I turn the cover over. It's stiff, and the binding creaks with age. The pages inside are crisp, though a little yellow around the edges, like the newspaper article now folded neatly in my purse. I turn a few, careful not to tear them. Black ink fills almost every inch. The handwriting has faded some, but remarkably, even after eighty-plus years, the script inside is completely legible.

My eyes see words I can hardly process. They steal the breath away from me. I look at Oliver, unbelieving. "It's hers." The script is loopy, lovely, and wide. I read aloud, and he moves to stand behind me, looking over my shoulder. "This is the diary of Lola Elizabeth Harrison." I turn to the first page. My mouth is dry. I wet my lips before reading on.

17th September 1927

I don't know where or how to begin. I've abandoned my child. It seems trivial to write something so awful on a piece of blank paper. These words would be better placed in an obituary, though my intention in leaving was to live. Still, the words feel too new and horrible to be true. I caught sight of myself in the train window, and for a moment I thought it was a stranger staring back. Grief and doubt have aged me in the hours since leaving my Elizabeth, and I wonder how I'll live with what I've done, and if I'll ever feel young again.

I stop. I can't believe it's here. Sitting at the hotel, thinking of the floral pattern stitched across the spine of this little book, I *knew*. I knew what it must be. That it was hers. That she existed. Now I hold the proof in my hands. What I didn't want to find was the truth my mother was so certain of, that she abandoned her daughter of her own free will.

Oliver wraps an arm around me. His mouth is close to my ear. "I'm sorry. I know you were hoping for something else."

I close the book and hug it to my chest. "It's stupid. I just thought, maybe . . ."

He presses his face against my hair. "I know." He releases me.

The book feels much heavier than it should.

"Don't you want to read it?"

I run my thumb across the cover. It might be made of thick cotton. I'm not sure. The needlework raises the flowers beneath my fingers. I look around the room for somewhere to sit and read.

Oliver lays his hand against mine and presses the book to my chest "Take it," he whispers.

"What?" I shake my head, confused.

"Take it with you."

"Oliver, I can't just . . . steal it," I whisper back.

"Why not?"

I open my mouth to make up an excuse but stutter on the words. "Because that's—it's not—it doesn't belong to me."

"If it doesn't belong to you, than who the hell *does* it belong to?"

I look at the book in my hands. This is my chance to find out what happened to Lola. "I'll just read it here."

"And leave it to sit unread and unappreciated for the rest of time? No one here's going to miss it, but it's your family story, your legacy. It belongs with someone who cares about her. Take it."

I'd never stolen so much as a dollar in my life before the achievement ribbon. Now I'm contemplating stealing a book from what is, essentially, a museum. I look around the room. It's deserted, lonely. I can't leave her, what's left of her life, here in this place. I open my purse and drop the book inside. We leave quickly, telling Carlan we need to get back on the road.

As Oliver turns onto the highway ramp, I find myself laughing, louder and longer than I can ever remember doing before. I'm a rebel, an outlaw, and it feels good.

***

Green Kentucky hills roll endlessly in front of us. Oliver takes a bite out of an apple, and it crunches loudly against his teeth. After leaving the Craig house, we decide to grab some provisions and find a quiet place to read Lola's diary.

The endlessness of the landscape is beautiful. Downers Grove is quaint by Chicago standards, with its little shops and manicured parks, but it's always full of people. After college I thought about leaving the city and the suburbs. For a few weeks, the idea of backpacking through Tuscany or the south of France consumed me. I even bought a few travel guides. Then something—I can't even remember what—got in the way. I don't know where those books are now. Lost at the bottom of my closet, maybe.

I sit on the grass between Oliver's legs. I've decided it's my new favorite way to sit. He offers me an apple. I bite down, and sweet juice fills my mouth. The book rests on my thigh, waiting for me to open it. It felt like an anvil in my lap the whole way here. I wanted to read it, and at the same time, I wanted to prolong the moment. I'm afraid of what more we'll find inside.

"I could get used to this." Oliver takes a sip from a bottle of beer.

"Me, too." It's not as hot out today, and there's a nice breeze. I could stay beneath this tree with him forever.

He nudges me with his leg. "You ready to read me a story?" He offers me the drink.

I take a sip and then another. "Almost."

We eat and drink in silence for a while. I close my eyes and rest my head against his chest. I haven't talked to my mom since leaving. What'll she say when I turn up with Lola's diary? Will she even want to know the truth? And what if the truth turns out to be everything she said? The first entry paints a pretty bleak picture. But I keep thinking about the initials carved into the tree. Whatever else she did, whoever she became, Lola was in love once. I can relate to that.

Oliver's arm reaches around me. He picks up the book. "You'll never know until you read it."

How does he do that? How does he know the questions that burn inside of me? I take the book in both hands, opening it carefully, and turn to the page with the first entry we read back at the house. It feels deeply personal to read someone else's private words. Like you're stealing something from them, which I guess I am.

"This is from the same entry." I read the words slowly so I can savor them.

This morning I gathered two dresses, a pair of silk stockings, my mother's patchwork blanket, and a few items from the bureau. I purchased this book from a man selling newspapers and oranges inside the station. I meant to buy the orange. I don't have much money, only what I've been able to sneak away from Dutch. I guess that makes me a thief as well. But my hand landed on the book, so now I sit hungry as I wait for the next train. I will use these pages as a diary. I don't know what will become of me or if I'll survive on my own, but it feels important to keep a record, if for no other reason than to remind myself why I left.

The parallel of her words with my own actions strikes me. I look at Oliver, and he inclines his head, urging me to continue.

18th September 1927

I've found a room in a lady's boardinghouse. It's not much, and nothing more than a single bed, a small desk and chair, and a bureau that's seen better days, but it'll do. The landlady, Mrs. Blanch, seems kind enough. She didn't ask many questions, which is good. What would I tell her, anyway? That I've run out on my husband and child? That I've got only enough money to last me until the end of the month? That after that, I'd rather live on the streets and starve than go back? I can't tell her these things. I can barely say them to myself.

21st September 1927

The wind coming off the Ohio has a chill. I'll need to buy a coat before long. I wanted to bring the wool jacket Mary Ellen sewed for me when I was pregnant with Elizabeth, but there was no room for it in my bag.

Elizabeth. I think of her more times than I breathe in a day. I wonder what she's doing now, if she's been crying for me? I hope Dutch will give her my letter when she's old enough to understand. I can't go back, I know that.

I went to the Seelbach Hotel to look for work as Mrs. Blanch suggested. The manager had a kind manner about him and promised to see me again a week from Thursday to discuss a job as a maid.

I've never been anywhere so beautiful. The hotel reminded me of a painting I saw in school. The walls and floor were made of marble. The railings on the stairs appeared to be built from solid gold. Every surface, every crack and crevice, glowed with an amber light. I wanted to stay longer, but I was afraid to be seen lingering.

I turn the page.

29th September 1927

I feel I can finally breathe for the first time since leaving. I've gotten a job! I smiled all the way back to the boardinghouse. It felt so foreign to me that I wondered if I were wearing someone else's face. I can't remember the last time I smiled or felt hope. I begin work tomorrow morning at five a.m. sharp. Mr. Kennedy warned me not to be late, and I don't intend to be. It'll mean rising before four a.m. but the money will keep a roof over my head. We're served two meals a day, for which I am eternally grateful. I've lost so much weight since leaving. I look like a child playing in her mother's clothes.

I pause, reading the passage again to myself. I'm torn between her excitement and my own sadness for my grandmother.

"She was a beautiful writer." Oliver's voice startles me. I got lost in Lola's words.

"Yes, she was."

His fingers play with a strand of my hair. "What is it?"

I shake my head. "It feels wrong to root for her, when I know what my Grams and her father must've been going through after she left."

He says nothing, just keeps twisting my hair around his finger.

"I don't know." I shrug against his chest. "It just makes me sad."

Oliver releases my hair and strokes my upper arm. "Keep reading. Let her tell her own story."

I run my finger down the page, following the last entry. He's right. If I want to understand why Lola did what she did, I need to let her words be the ones I hear. The rest—my grandmother's pain, my mother's resentment, even my own hope that Lola's story will somehow give me courage to change my life—all of those voices must be quiet.

THIRTEEN

9th October 1927

I had the day off and decided to take a walk. I thought the people here would be different than the ones in Chicago. But they're the same. They move through the streets hurried and restless, and when they look at me, they look straight through me. I'm so dreadfully tired of feeling invisible.

What if Dutch was right, and I'm useless and stupid and I'll never be anything more than the woman who cleans his shoes and has his babies? What if, after everything I've given up, I still die alone in this room with the cracked window and threadbare blanket? I wake up crying, terrified that his words are true. But I had to try. I had to leave before I became nothing at all. I couldn't live a whole life existing only in the shadows.

It seems to me now that hope is a terrible thing. It's the only emotion that pushes you forward and holds you back at the same time.

28th October 1927

I saw a little girl in the street today that looked so much like Elizabeth. I ran to her and called her name. She had lovely blonde hair, but her eyes were blue instead of brown. Her mother pulled her away from me. I stood in the street until a man led me away. I can't remember his face. Hers is the only one I see. I thought it would become easier. I've been keeping busy at the hotel, and I help Mrs. Blanch with the housework three nights a week. But Elizabeth creeps into every thought . . .

11th November 1927

There was a man on the street in front of the hotel today selling ladies gloves. I thought maybe they were cheap imitations of the fine ones I see on the women in the Oakroom, but they were lovely and soft. He wanted five dollars a pair. I handed them back so quick you'd think they had burned me. I explained to the man that I couldn't afford them. He told me I reminded him of someone he loved very much, and if I would only smile at him, he'd give me a pair for free.

His request was so ridiculous, the smile came to my face without consideration. He handed me a pair of blush-colored gloves without another word. I tried to give them back, but he said the exchange was to his benefit. He wouldn't take them. I told him it wasn't right, selling a pair of leather gloves for a smile. He looked at me with such affection, it nearly broke my heart. He thanked me.

He left me in a daze.

I tucked the gloves into my apron pocket and joined the others for work. The weight of them against my thigh felt like a secret. Like something private and dear. I wore them home, and my hands didn't sting from the cold.

A man in a long black coat tipped his hat at me as I passed, and I bowed my head at him, unable to hide my smile.

I placed the gloves in the top drawer inside the folds of the tattered old shawl I wore when I arrived here, nearly two months ago. I stayed at the dresser for a long time, admiring the stitching and the evenness of the color. They're the first thing I've ever owned that makes me feel special.

22nd November 1927

A policeman came to visit Mr. Kennedy as we sat down to lunch today. He looked at me several times. I was sure Dutch had reported me missing, and the police had come to take me home. I knew Dutch wouldn't be able to let me go so easy. But the man left without saying a word. The whole situation made me feel jumpy and nervous.

I came back to my room in a panic, wondering what I'd do if my husband came to collect me. I think I'd throw myself in the river before I'd let that happen.

Wake up, light the stove, cook the breakfast, sweep the floors, beat the rugs, wash the clothes, peel the potatoes, iron his shirts, sew her dresses, make the dinner, clean the dishes, fill the bath, wash his hair, trim his beard, lie beneath him . . .

I won't die if they take me back. I was dead when I left.

1st January 1928

Mrs. Blanch shared a glass of her good cider with me at midnight. It was nonalcoholic, of course, but I imagined it otherwise. We toasted to our good health and that of our families. She doesn't know my true circumstances, of course. Shortly after I arrived, I told her my brother had sent me from Chicago to find a job and a suitable place to live before he and his wife would come to join me. I made up an elaborate story about him trying his hand at insurance and his wife and I being old schoolmates. I think she must know by now I wasn't being truthful, but she toasted them anyway.

As I sit in my room during the first hour of the New Year, my thoughts turn to Elizabeth. I've written her several letters, but none that I can mail. Dutch would only burn them. For some reason the turning of one year into another has given me more courage. I've made it on my own out here. My back and feet ache from the long days, and my hands are pink and cracked from soap flakes. But those things don't bother me. I'm living for me now. Every ache and pain is mine alone.

3rd February 1928

A funny thing happened. Mr. Kennedy asked if I would assist him in set-ting up the decorations for a party in the Rathskeller tonight. I've never been inside the room before today. I was amazed at its size and the beauty of the tiled floors, arched ceilings, and ornate sconces. There are sculpted pelicans in the pillars. Can you imagine?

A man dressed in a tailored navy suit came down as I was arranging the flowers. He handed Mr. Kennedy a list and turned to leave, but he stopped when he saw me. I kept working, but I heard him inquire after my name.

At the end of my day, Mr. Kennedy called me into his office. I was nervous he'd somehow found out my secret, but all he asked was whether I was happy with my position in housekeeping. I assured him that I was.

He said he felt perhaps my talents were wasted; perhaps I should be working as a cigarette girl in the Oakroom instead. I was shocked and could only ask if he meant me?

He called me a lovely girl, which made my face grow hot and my hands sweat. I know what they say about the girls who work in the clubs and restaurants. They're wild and unrespectable. Flapper girls. I asked if I could think about it, and he gave me until the morning to decide. Before I left he told me the new position would come with a raise in income, and that I could expect to earn as much as thirty-five dollars per week!

The truth is, and you are the only one to whom I can tell the whole truth, I wonder why I left Illinois if not to do something exciting and maybe a little dangerous.

I'd just turned seventeen when I married Dutch because of the baby. I didn't know him then. He told me he would take me everywhere I ever wanted to go and show me everything I wanted to see. But he lied. All he ever wanted was a slave to keep his house and a whore to warm his bed.

I know as I write this that I will go to Mr. Kennedy first thing in the morning and accept the job. I want to live fully and laugh loudly and be young again. If I don't strive for those things, all of this was for nothing, and I've lost Elizabeth to fear rather than possibility.

9th February 1928

My hands are shaking so badly, I wonder if I'll be able to make heads or tails of what I've written. Tonight was my first night in the Oakroom. The costume is a black satin dress that falls just above the knee with sleeves tight past my elbows. White crocheted silk dips beneath my collarbone in a V shape. I have never in my life worn anything so daring. Thank goodness I thought to pack the silk stockings Mary Ellen gave me as a wedding gift.

I was worried the other girls would think me an ugly duckling or a country bumpkin, but they're a kind and happy bunch. One of the girls, Kristine, even helped me pin my hair back in waves so it looked as though I had the same short bob as the others.

I was so nervous, I nearly burned the first man to ask me for a light. I managed somehow. A couple of men reached to touch my legs as I passed, but most were polite and respectful, and all of them tipped. By the end of the night, I had more than seven dollars in my apron. I was nervous about walking home with so much money, but Kristine told me to keep it in my shoe. She said that way, if I was accosted, they wouldn't think to look there and would let me go. It made getting home a little sore, but spreading the green and silver out on my bed was worth it.

I've hidden it and I won't write where in case this book is found.

I'm so happy I could scream. For the first time since I was a girl, I feel like all I ever wanted could happen. I don't know how I'll sleep tonight.

15th February 1928

Yesterday was Valentine's Day, and the hotel lobby and all the rooms were transformed with red and white roses. I felt a bit morbid amongst the holiday splendor in my black hat and coat, but I didn't want anyone seeing my new hairstyle until Kristine had a chance to freshen me up. On Sunday, she took me to the apartment of a friend of hers. She said her friend "has eyes as sharp as scissors."

Her friend's name is Dora, and she answered the door in nothing but a peach slip and an open dressing gown. I was a little shocked when she offered me a drink. It was hardly past two o'clock, not to mention it's illegal!

But Kristine said it's illegal only if you buy it or sell it. We can drink it all we like.

I didn't want to look like a ninny, so I took some in a small crystal glass. I've had alcohol only once before when I was still a girl in school. It tasted like expired medicine, and I spit it out. Dora's sherry tasted tart, and it was hot in my throat, but I swallowed it, not wanting to seem rude.

I asked Dora how she came to have it, and she said a man she sees socially knows a bootlegger from near Bardstown.

I didn't take the cigarette she offered, but I did finish my drink. It gave me a warm, pleasant sort of feeling. I wonder now if she gave it to me so I'd relax about my hair. After a second glass, I hardly knew what was happening. It wasn't until I woke up yesterday morning and looked in the mirror that I remembered about it at all.

The other girls complimented me on the way my dark curls, now short and close to my head, make me look like a modern woman. A famous writer who comes in from time to time told me I looked like a heroine sprung from his imagination. I think I must have blushed brightly, because he looked a little embarrassed when I was next at his table.

The evening was long and full of dancing. Bursts of laughter were everywhere through clouds of blue smoke. I smiled so much my face feels swollen.

It's early now; the sun hasn't risen, though there's red on the horizon. I really should get to bed, but I find, more and more, that sleep is impossible after a night among such jollity and decadence. I wish I could go back and stay in those hours forever.

29th February 1928

Today I have no happy words to write. I rose to assist Mrs. Blanch with lunch, and she asked if I might make a lemon tart for dessert. The smell of sugar and lemon reminded me so much of Elizabeth, I had to run to my room and burrow beneath the covers. I try so hard to put her from my mind. I feel like a wretched coward for leaving her as I did. I should have taken her with me. I should have risked it in order to be with her now.

But I was scared. I didn't know how or if I'd be able to make any money, and the threat of starving to death was all too possible. I was prepared to take the risk myself, but not for my little girl.

There are so many grand things in the world. So much to do, see, and feel, but they'll never make me whole. How can I be, when I left part of myself behind?

19th March 1928

When I was very young, I had a nightmare about a masked man who came to take my family away from me. I remember waking sweaty and scared with my mother's hand on my back as she tried to calm me down. She whispered it had been a bad dream, but it felt so real. Even now I can recall how my voice cracked and pleaded with the man to bring them back. I was afraid of being left alone in the dark.

Last night I had the dream again, only this time the masked man was not taking my family. He was taking me away from Elizabeth. I fought him, but he was so much stronger than me. I tried tearing the mask from his face, but it wouldn't come off, as though the mask itself was his face, dark and void of eyes or mouth. Elizabeth reached for me, her little fingers outstretched, desperate to touch mine, to bring me back to her.

I woke up as I did all those years ago, sweating and shaking with sobs. I couldn't return to sleep after. A painful uneasiness settled in my stomach and lingers even now, with the sun touching the corners of the window. Perhaps it's an omen of something bad. Maybe it's a mother's intuition, and something terrible has happened to my little girl.

My dream followed me out of the night and into the day. I don't think I'll help Mrs. Blanch this morning. I think I'll return to bed and hope for nothingness.

12th April 1928

The air is warm and sweet today. I went to the waterfront with Kristine, and we got bags of roasted nuts and lemonade. She said I need cheering up and has made me promise to go dancing with her tonight. I've never been to a club before, at least, not as a patron. I told her I didn't have anything appropriate to wear, and she said not to worry. She has lots of pretty dresses that will suit me. She was so excited over the prospect, I could hardly say no.

I've just dusted my face and shoulders and expect her at any moment. The dread, which has sat like a pit in my stomach for weeks, feels a little smaller today.

I wonder what the club will be like. What kind of women and men will be there? I'm twenty-five but feel like an old hen next to Kristine, with her golden hair and ruby-colored lips. I don't have any designs beyond standing in a corner all night, though my imagination can't help but wonder what it would be like for a man to ask me to dance, to be twirled until my dress spins out around my knees and I fall over from laughter.

13th April 1928

I don't know where to begin. Last night I stepped off the streetcar and into a dream. The club was warm and filled with the sweet perfume of cigars. Everyone had a drink in their hand, a real one, so I got one, too. People were crashing into one another, but no one seemed to mind. In fact, no one seemed to walk! Everyone was dancing, twisting and kicking, stomping and sliding across every available surface. It reminded me of a picture show I saw, and I told Kristine. She agreed it was an especially good crowd and introduced me to her friends. A girl in a green-and-gold dress laughed at my face. I think she must've seen my awe at being there. Then she embraced me like a sister and kissed my cheek.

After that, a man took my hand and twirled me around. I thought I was going to lose my footing, but there was always someone beside me to keep me propped up. Kristine danced the Charleston and another dance with a funny-sounding name. I joined in when I could, but I was so overwhelmed I couldn't follow for long. The band played jazz. They sat high on a stage in the back. Their faces changed, contorted in both shape and color as they played. The notes they cast never seemed to land. A man whispered in my ear that I was beautiful. He pulled me in for a dance and spun me around until I forgot I was ever sad or lost, or lonely.

26th April 1928

The most amazing thing! Kristine and I have been asked to join a group of dancers that performs in the Rathskeller on Friday and Saturday evenings. I hardly knew how to respond, the invitation was so unexpected. Kristine said yes right away and included me in her acceptance of Mr. Kennedy's offer. She squeezed me in a tight hug after we left his office and laughed when I asked her if it had actually happened.

Showgirl. The word looks made up. Can something be real if it feels impossible?

29th April 1928

The past few days have been like something off a film reel. I've been coiffed, dressed, fanned, and flirted with. The black-and-silver dress, its tassels dangling, tiered like many thin church ropes, hangs in the center of my open closet.

We had only two days to learn three dances, and to my astonishment, I've picked up the moves quickly. Even Kristine, who is a natural dancer, didn't learn the steps as fast as I did. There are four others in our group. One of the girls looks like Clara Bow, with big bedroom eyes and a round mouth. Her name is Jezebel St. James. At least, that's the name she gave me. She asked my name and when I told her, she laughed.

"Showgirls don't have names like Harrison."

I wanted to say that wasn't even my real name, that my real name was McConnell.

"You need something romantic. Something that'll make the men fall in love and the women fall over in jealousy."

I think it's fitting that I come up with a new name. I've left everything else behind. But another part of me doesn't want to give away more of myself than I already have. The part that wants me to stay the same for Elizabeth. How will she ever know me again if I have a new name, a new face, and a new life?

Lola LaBelle. I'll keep my first name for her. One day when we meet again, she'll still know me. I'll keep that much of myself for Elizabeth.

12th May 1928

A man caught my attention in the crowd tonight. His clothes had the worn appearance of the country, and his boots weren't black and shiny but brown and scuffed with mud. He was speaking with Thomas Jury, who manages the bar—and the things behind the bar we're not supposed to talk about. We were dancing, turning like the blades of a fan, when he looked up and our eyes met. He had the bluest eyes I've ever seen. They looked like a piece of glass I saw once in a window display at Marshall Field's.

I could hold his gaze for only a second. By the time I came back around, he had gone. I thought maybe he hadn't been there at all, that his eyes had been a trick of the low light, but as I was leaving with Kristine and Dot, I saw him again. He was leaning against the bar, and as we passed he removed his hat and inclined his head toward me. His hair was thick, unruly, and as black as an oil slick on the road. He smiled, and I stepped on the back of Dot's heel. I don't know how to put it in words.

He shook me off balance.

17th May 1928

Michael Craig. His name is Michael Craig.

FOURTEEN

Blue glass. The words nearly stopped my heart. I close the book, keeping one finger against the spine to hold my place.

"What?" Oliver shifts so he can see my face. "What's wrong?"

How do I explain it to him, when I can't make sense of it myself? "It's the words she used to describe his eyes. Blue glass. She said his eyes reminded her of blue glass."

He stares at me, not understanding the significance of what's been uncovered.

I look at the book in my hands. "My Grams was obsessed with blue glass. It was all over her house."

His eyes fall to the diary. "And you think—"

"I don't know what to think." I drum my fingers across the cover. "But it seems like too big of a coincidence to—"

"Be a coincidence, yeah," he finishes for me. "You said your grandmother never saw Lola again. If that's true, how could the two things be connected?"

"I don't know." Something's out of order. I open the diary back to the page I left off on, and continue reading aloud.

25th May 1928

A cluster of white gardenias tied with yellow ribbon was lying on my dressing table after our last dance of the night. My name was all that was on the note, but I know who must have sent them. Michael was there again. He was wearing a brown suit jacket and had a crisp white shirt on underneath. He wasn't wearing a tie, as the other men do, and he held a black fedora against his knee. He must've run his hand through his hair a few times because it was sticking up in places.

I looked everywhere, at the other men and women in the crowd, but my eyes were never long off his. Blue eyes made of sapphire glass. I was nervous to leave the dressing room. I was sure he'd be there, waiting to see if I got the flowers, but he was gone when I came out. I asked Kristine to stay back with me, just in case he hadn't left the hotel yet, but he never returned and after half an hour, she said she had to go.

I brought a mason jar from the kitchen pantry and filled it with water. The petals of the gardenias overlap each other like the silk petticoat my primary teacher wore beneath her plain black dress. The scent is exotic. It transports me to a place I've never been, somewhere warm and beautiful.

I tied the yellow satin around my head. It feels forbidden to sleep with something a man gave me. Dutch never gave me anything. He only ever took.

I know my dreams tonight will be overrun by thoughts of Michael. I wonder when I'll see him next, and why he left as he did.

26th May 1928

He left another bouquet of flowers, white daisies bleeding purple from the center. I had to ask Mrs. Blanch for another jar and confess to the one I borrowed last night. She said I had better be careful, that I didn't want to invite any untoward behavior from a man I didn't know. But I caught her smiling when I looked back over my shoulder. No matter what she says, I think she's a romantic at heart.

The daisies were held together with a pink ribbon. I've twisted it around the yellow and used them to tie back my hair. I stood in front of the mirror for a long time, admiring the colors against my dark curls. His note lies next to my hand as I write this. "For you," is all it says. I never even saw him. I wonder if he's a magician, and all of this is some elaborate illusion.

1st June 1928

My room looks like the inside of a florist's shop. Every day this week, I've found a bouquet of flowers waiting for me at the hotel. I had Tuesday off, and he must have known. Instead of turning up at work, a dozen red roses were delivered to Mrs. Blanch's front door.

She turned fuchsia when the boy asked if they were for her. I could tell she wanted to scold me for whatever it is she suspects me of doing, but she didn't have the time to spare on a lecture. It's hard, being alone. I think deep down she's happy there's someone out there who wants me.

I've spread his notes across the small desk. The same words over and over. "For you." "For you." "For you."

3rd June 1928

He kissed the back of my hand. I was stepping off the stage, and he took hold of my fingers. He materialized at my side as though he'd always been there. I hadn't even seen him in the crowd. I couldn't say a word, only watched as he brought my hand to his lips. Even now, hours later, I could swear the hall was empty but for us. He introduced himself and I said, "I know." It came out in a whisper.

I walked with him to a dark corner. The basement was busy and crowded with workers and customers, but I can't remember them. My eyes and ears saw and heard only Michael.

He stood in front of me and removed his hat. I felt his fingers twitch. I think he wanted to smooth out the dark hair he'd revealed. His eyes were slow to meet mine, but when they did they were the same brilliant blue I first discovered.

I found my voice and thanked him for the flowers. He ran his thumb across my knuckles. I shivered and he wondered if I was cold. I told him I was hot and fanned myself. He inquired after my health and happiness, and I assured him both were satisfactory.

Then he leaned in close and said that I was beautiful. I watched his lips form the words, and I said, "So are you." He seemed completely untroubled by the pounding of my heart, which I was certain he could hear.

We spoke several minutes. He and his brother come from Anderson County every weekend to do business with the hotel. It was on my lips to ask the nature of the business, but I stopped myself. I already know. Kristine told me the night I first laid eyes on him. He's a bootlegger. A merchant of bottled amnesia for people thirsty to forget.

I had to get back and change into the red-feathered costume for the last dance of the night. Michael asked if he might escort me home after I was done. I wanted to say yes, and, had the music been lower, my heart would have answered for me. But in the back of my mind, I knew it'd be a mistake. I'm still a married woman. The thought of Elizabeth, of the sweetness of her breath on my cheek as I kissed her good-bye, helped me pull my hand from his.

The flowers are gone now. I've shoved them inside the bin behind the house along with his notes and the ribbon, all except the yellow one. I'm going to keep it in this book, as a reminder of how it felt to be admired.

I flip through the pages gently, but no ribbon falls out.

Oliver looks around us. Dark clouds have begun rolling in, and the wind has picked up. "Come on. Let's get out of here before the weather turns."

We put the bottles and wrappers from our picnic into a plastic grocery bag. Fat raindrops begin to fall as we arrive at the car. I wipe a drop of water from the cover of Lola's diary. Oliver climbs into the driver's seat. It's amazing how fast we've sunk into the routine of him driving. There've been moments during this trip when I've felt like we've been together for years, rather than days.

His fingers find my chin and tilt my head up. "What's going on inside that big brain of yours?"

My smile is weak. It isn't fooling either of us. "I'm just processing."

"It's okay for you to feel however you feel, Wynn."

"Is it?" I'm not so sure. Lola's diary has hinted—strongly—at her reasons for leaving as she did. Will her reasons be worth what she lost, what she left behind, if her story has a happy ending?

He starts the car along with the windshield wipers. The rain is coming faster now. "Yes. You are entitled to make up your own mind about everything. Just . . ." He pulls us onto the main road, letting his sentence go unfinished.

"What?"

He looks apprehensive. "Don't let this story affect what you want for your life."

"Why would I do that?"

He keeps his eyes focused on the road, which appears every three seconds as the rain is wiped away. "I know you think you have a connection with Lola—"

"I do have a connection with her."

"—but you're not her. Your decisions, what you want for your life, they're different. I just want you to remember that."

We drive in silence on the highway. Our hotel for the past few nights is nearly forty minutes from here. There's no point in turning around just to check in all over again, so Oliver points us in the direction of the next closest town. We'll be going home tomorrow. Back to our jobs, our families, our separate lives. I know he wants to keep seeing me, and I have no intention of letting him slip through my fingers, but the past four days have been like something out of Lola's diary. Something I can't believe is real.

From the corner of my eye, I watch him drive. He has a small tattoo on his arm, right at the place where the sleeve rests on his bicep. I've spent a lot of time looking at the words inked there: "Be Brave." He says they remind him not to give up.

I lean my head against the seat and stare out the rain-splattered window. There's a whole world out there, passing me by. Is that how Lola felt before she left? It seems so. Sometimes I forget other places exist at all. As if they fail to be real because I can't see them or walk on them. I want to go to those made-up places. I want to leave and not be held back by duty or guilt.

I want to be brave. Like Oliver. Like Lola.

***

Oliver snores softy beside me. I crawl out from under the covers, finding his T-shirt and boxers on the floor. Taking them off earlier was infinitely more fun than putting them on in the dark. I tiptoe across the room and open my purse. The embroidered cover of Lola's diary is easily discernable. I pull it out, careful not to disrupt anything around it that might make noise. I turn the doorknob silently and step into the brightly lit hall of the hotel.

It's just after two a.m. No one else is around, so I sit with my back to the wall. I felt drained by the time we got here. I needed time away from the words in the diary, and, if I'm being honest, I wanted to finish reading Lola's story on my own. I know I wouldn't have made the trip at all if not for Oliver, but the more I read, the more I want to keep the words to myself. There's a connection between my great-grandmother and me. One that I felt, without knowing it existed, long before her article ever made its way out of Grams's book.

I thumb through the pages—secretly hoping the yellow ribbon Michael gave her will appear.

14th June 1928

He was there again tonight. He's always there now. Dot told me I should say something to Mr. Jury, but I doubt that'd do any good. A bootlegger is far more valuable to a speakeasy than a silly dancing girl. I've tried ignoring him but he refuses to let me. Jezebel noticed the way he hangs around. She's taken to flirting with him after the show. To my delight, he seems completely uninterested. Still, I wish he'd stay away. Every time I brush past him, I feel like a weather vane caught in a storm, turning toward the pull of lightning.

23rd June 1928

I'm worried he's uncovered my secret somehow. He was waiting on the street corner in front of my room this morning. I didn't want Mrs. Blanch getting suspicious, so I slipped out the door and walked past him, motioning for him to follow. When I turned the corner and looked over my shoulder, I was caught off guard by his closeness.

There weren't many people about at that hour, but I worried about being seen, so I ushered him into an alcove in front of an auditor's office. I asked what he meant by showing up at my home. He told me I hadn't left him any choice. "You can't drive me away," he said. I told him it was no good, that he was wasting his time.

He asked if I was ready to stop running; I asked from what?

He pushed a lock of hair behind my ear and said, "From everything that's behind you."

He can't know about my life before. No one knows what I've done, but I saw understanding in his eyes. He knows I'm hiding from something, and now I know he is, too.

5th July 1928

I'm writing from a different room today. The floors are unfinished and full of splinters. Three of the walls are robin's-egg blue, but the sun from a western-facing window has bleached the fourth almost white. I tried the bed in the corner. It creaked loudly when I went to lie down, but it's been made up with fresh-smelling linens.

A vase of wildflowers sits next to me on the desk. This is my home now. I still can't wrap my head around what's happened.

Last night began like any other. Then, an hour past midnight, we changed into the red, white, and blue costumes for the holiday dance we rehearsed last week. The city put on a fireworks show over the Ohio, and men and women had just traipsed back inside, no doubt to toast the eighteenth amendment.

I looked to see if Michael was in the audience. He hadn't been there since our argument on the street. Kristine told me not to worry, he'd be back around. I didn't tell her I wanted him to stay gone.

The band had just struck the first few notes when men in dark suits arrived, flanked by policemen in blue. They stormed into the Rathskeller like a swarm of angry yellow jackets, waving guns and yelling orders.

Some of the girls screamed and turned hysterical, running for the door. Kristine grabbed my arm and led me through the mass of people fleeing arrest. She pulled me into the servants hall that separates the basement from a series of tunnels beneath the hotel.

She changed her mind at the last minute, perhaps thinking, as I was, that the tunnels would be teeming with Prohibition agents. We doubled back and ran for the stairs off the lobby.

A young policeman was stationed there. He held a pistol at his side and his forehead wrinkled in surprise when he saw us. I thought we were done for. For the first time in months, I was truly terrified of what might happen if I was forced to reveal my true name. In the space of five seconds, I saw my new life being ripped away.

Then Kristine flashed him a smile and did a little shimmy. She dropped my arm, put her hands over her head, and swayed her hips from side to side like a snake charmer. I wanted to laugh it was so ridiculous.

The young officer's face transformed from confusion to enchantment. His lips curved into the most begrudging smile I've ever seen. He raised an eyebrow at her and nodded for us to move past him. She placed a kiss on his cheek as we ran past him for the stairs. His eyes lit up like the fireworks outside.

We made our way to the back entrance of the hotel, avoiding the lobby. There were men stationed on the street, so we skimmed the building. I prayed the shadows would conceal us until we could make it around the block. That's when a green car with a tan leather roof folded up behind the backseat screeched to a halt just feet in front of us.

Michael Craig and a man I didn't know called for us to get inside.

Kristine hopped in straight away, but I hesitated. Adrenaline urged me forward, but I knew getting into that car would mean running again. I'm so very tired of running. Michael and I stared at one another for no more time than it takes to draw a single breath. His lips hinted at an adventure that convinced me to take his hand.

We drove Kristine to her apartment. She laughed the whole ride there, sitting atop the compressed roof so she could feel the wind on her face as we sped down deserted streets. I jumped out of the car when we pulled up to her building and hugged her fiercely. She thought it was funny. She said they'd keep the place shut down only a couple of weeks, and then we'd all be back to work.

She didn't know I had no intention of ever coming back. The risk of being caught and exposed is now too great.

Michael and his brother Jimmy, a sweet young man with a badly scarred face, stayed with the car as I snuck through the front door of Mrs. Blanch's house. It was before three a.m., but she's a light sleeper and I couldn't bear the thought of having to tell another person good-bye for the last time. I brought so little with me, and I've accumulated so little since, it took only ten minutes to pack everything I own into a bag and a duffle made from my bed linens. I wrote Mrs. Blanch a letter thanking her for her kindness and placed a ten-dollar bill between the folds.

We made it to Lawrenceburg just as the sun was rising. There were a few people milling about. I faced forward, hoping they wouldn't notice me. Now, as I look around my new room, I can't help but compare it to the one I left. The bright sunlight and soft colors are pretty and pleasant. It doesn't feel like mine, as the room in Mrs. Blanch's house had begun to feel, but there's a presence here that soothes me. I can't quite put my finger on it, but when I woke up after a few hours' rest, I thought, maybe, it was hope.

6th July 1928

Today I met Michael's oldest brother and his wife, Cecelia. She's very pretty and a few years younger than me. She's the one who put the flowers in my room. I don't know how she knew to do it, how she knew I was coming, but I sense she's wise beyond her years. She has two black-haired little girls. One is still in diapers, and the other toddles around the yard on legs too short and chubby to provide much balance. I gave her a blue flower I found on my walk this morning, and she squealed in delight. It made my heart ache for Elizabeth.

I wonder where she is now, what she's doing? I have some money saved in the fake bottom of a wooden box I bought at a nostalgia shop in Louisville. Maybe I can earn more here, somehow, and finally go back for her.

Michael and his youngest brother, Patrick—or Patty Cake, as they call him—left early this morning. Cecelia told me they had business to attend to in Chicago. I asked her about Michael, but she told me only that he's had a hard time of it and that he'd tell me everything when he was ready.

I've been snooping around the grounds some. If Michael and his brothers are running an illegal still, they've hidden it well. All I see are acres of soft wheat and green grass. There's a forest of sorts on the far end of the property. On my walk, I noticed a path leading through the trees, worn down by boots. Perhaps I'll snoop there next.

10th July 1928

Michael and Patrick arrived back at the house last night. I was in the kitchen, helping Cece prepare dinner, when they walked through the back door. I've barely spoken to him since he rescued Kristine and me from behind the hotel. He asked how I was doing and if everyone's been treating me right. I thanked him for what he's done, and he nodded and removed his hat. I took it and hung it on a nail in the hallway. The felt is tattered in places. I might try to fix it for him if he'll let me.

This morning he offered to give me a proper tour of the farm. I wanted to change—I still had on the housedress Cece loaned me for helping with the chores—but he insisted I looked fine. We walked very close to one another. The backs of our hands connected a few times, and I had to turn my head away, embarrassed by the blush I felt spreading up my neck. There's an old barn behind the house and he showed me where they played as children. A broken sawhorse made to look like a pony sat in the corner, half-buried by a bale of hay. I asked if it was a happy place to grow up in. He got a far-off look in his eyes, as though there was something painful in those memories.

We talked about my time at the Seelbach, and my wonder at the city in general. He didn't inquire about my past, and I didn't offer anything. I'm not sure what he'd think about me if he knew I left my family. I asked about his brothers and parents. Both his mother and father died of the Spanish flu. His oldest brother, Daniell, was only eighteen when it happened. I think Michael must respect his brother very much for the way he kept them all together.

As we walked back to the house, he plucked a pink flower from the bush by the mailbox. He tucked it behind my ear and looked at me a long time. It didn't make me uncomfortable, as silence sometimes does. There's a calmness to him, an empathetic light behind his eyes that I've never seen in a man. He hides his true character well beneath the careless smile and badly behaved hair, but I can see it.

As I made to walk upstairs to my room, he touched my arm. He told me I could have a home here if I wanted it.

Home. The word has never held much stock for me. My father was drunk more often than he was awake. My mother, lovely and soft as she was, wasn't strong enough to protect me. The first time I thought of running was the day of her funeral. I couldn't stay alone in the house with my father, but I had no money or means of travel. Dutch became my escape. He was so handsome in his woolen tunic and cap, and I was so very young. He gave me one of the bright medals pinned to his chest the first time he took me out. It was for courage under fire.

I've tried not to think much about him these last ten months. It's funny. I can hardly remember his face sometimes. What I can't forget, what I'll never forget, is the blankness of his stare when he looked at me, like I didn't exist. Sometimes I would bury my face in a pillow and scream, just to prove I did.

FIFTEEN

1st August 1928

I've done something I shouldn't have. I followed Patrick into the woods early this morning, just after sunrise. Cece warned me about snooping, but I had to see for myself where Michael goes off to each day. Patrick walked almost an hour and nearly caught me once. I hid behind a tree trunk and held my breath until his footsteps started up again. I watched him bend low and walk hunchbacked through a bramble of little trees. When I came out on the other side, I could hardly believe my eyes.

A building five times the length of this house has been constructed in a clearing in the forest. I wasn't altogether sure it was a building at first—it looked more like an oddly shaped hill—but I saw steam rising through the vines and flashes of red and gold beneath a cluster of green leaves.

Michael wasn't there, but his brother Daniell was. So were Thomas, Elijah, and that skinny Eby White from the house down the road. I hid in a hollow spot in the bramble and watched them check big, round kettles made of shiny orange copper.

It's not like I didn't know the Craig brothers were moonshiners, but it feels wrong that I've uncovered Michael's secret when I have so many hidden away.

I tripped and fell and nearly tumbled halfway down the ravine on my way back. I cut my leg, and it hurts terribly. I'll have to ask Cece to help me clean it properly after supper. I can tell I didn't do a good job on my own this morning. It burns beneath my dress. Wouldn't it be a funny thing if I were to die from a scratch after making it so long on my own?

3rd August 1928

I confessed about following Patrick into the woods. Cece thought the cut on my thigh looked infected, so she went and got Michael, who called the doctor for me. The antiseptic brought tears to my eyes, but it was nothing compared to the sharp pain of his needle. He had to sew the wound shut with a series of tiny stitches. I'll have a scar there for the rest of my life.

After the doctor left, Michael came to see me. I was so ashamed and embarrassed, I could hardly look him in the eye when I told him how it happened. He sat beside me on the bed and turned my face toward his. Then he kissed me. When I opened my eyes, I saw that his were focused on my lips. He told me I scared him, and I said I was sorry. He touched his forehead to mine and took a deep breath, then kissed me again. I keep touching my lips, trying to remember how his mouth felt pressed against mine.

I'll put an end to things here. I hardly know what I'm writing anymore, I'm so happy. I'll just say this: my leg doesn't hurt at all now.

31st August 1928

I've been reading my last entry, and I can't help but smile at the memory of that kiss. There have been so many since that afternoon.

11th September 1928

Michael took me to the cemetery today. His wife and infant son are buried there. They share a grave. He couldn't bear to part them from each other.
I held his hand while he told me their story. Her name was Shelby and she had red hair and blue eyes. Their son never drew his first breath. Shelby had a difficult pregnancy and had to stay in bed for months. She went into labor some weeks before she was due. The doctor convinced Michael to stay outside and wait for the baby to come.
He didn't cry as he told me what happened next. He just sat down on a concrete bench inside the cemetery walls and pulled me onto his lap. I wrapped my arms around his neck and combed through his hair with my fingers.
He never got to say good-bye to his wife or hello to his son. They were both gone by the time the doctor emerged from the house. I held him tighter then. I know what it's like to lose your child. Maybe not in the same way, but I feel the pain of her absence nonetheless.
I want to tell him about Elizabeth, about my life before Kentucky, but the thought of losing him scares the truth from my lips. He's taken to kissing me good night in the hallway between our rooms. I was shy at first, worried what his brothers or Cece might think, but they never seem to pay us any attention. It was especially difficult to pull away from him tonight. I know the cemetery upset him, and I wanted to do something to take his mind off things. When he turned to leave, I pulled him back and placed a kiss on the cotton over his heart.

I've fallen in love with him. With his blue eyes, funny hair, and big smile. He's given me a real life again.

25th September 1928

Michael took me to the stills today. He made me promise not to venture out on my own again. The cut on my thigh is fully healed, but there's a pink, puckered scar to remind me of my promise. He explained the entire still operation. How the mash is made to how the whiskey is triple distilled and bottled. I admit I was impressed. The process is complicated and handled with great care. I didn't ask about the money. All things in time, I think.

On the way back through the woods, he spun me around and pressed me to a tree. His eyes were dark and hungry, and he claimed my lips with a new kind of kiss. He asked if he could come to my room tonight. I said yes, so here I wait. The brass clock on the mantel downstairs has let out the first of twelve chimes. He'll be here soon. I thought writing would help to steady my hand, but it's only hastened my excitement. I want him. I want all of him.

26th September 1928

There are no words, there is no time to explain the joy I feel. I said I loved him, and he said he already knew.

"When?" I asked.

"When I took your hand to help you off the stage."

The cheek of him! But I couldn't deny it. He captured my heart from almost the first minute.

29th November 1928

It's been so long since I've written! Life with a bootlegger. It sounds like the title of a penny novel rather than my life, but that's exactly what it is. Today is Thanksgiving and all the boys are coming over for a proper family meal. I'm wearing the new red dress Michael had made for me in Lexington. The waist is trimmed in white lace and there's a string of fake pearls attached to the collar. I've been admiring myself in the mirror for too long. Cece will wonder what's happened to me. Poor Cece, she's having a terrible time of it lately. Daniell's gone off on a bender, and she's stuck here all alone caring for the little ones.

I help as much as I can. Every day Sophia's sweet face and brown eyes remind me of my Elizabeth. It's been more than a year since I left. I wonder how much she's grown and if she looks any different than the little girl I remember. Michael caught me crying two days ago. Sophia had lost her favorite rag doll in the yard, and I went to help search for it. When I found it lying alone in the tall grass, it made me so incredibly sad. I hugged it to my chest as if it were my own real baby. I used to cry for her. I worried that she was scared and hurt by my absence. Now I cry for myself, for the emptiness that never gets filled up, no matter how much love Michael shows me.

Suddenly I don't feel much like celebrating or wearing a pretty dress. I think maybe I'll stop writing for a while. It's too easy to remember when I don't have to pretend I'm someone else.

4th April 1929

It finally feels like spring. I felt like a walk and decided to take you with me into the woods. Reading through all of my old entries, I can't believe how much life has changed. The winter was long and cold and I'm desperate to stay outside and breathe the fresh air.

Life in the house has gotten complicated. Daniell and Michael have been at one another's throats for weeks now. I think Daniell's jealous of him. Michael is a leader and the men listen to him, respect him, and follow his directions without argument. Except his oldest brother, who does almost nothing but argue.

I heard Daniell tell Patrick that he thought Michael needed to be reminded of who is oldest. I wanted to say something, but I don't want to stir up more trouble. Besides, Daniell still doesn't trust me. I don't want him looking too hard at my past.

I still haven't told Michael about Elizabeth and Dutch and everything back in Illinois. I'm in so deep now, I just can't seem to find the courage. But I'll need to tell him soon. He's been asking more and more questions. He wants to know about my family and my life before the hotel. I'm as honest as I can be, but am always careful to not reveal too much. I can tell he sees this. He's been so patient with me. I owe him the truth.

Cece has been a godsend. She and the girls kept my spirits up when all but Patrick headed to Chicago for three weeks in January. Michael's got some new business there. I was worried they'd be caught and thrown in jail or get into trouble with the gangsters we read about in the paper. He called a few times. He sounded tired and not himself. It was such a relief when I heard the car turn onto the drive one afternoon. I've grown to think of him as my husband. But not the kind I'm used to. One that takes care of me and loves me. More than that, he's given me a reason to believe that the life I wanted, the one I sacrificed everything to have, is possible. A meaningful life that includes laughter and joy and promise.

I was sure I was pregnant last month. I was late getting my monthlies and my breasts were sore and swollen. I didn't say anything, partly because I wanted to be sure and partly because I was afraid of how Michael would feel about it. We're not really married, after all. A week later I woke up to terrible cramps and ruined sheets. I admit to feeling relieved. The thought of having another child terrifies me. When I got pregnant with Elizabeth, I was just seventeen. Dutch was delighted and, for a while, I was, too. Then we got married and I was finally free of my father's house and all the bad memories there. But things soon changed.

It took only a few months after her birth for me to realize my dreams were over. All those ambitions I had as a girl were out of reach. I was smart, I could've gotten a job and earned a living. But Dutch wouldn't allow it. I was popular, too, but he didn't care for my friends and once we were married, I wasn't allowed to see them anymore. He suffocated me. Not slowly, the way a gas leak can, but quick and painful. There were nights he'd lie asleep beside me and I'd swear I could feel his hands around my throat.

I thought once the baby came his needs might diminish, that he'd allow me some room to breathe. But, if anything, he became more demanding of my efforts, my body, and my time. Every day began and ended the same, with me attending to everyone but myself. I loved Elizabeth. I cherished every moment of quiet I could find with her, but they were few and far between. By the time I made up my mind to leave, it was a relief. What a terrible thing, but it's true. It was a relief to know my time as a wife and mother was over.

How can I ever tell Michael what I've done? How selfish I've been? He won't understand. No one would. I traded being a mother for being a person, one with a life in front of her. But the price was high. How can I ask him to forgive me for what I've done, when I'll never be able to forgive myself?

10th April 1929

I'm waiting for Michael to come home. I acted foolishly today, and I'm afraid it's put me in Daniell's path. Cece, Sophia, and I were in the kitchen preparing dinner and he came in, stupid and stinking with 'shine. Sophia had left some wooden blocks on the ground, and he tripped over them and *fell into the table. I knew what he was going to do before he took a single step. His eyes fixed on Sophia with a cutting rage.*

All these months, I've tried so hard to keep from getting involved, but I couldn't let him hurt that little girl. I stepped between them and shoved him backward with all the strength in my body. He fell into the wall and looked at me for a minute. Then he laughed and pointed a dirty finger at me. He said I'd regret it and called me a whore.

I don't care about the insult. My father called me worse when he was drunk, but the expression on his face . . . He's going to find a way to destroy me. I can feel it. I can't wait for the earth to fall out from beneath me.

Tonight I'll tell Michael everything and hope he can forgive me for what I've done.

12th April 1929

It's over. My secret is out, and now I wait. Michael left the house after I told him, and he hasn't been back since.

I've confessed everything to Cece, too. I needed to explain it to her, in case these are my last days at the house. She held me while I cried, and I think she cried a little, too. Maybe because she knows what it's like to feel trapped and hopeless, maybe because she lost faith in a person she thought was her friend. I don't know.

I held onto her until all my tears were spent. I cried for myself, for Elizabeth and Michael, and for her, too. I see so much of myself in Cece, but she could never do what I did. She could never leave her babies with a man like Daniell. He'd kill them just to spite her. At least Dutch loves Elizabeth. I know he'd never harm her. I don't think Daniell has ever looked twice at his girls.

I can't bring myself to pack my things, even though I know Michael may come back and throw me out. At least I had his love for a time. His true love. No one can take that from me.

15th April 1929

Michael got home sometime late in the night. I thought I heard a noise and went down to the kitchen. There he was, sitting at the table with his old hat in his hands. He looked at me and I was sure he was going to tell me to get out, that he didn't love me anymore, but he got up and wrapped his arms around me instead. I tell you I wept for joy then. I held him so tight, it's a miracle he could breathe. He apologized that it took so long for him to come home. He said, "I don't care about your past. I love you. I want you to be my wife."

He took my hand and led me upstairs to my room. The window wasn't letting in much moonlight, but I could see his eyes. They were full of love and compassion. I couldn't stop crying as he made love to me. We held each other for a long time after. This morning I watched him sleep until the sun came up. His beard is scruffy and as black as his hair, but his heart is pure. He's saved me.

30th August 1929

Today is Elizabeth's ninth birthday. Michael took me to Lexington last week, and I bought a silver necklace with blue glass in the shape of a teardrop attached to it. He's promised to try to figure out a way to get it to her.

Since coming out with the truth, I've been thinking of ways I might return and bring Elizabeth back with me. I just don't see how.

Dutch would never let me take her, and no court is likely to let a woman living with a bootlegger have custody of a little girl after she abandoned her, as I did.

Perhaps I'll write to her. Maybe I can convince her that I'm sorry. I think she'll like the necklace. It's the same blue as Michael's eyes.

12th October 1929

He's done it. I don't know how, but he managed to get the necklace and my letter to one of Dutch's sisters, Kate. And he brought back a letter from her to me. It said:

"Dear Lola, It was such a relief to know you're alright. Dutch didn't tell us about your letter until weeks after you disappeared. At first I was worried harm had come to you. Now I hear you're safe and happy, and I'm grateful. Whatever happened, you became my sister the day you married that poor soul I call brother. Your friend has given me a letter and a necklace for Elizabeth, and I promise you I will get it to her somehow. It'll require secrecy. Dutch doesn't speak of you at all anymore. When he lets something slip, it's vile and unkind. But I promise I will get it to her. She's turning into a lovely young lady. She has good marks at school and a few new friends since you've been gone. She is different, though. I debated whether or not I should say, but she's become a little cold and formal like my brother. I know it may ache your heart to hear it, and I tell you not to hurt you but to speak honestly about what your absence has caused. Maybe if you were to return, some of that coldness would give way. Please think about it. All my love, Kate."

My heart did ache reading those words. I don't want Elizabeth to lose the childish wonder I gave up everything to get back for myself. But I have hope.

29th November 1929

No further word from Kate. Michael was in Chicago two weeks ago and left her, in a post office box he rented for our correspondence, a new letter and a doll that I made. Perhaps she hasn't had time to pick up the mail. It's torture to wait.

8th December 1929

Michael brought me a letter this morning. It was from Elizabeth. I recognized her tidy penmanship right away and began crying big, happy tears. She still makes her r's the same way, even though the rest of her letters have become more refined and mature. Her note was written with great care. It broke my heart to read it.

"I don't wish to hear from you," it said. "Father says we should think of you as dead, and that's what I do. Please don't write to me again."

There's a pain in my chest like it's been torn open. Not even Michael's sweet, comforting words can help.

14th May 1930

I don't know why I bother keeping this journal. I can't bear to read anything I've written. It only upsets me. But there are rare days when I need to get everything out and I have no one to burden with my words.

Michael and I just came back from the lawyer's office. I petitioned Dutch for a divorce over Christmas. He refused. I can't imagine why. It's not like I'll ever go back to him. But he won't give up his hold on my life.

The lawyer says it's no use unless he agrees. Michael was upset. He's said before that he might just drive up there and confront Dutch. But all that would do is land Michael in jail. We need him here.

There was a raid a few weeks ago on the house and farm. The sheriff came out with a Treasury agent to investigate a claim the boys were in the business of moonshining. Of course they didn't find anything. Michael's too smart for that. There's no way they'll ever find the stills. They're too well hidden in the woods, and none of the boys would dare speak against him.

Tomorrow he's promised to take me on a picnic to celebrate our sinful love. I giggled when he called it that. I guess if I can't be his wife on paper, at least I can be his wife in spirit. I already am, really, but he wants to make it official. I have a feeling that means a lot of kissing under the open sky.

26th June 1930

Cece lost the baby. She was four months along this time. I think maybe Daniell caused the miscarriage, but she won't say. I see the bruises on her arm, and she flinches whenever he comes home drunk. Michael confronted him about it, and Daniell was so angry. I was worried he might do something violent. He's left the house for now. I hope for Cece and the girls' sake he never comes back.

4th July 1930

Michael is taking me to Chicago with him when he and Jimmy head out in the morning. Good old Jimmy. He's like a true brother to me. We're staying only two nights. One of the nights, the boys have business with some clubs up there.

I've hatched a plan, and I hope Michael won't say no. I'm going to go see Kate. She sent a letter a few weeks ago and said Dutch would be traveling for business this week and that Elizabeth would be staying at their house.

It's my first real chance to see my daughter in nearly three years. I made her a dress out of the green-and-yellow-checkered frock I wore to tea at Mrs. White's house last month. I hope I've guessed her size right. I'm so excited and nervous I can't sit still. I know it's silly, but I hope if I do see her, she'll be wearing the necklace I bought. It makes me feel connected to her somehow.

5th July 1930

Michael and Jimmy left twenty minutes ago. They won't be back until late. The concierge at the front desk was able to come up with some wrapping paper and a red ribbon for my present to Elizabeth. Michael isn't sure it's a good idea but says he can never say no to me. Anyway, I've made up my mind.

Kate's house is about forty minutes from the city. Michael's agreed to take me there at nine tomorrow morning. I'm glad for the solitude tonight. I'm sure I'm no fun to be around. My nerves are completely frazzled. So many questions running through my mind! Will she be there? Will she want to see me? Will Kate let her see me? Will she remember my face?

6th July 1930

Today was the best and worst day of my life. Michael and I arrived at Kate's house just before ten. I knew immediately Elizabeth was inside. I could hear her voice through the open windows. She always had such a lovely voice.

I was shaking so bad as we walked up the drive, Michael had to put his arm around me to keep me from falling over.

Kate's youngest, a little boy with red hair and freckles, answered the door. I couldn't believe it was the same little Tucker I held just hours after he was born. He didn't remember me, not that I expected him to.

Kate came to the door in the same brown housedress she had on the last time I saw her. She looked stricken at first. She just stared at me from the other side of the dusty screen. Then she cried out and threw the door open and wrapped her arms around me. We both sobbed into each other's shoulders. I forgot Michael was there until she asked his name.

I think she thought he was very handsome. He is, especially in his new green suit and tan hat. His hair was adorably untidy when he took it off to introduce himself.

She invited us inside, and the first thing I noticed was how quiet everything had gone. No singing, no kids yelling and running around. Kate's husband, Jonah, was out helping a neighbor, and I'm grateful I didn't have to see him again. He's a nice enough man, but looking into the eyes of the people you hurt is draining. I had to save up my strength for Elizabeth.

Michael and I waited in Kate's little sitting room when she went to get her. Every minute that passed was a torment. I'd almost given up hope she would see me when, suddenly, there she was.

Her blonde hair was plaited down the middle and her white dress was crisp and proper. She's a lady now. I know Kate must've told her who I was, but I still said, "It's me, your mama."

She didn't say a word, but Kate persuaded her to take a seat on the chair opposite mine. I handed her my present, but she wouldn't take it.

Kate accepted it and placed it on the floor. Elizabeth looked at Michael. Her eyes reminded me too much of Dutch's.

I wanted so badly to wrap her in my arms, but I was worried about expecting too much of her. So we sat and I talked. I asked her questions and after a while she answered. She said she was fine and that she was doing well in school.

I asked if she'd gotten the necklace I sent. She blushed and looked away. Then she said she'd given it to a friend. I admit, it hurt me, but I also know I've hurt her greatly and shouldn't be surprised.

When I introduced Michael, she nodded stiffly at him but wouldn't say a thing. He told her how much I miss her and how often I speak of her. She looked at me with such pain in her brown eyes. It felt like an arrow to my heart.

I got on my knees and told her how sorry I was and that I loved her. I reached for her hand, and she let me take it for a moment. I felt her soft skin and the pulse in her wrist before she slowly took it from my grasp. To feel her again, to touch and see her with my own eyes, was the greatest joy I've ever known, no matter how short a time it was.

I promised to keep writing to her and to visit again. I couldn't keep from embracing her as we left. I had to feel her one more time and try, somehow, to show her how sorry I am.

She didn't push me back, and I felt her body relax against me some. It's the best she could do, and I understand.

We're at the hotel now and I keep replaying the meeting in mind. I wish I had said so much more. I don't know when I'll see her again, but I know I will. My heart feels light and heavy at the same time. I got to hold my baby. It's enough for now.

Light is touching the sides of the curtains as I sneak back into the hotel room. I lower myself to the bed, careful not to make noise. Oliver's back is to me, and I'm glad. I'm too tired from the hour and everything I've read to talk about any of it right now. My eyes are heavy, but I fight sleep. I keep thinking of Grams's hands. Of how warm and strong they were. There was so much love in those hands. Yet she was unable to forgive one of the people in this world who is supposed to love you most.

I turn my face into the pillow. I don't want to dream tonight.

SIXTEEN

"Wynn."

I turn my face into the pillow, ignoring the voice calling to me.
"Hey."

A kiss on the side of my head.

"Time to wake up, beautiful." Oliver's voice is insistent.

I roll over, taking the covers with me, but he pulls them away.

"Come on, we've got to check out in like ten minutes."

I crack open one eye and follow his movement around the room.
He's dressed and ready to go. I didn't make it to bed until after four.
I turn my head toward the clock on the nightstand. It's almost ten.
"Why'd you let me sleep so late?" I ask, stretching.

He kisses me as I pass him on my way to the bathroom. I've never
been a big fan of morning kisses, but he doesn't seem to mind, and I'm
not in a position to turn down a kiss from Oliver Reeves.

"I thought you could use it. I knew you were up late."

The look on his face tells me he knows exactly what I was up to
last night—or was it early this morning? I lock myself in the bathroom
and stare over the sink at my reflection. My hair is a tangled mass; there
are bags beneath each eye and what looks suspiciously like a pimple

forming on my chin. We're going home today. The spell has officially broken.

I brush my hair and teeth quickly and rub some moisturizer on my face. I don't bother with makeup. He's seen me naked. I doubt he cares whether or not I apply mascara for the five-hour car ride. When I step back into the room, he's gone. My suitcase lies open across the mattress. I swap out Oliver's shirt and boxers for a blue sleeveless blouse and shorts and slide my feet into my Keds, which are on the floor near the small desk.

The door opens, and Oliver reappears with a white paper bag in one hand and a manila envelope in the other.

"What do we have here?" I reach up to distract him with a kiss, pulling the paper bag from his hand.

He points at me. "Devious."

Two glazed donuts are inside. I remove one and take a large bite. The flaky sugar sends a moan through my full mouth. "So good," I mumble.

He zips the suitcase closed, sticking the envelope beneath his arm.

Three bites and the donut is gone. I offer him the bag, but he shakes his head.

"I already had some. Those are for you. Because you're sweet." He smiles, proud of himself. "See what I did there? With the sweet thing?"

I kiss his lips, unhampered by the grin on mine, and follow him toward the door. I try to swipe the envelope, but he's too quick.

"Sorry, too slow," he teases.

"What is it?"

"This"—he holds the envelope over my head while I jump for it—"is a surprise."

"Ooh. Yeah, we haven't really covered this yet, but, uh, I'm not a big fan of surprises."

"Really?" He looks at me skeptically.

"Yeah, you could say I've been a victim of some bad surprises in my life."

"Such as . . ."

We step into the hall and I check my purse to make sure the diary is still safely tucked inside. "Such as finding my sister making out with my boyfriend in a closet during a game of seven minutes in heaven—"

"Tabby?" he asks, pushing the down arrow on the elevator button.

I tilt my head toward him. "You'd think, but no, it was actually Franny."

"That is surprising."

We step into the elevator and Oliver presses the button for the lobby. "Oh, that wasn't the surprising part."

"No?"

"No. The surprising part was that she married him."

Oliver laughs loudly in the confined space. It bounces off the walls. "You're kidding me."

"Nope." When we arrive, the lobby is full of guests checking out or enjoying a late breakfast. "So you can see why, when you say surprise, I'm cautious."

He places my suitcase and his backpack on the ground near his feet and removes the wallet from his back pocket. I begged him to let me pay for at least half the expense on the first night of our trip, but he insisted on covering everything. He told me it was a small price to pay for allowing him to tag along, and besides, he's got more money than he knows what to do with. My own bank account is abysmally low on funds, so I didn't argue.

I keep my eye on the envelope as we make our way through the parking lot. "Oliver?"

"Yes?" He pops the trunk and places the bags inside.

"What's in the envelope?"

He sighs but doesn't hand it over. I watch him climb into the driver's seat before I open my door and do the same. He tucks the envelope between the seat and console on his side. "It's a surprise and not a bad one."

"At least give me a hint."

He puts the car in reverse. He's so good at deflecting me. "It's some research I ordered from Frankfort."

It's on the tip of my tongue to ask who we know from Frankfort when it occurs to me. "The kooky receptionist?"

He nods and turns the car onto the highway that will take us most of the way home. "I called in a supersecret rock star favor."

I raise my eyebrow at him, interested to hear how much the pretty—though possibly certifiable—receptionist was bought for.

He smiles, and my eyes go straight to the chip in his tooth. "Don't look at me like that. I just had our agent send her some Lumineers T-shirts."

"She didn't want Multitude swag?"

"Oh God. I don't think there's anyone left on this planet that would want our crappy band T-shirts. I certainly don't."

I stare at the envelope a little more but decide to let it rest, for now. We listen to two of the CDs he made for the trip and enjoy our final hours alone together. As we pass Indianapolis, Oliver asks me to tell him what I uncovered in the diary last night. I tell him everything. How Lola went to live with Michael and his brothers. How she and Cece became close, about Daniell's jealousy, Michael's wife and son dying, and finally about Grams. How she'd seen her mother, spoken to her, how Lola even held her.

"Do you think your mom knows about that?" he asks, one hand slung casually over the steering wheel.

"I don't think so. When I talked to her last week, she seemed pretty confident Lola had never tried to reach Grams after she left."

"You think it'll change your mom's opinion of her grandmother? Knowing she at least tried to make up for her mistakes?"

I watch the buildings grow smaller out the window as the city and suburbs fall behind. "I don't know. Maybe."

He's quiet for a while, then asks if I'll read the rest of the diary to him.

"Now?"

"You got someplace better to be?" he asks.

He reaches over to run the backs of his fingers against my cheek. He's so patient with me. So genuine. I didn't think it was possible to be more infatuated with him than I already was, but I was wrong. Spending this time with Oliver has given me new insight into my feelings pre-Kentucky. I always fancied myself in love with him. But what I felt before is nothing compared to what stirs inside me now. If that was love, this is something considerably stronger. Or maybe I've just never been in love before and didn't realize how powerful it can be. I look at him and a lot of times, it's like the wind's been knocked out of me.

I take the diary from my bag and turn to the end. Only a handful of unread pages remain. As excited as I am to find out what happened next, I don't want the story to be over.

18th August 1930

Michael and I promised ourselves to each other yesterday. We can't officially marry, since Dutch refuses to agree to a divorce, but we wanted to do something formal to vow our love to one another.

Cece made me a beautiful ivory cotton dress and stood beside me as we pledged our lives to each other under a tall oak tree near the stills. It was just the four of us, Michael and me, Cece and Jimmy. It was enough.

I love this man more than I ever thought possible. He's saved me, stood by me, helped me when I needed it most. His love has never failed, never faltered. I vowed to never love another, and I know I never will.

24th December 1930

It's Christmas, and Patrick's gone and gotten a proper tree for the house. Sophia and little Maybelline helped Cece trim the branches while I baked a pudding for dinner tonight.

It's been pretty merry around here, even with Daniell back home. I'm excited to give Michael his Christmas gift. It's a gold ring I bought from the Sears catalog last month. I spent pretty much every dollar I had to get it, but I think he'll like it. I haven't taken my own band off of my finger since he placed it there four months ago.

With the winter coming, the boys have been busy building up a supply of apple moonshine to keep us in cash until spring. Moonshine whiskey isn't meant to be stored, but the apple stuff tastes better the longer you let it sit. They've been accepting orders for it for a few months. I've been helping with the books a little. Michael says I'm the only one he trusts to keep it straight.

I think he's starting to warm to the idea of me helping more with the business. He thinks it's too dangerous, but that's what I enjoy about it. Every day, my new life feels like an adventure. Some days are hard, but I feel alive and feel like all things are possible. I wouldn't trade hope for anything in the world now.

11th February 1931

There was a new Prohibition agent sneaking around town last week. Eby said his name's Murphy and called him something I won't repeat. Michael says we should go on with business as usual but be more cautious. I guess this Murphy ran down a couple of local boys on their way to Louisville three days ago. Knocked them right off the road in the middle of the night.

Daniell wouldn't let up about it. He says the agent's got a car as fast as any of the moonshiners, except us. Elijah is a genius mechanic and he got the old Ford running like a rocket. I don't think there's a car anywhere that could outrun it. I hope it stays that way.

For now, Michael's having the boys take a different route out of the county on every delivery. They're also leaving at different times of the night to try to keep a step ahead of Agent Murphy and the sheriff's boys.

I've got the books sorted out and am worried about how long we can keep up with the demand without getting caught. With the talk of repeal, we may not have to worry about that much longer.

3rd April 1931

Kate's written and said Dutch may grant my petition for divorce! He met a woman and wants to marry her. Kate says she's a widow with two young sons. I replied that she can have him!

I told Michael, and he picked me up and spun me around the kitchen. We were still kissing when Cece came in and caught us ten minutes later. I'm so happy I could burst. I'll be able to truly marry the man I love and take his name. Can this really be happening?

I'm so scared Dutch will change his mind. I'm tempted to drive up to Chicago and chain the poor woman naked to his bed. I really shouldn't think those things, knowing Dutch as I do, but I'm just so happy! Mrs. Michael Craig . . .

24th April 1931

Michael came back from the lawyer's this afternoon with the divorce decree. Dutch won't allow me to see Elizabeth, but he is finally granting me the divorce.

I know I can win Elizabeth back. I just know it. Michael said Prohibition is going to end soon, so he's going to use the money we've saved and the money he'll make this year to start a hardware shop in Bardstown. Once he's established himself as a respectable businessman, we'll be able to go to court for visitation rights.

I've got to go and help Cece with the wash. I think I'll bring the paperwork for her to read. She's been very low lately. I think it'll cheer her up to know Michael and I will be truly married soon. She already feels like my sister. I can't wait to make it legal.

1st May 1931

Agent Murphy came to the house today with another Treasury agent and Clive Melling from the sheriff's department. The young Treasury agent didn't say anything; he just leaned against the car and looked at Murphy in awe.

Daniell didn't help matters by spitting at the agent's feet when he stepped onto the porch. Cece and I were watching from the window. When the agent saw me, he smiled and tipped his hat in my direction. Michael saw, and I could tell he was worried. He doesn't want me involved in any of this business. Soon, though, I'll be his wife, and it'll be my right.

Agent Murphy didn't come inside, but he told Michael he knew they were hiding a still in the woods and that it was only a matter of time before they found it.

Before he left, he asked my name. It sent a chill up my spine. Michael told him it wasn't any of his concern. The agent smiled and said I was lovely and that Michael was a lucky man. After he left, Michael went up to our room and stayed inside alone until dinner.

We should be happy and celebrating getting married soon. Instead, a gray fog has settled over everything. Uneasiness hangs in the air like the threat of a wolf outside the door.

I can't stop hearing the agent ask my name. His voice was oily and quiet. It reminded me of a weasel. What makes it worse is Michael. He's nervous about something, and it's not like him. Everyone is on edge.

26th June 1931

Kate sent me a letter. She says Dutch told Elizabeth that Michael is a bootlegger. Was I a fool to think she'd never find out? The thought of losing her now, after I'm so close to being able to see her again, twists me up inside.

22nd July 1931

Michael and Daniell came to blows this afternoon. Daniell got drunk and went to the stills in the middle of the day. Not entering the woods during the day is the one rule Michael has insisted never be broken, especially now that we're being watched so carefully.

Anyone could have followed Daniell, and we all would've been carted off to God knows where. Daniell rushed Michael, and they fell in a heap on the floor. Michael's nose was bleeding terribly, and Daniell got a cut over his right eye.

Poor Cece. She looked so frightened when he got to his feet and set his eyes on her. He knows he can't beat Michael in a fight. His wife is another matter.

I've got to find a way to protect her and the girls. I can't do anything for Elizabeth right now, but I can sure as hell step between a drunk and his innocent children.

29th July 1931

A gangster from Chicago propositioned Michael for the largest sale of whiskey we've ever had. Over twenty barrels!

I suppose there are still people in the world who have money and nothing good to spend it on. I should be grateful if I want us to keep living as we do. But it worries me. This man is notorious for his connections to crime in Chicago and Detroit, and it's a tremendous amount of alcohol for us to move. Michael says we can do it.

It'll clean us out, but we'd have enough money to build the hardware shop and get the family out of this business for good.

The boys are all at the stills now, prepping the mash and checking the stock to make sure everything will be ready.

A courier came by an hour ago to drop off the final paperwork for my divorce. A week ago I could think of nothing else. Now I find myself wanting to hide it. If we're going to get through the next couple of weeks, Michael needs to be focused. He can't worry about me and take care of the family at the same time. I've placed it in a drawer for now. I've waited so long already; I can wait a little longer.

8th August 1931

I ran into Agent Murphy in town. He took my hand and kissed the back of it. I wanted to wipe it on my dress. He said I should leave Michael while there's still time, that he's going to drag me down.

I turned to walk away, but he grabbed my arm. I don't think I've ever seen such hate in a man's eyes. He called me by my real name, and I gasped. No one but Michael and Cece know my name from my old life.

I shook his hand off me and ran for the car. Jimmy was waiting, and I was shaking so badly I had to tell him what happened.

One other thing Agent Murphy said that's had me on edge: "Be careful out there. These woods are full of snakes."

What did he mean by that?

16th August 1931

Michael's leaving in a few hours to deliver the order to his man in Chicago. They're supposed to be meeting somewhere in the middle, but he won't tell me when or where. I'm terrified. He's tried reassuring me everything will be alright, that he's got a plan, but I have this horrible feeling.

Tomorrow is the anniversary of our commitment to one another. He's promised to be home in time to celebrate with me under our tree. I wish I could believe him. Agent Murphy's words keep playing in my mind. I told Michael what he said, but he just shook his head and said not to worry.

I think I'll ask Cece if I can sleep in her bed tonight. Daniell's been back a month now. Though he hasn't been exactly kind, he's at least been in agreement with Michael. He wants his cut of the money. Not that he'll save any. It'll go straight to alcohol and women. He's a lowdown boozehound if there ever was one.

I wish I knew what Michael's plan is. He must have one, he always does, but I feel like there's a piece missing.

I begged him to let me come along. The police are less likely to pull over a woman driving at night than a man, but he won't even discuss it. I love him so much. What will I do if something awful happens?

17th August 1931

Cece, if you're reading this, thank you. Daniell and Patrick have been brought in for questioning. I only hope you'll have enough time to get yourself and the girls out. I don't know what's happened to Jimmy, only that Michael says he'll need to stay away for a while.

They turned me loose early this morning but Michael is with his brothers at the Bardstown County jail. Please don't worry about us. Everything is going to be alright. Michael set it up. I still can't believe it. I won't be around for a little while. I'm going to hide until all of this has blown over.

I'm burying some money under "our" tree for you. Take it and the girls and run as far away as you can. You have been better to me than I deserved. However I can repay you, I will. Send word through Kate when you're settled.

I'm leaving this diary behind in case they ever question your role in any of this. You alone have been innocent, and I hope my faithful notes on life here over the years will help you, should you ever need it. I know you'll keep it safe until we're together again.

I love you so very much.

X, Lola

SEVENTEEN

I close the book carefully, as though it's a precious thing. And it is. Lola's last entry wasn't written in the same neat hand used in the rest of the diary. It's slanted and rushed. I think she was scared about being on her own again. I knew from the article and from Eby's story how that night was going to end. Still, as I read her words, I was hoping he and the article had been wrong. I wanted Michael to get away and them to be together. Not knowing what happened next—where she went to hide and what happened after—upsets me.

Oliver takes my hand. "You okay?"

I play with his fingers in my lap. "Yeah. I think I was sort of hoping that they'd make it out together, somehow."

"I know. Me, too."

The car hums, nearly silent, as we pass a series of small towns. We'll be near the tip of Lake Michigan soon, and then home.

"You said Lola never divorced her husband, didn't you?"

I think back to the conversation we had during the drive to Kentucky. I told Oliver about the argument between me and my mom and the little she knew about Lola. "No, she didn't."

He makes a thoughtful noise and rubs a hand over his hair. "But in the diary, she talks about the paperwork being almost finished. So if they never got divorced, what happened?"

I turn the pages, looking for Lola's entries on the subject. My mother had made it very clear that Lola left my great-grandfather alone to raise Grams. What happened to Dutch and Lola between August of 1931 and the midsixties when Grams's father died? Why *had* they never divorced? And why was Lola's diary still at the Craig house if she'd entrusted it to Cece? Had it made its way back there, or did Cece never take it in the first place? I let the questions stew. But another bothers me more.

"What I'm more interested in is what happened to her and Michael after he went to prison. I wouldn't even know where to begin to look. She said she went into hiding."

"Now that"—Oliver pulls the envelope holding my "surprise" from the side of his seat—"I may be able to help you with."

I take it from him. It's light.

He answers my question before I ask it. "Michael Craig's death certificate."

"Oh." I don't know why it shocks me. It's not like I was expecting him to be alive. But having been introduced to him through the article only a couple of weeks ago, the news feels sudden. I pinch the brass closure together and open the top of the envelope, then remove a single sheet of paper. The certificate shows Georgia as the state of death. His name has been written in neat handwriting, along with his place of birth—Lawrenceburg, Kentucky—birthdate—January 2, 1899—and then his residence when he died.

I gasp and feel the car swerve as Oliver looks from the road to me. "What?"

I cover my mouth with my hand, reading more. "Did you look at this?"

"No, I wanted it to be a surprise for you."

He must be able to read the expression on my face because he curses under his breath. "What is it? What does it say?"

I place a hand over my heart, which hurts. "It says he died in 1932 at the United States Penitentiary, Atlanta. The cause of death is listed as acute pneumonia."

All hope I had for Lola's story ending happily flees with the paper in my hand. Michael Craig never made it home again.

***

"We're here." Oliver parks along the curb in front of the thrift store that takes up the lower level of my building. We step from the car into the bright early evening sun. My shirt rises as I stretch. The old building looks shabbier than when I left. Maybe I'm just seeing things through new eyes. We were gone only a few nights, but it seems much longer.

He lifts my bag from the trunk and sets it on the sidewalk by my feet.

"Hey." He stops a foot away from me. "I'm sorry about my truly terrible surprise."

I try to smile, to reassure him I'm fine, but I know it falls flat. "It's okay. It's better than not knowing."

"I promise," he says, moving some hair away from my face, "I'll never surprise you like that again."

His joke breaks the ice, and I reach to wrap my arms around his neck.

He tightens his arms around my waist and lifts me, bringing me up to match his height. Kissing him has become easy, natural. It's hard to open my eyes once he pulls away. When I do his lips are rosy from our good-bye. He looks happy.

"Thanks for the lift." I wiggle my shoes in the air behind me.

"Wow. We need to work on your joke-telling skills." He sets me back on solid ground and I find it overrated by comparison. "What're your plans for tomorrow evening? I'm thinking dinner, maybe a movie?"

A little part of me was afraid that, once we'd crossed the Illinois state line, he'd come to his senses and wonder what he's been doing with me. I'm glad to be proven wrong.

"I don't know. I've got to check in with the family and tell Lucky I'm back. I wouldn't put it past him to schedule us both for work the minute he knows we're in town. That is, if we both still have jobs. Which reminds me. How long are you planning to stay?"

"Not sure. But"—he leans over and places a hand on the brick wall behind me—"there's a girl here I'd like to see more of." He kisses the side of my mouth, then backs away and rubs his hands together. "Alright. Call the parents, put off the boss, then meet me at the school at eight tomorrow night."

"The school?"

"Yeah." He grins. "It's kind of our place, I think."

"You don't have another surprise, do you?"

"I'll be honest. I'm sort of looking to redeem myself now. I can't have you walking around being afraid of surprises. That's no way to live."

I watch him over my shoulder and just as I'm about to place my key in the lock, it occurs to me he doesn't have a car. "Wait, how're you getting home?"

"I'll walk."

"But it's at least two miles from here."

"Where was your concern Saturday morning?" He winks. Walking back, he takes my hand. "I like to walk. It gives me time to think. And you've given me plenty to think about." He kisses the skin below my knuckles. "Thank you."

"For what?"

"For letting me come along."

"I should be the one thanking you. I never would've gone if you hadn't made me step into your time machine." I try to say things I know will make him smile just to see the chip in his tooth.

"Anytime," he says. "And don't worry. We'll find out what happened to Lola."

I lower my eyes to the ground. "I wish I could believe that."

"What? You don't believe in our amazing investigative skills?"

"Oliver . . ." I raise my head. I don't want to seem argumentative, but after reading those last entries in her diary and discovering Michael never made it out of prison, I'm afraid of what else we'll find. Knowing that all those things she wanted for their life together never came true feels like a fresh wound. "Maybe it's better not knowing."

"Come on, Wynn." His voice is tinted with frustration. "Don't give up now."

I raise my shoulders and lift my arms from my sides. "I'm not giving up. I just have no idea how we're going to find her. We've already been through pages of census records and social security information. And we don't know where she went. For all we know, she changed her name again."

"We'll dig deeper."

I release a frustrated sigh. "Oliver, I'm so grateful you came with me and that we found her diary. Getting to read part of her story in her own words was amazing, but—"

He takes my chin and forces me to meet his eyes. They're light today. "What're you afraid of? Why is it so difficult for you to believe anything is possible?"

"She's gone. She never wanted to be found in the first place. Maybe her story should end with the diary."

"Wynn—"

"I know what you want to hear." I pull on his wrists until he lets go of me. "And I have so much more faith in what *could be*, now. Because of you." I touch a spot on his chest. "I really am grateful. But I'm also more certain than ever that chasing dreams instead of real life is dangerous. I mean, my God. After everything she gave up, everything she put herself through, to end up losing Michael . . . Look at the consequences she had to live with. Wouldn't it have been better if she'd just stayed with her daughter? At least she wouldn't have ended up alone."

He turns away, running his hand down his face. "I thought you understood her."

My head jerks back a little, recoiling from the sting of his statement.

"I know you're afraid, Wynn. You're getting a picture of the way Lola's life turned out, and it isn't what you imagined it to be. But look at what's happened between *us*. Did you think *that* was a possibility? Because the odds of us getting together after all this time weren't great."

"What's happening between us is totally different from finding out what happened to her."

"No, it's not."

"Of course it is!" My voice is more high-pitched and accusatory than I intend. "Lola has probably been dead for decades. She ran away. She vanished. Maybe it was to survive; maybe my mom is right and it was because she really was just a selfish person. Whatever the reason, she's gone. We"—I move my finger between us—"are here together. Now."

He grips my upper arms. "You've read the words. You know there's more to her than what she did. And I've spent the last ten years regretting the chance we never took. *Ten years.* You could've been gone by now. You could've been married, had children. You could've been a missionary in Timbuktu, for all I knew. But I came home and you were still here. It was like time stopped where you were concerned."

His words hit a dark place inside me. A familiar place. Suddenly it's like the last five days never happened. "Time didn't stop. I just didn't move along with it." I break away from him and grab the handle of my suitcase.

"That's not what I meant, and you know it."

I turn the lock to my building with my key, and it clicks audibly. "I know."

"Wynn."

I look over my shoulder. I hate that he sees the doubt in me. "It's fine. I'll be okay. I'm just tired."

"Will you meet me tomorrow night?"

I drag my bag across the threshold and remove the key from the door. "I don't know. I need to check in with everyone, see what's going on. I'll call you."

"I'll wait for you."

I close myself in the dim stairwell. I want to smile at the irony. It's always been me waiting for him.

***

A cardboard box sits on the kitchen table when I step into the apartment. A sheet of paper lies faceup on the closed top.

We finished cleaning out the house while you were away. I thought you might like these. Call me when you get in.

Love, Mom

I pull the flaps and open the box. There's a bundle of cards, both handmade and store-bought, resting near the top. They're cards I gave Grams over the years. I didn't know she saved them. A sharp pain pierces my chest. I place the cards on the table and root through the box, looking to see what else my mom saved for me. Pictures of my sisters and me as kids, a badly constructed pillow in the shape of a pair of lips from ninth-grade home ec, a folded-up map, and a vase made of blue glass.

I remove the vase and turn it over in my hands. I can't believe—because of all those years of resentment and bitterness—that my grandmother chose to surround herself with something so clearly inspired by her mother. I wonder if Grams knew why Lola loved blue glass? Grams met Michael. Did she see the resemblance to his eyes?

I take the cards and photographs to my bed and spread them out. Mom must've made my bed. She can't help but clean up after us, even in our own homes. I pick up a card made of red construction paper. There's a pink heart glued to the front with the word "Love" spelled crookedly in childish handwriting.

> *Dear Grams,*
> *You our the best granmuther in the hole world.*
>
> *Love, Wynn*

Really, Mom? Trying to guilt me into giving up the ghost of Lola, literally? I push the cards into a pile and walk to the bags I left by the door. Lola's diary sits on top of my wallet inside my purse. I bring it back to bed with me.

If anything, I'm more conflicted about who this woman was and why she did what she did. She's not the monster Franny makes her out to be. She was just a young woman scared of what her life had become and of what it would be if she stayed. I understand that part. I can relate to that fear. And I don't dispute that she acted selfishly. She hurt Grams, and for that, it's difficult for me to forgive her.

But she was also brave. She wanted her own life. One that was big and full. Can I blame her for that? I think what I fear most is the unknown, when what I should be afraid of is the undone. Lola risked everything for a life she wasn't even sure she could have. Could I do the same? Could anyone?

Lola and Oliver saw their paths clearly. They didn't falter or turn away from the chance at a bigger life. But where did it get them? Lola ended up losing everything a second time. Oliver followed his dream, only to find it wasn't enough. He wants me to believe anything is possible, but that's not how life works; it takes as much as it gives.

I press my fingers to my temples and shut my eyes. Leaving Kentucky without knowing what became of Lola wasn't what I wanted, especially after discovering so much of her story. What am I going to say to my family about all of this? My mother and Franny need to know that their version of Lola is wrong. Whatever poor choices she made, her story deserves to be told. She's our family. If we don't remember her, who will?

I open the book. Her words echo softly off the page. I trace the sentences with my fingertip and realize the voice I'm hearing is my own. Am I like her? Some days I want to do what Oliver would have me do. Leave and never look back. Go, seek, find, journey from one experience to another. No fear. No regret. Just freedom to be whoever the hell it is I'm meant to be. Some days it seems like that's all I've ever wanted.

But it's never that easy. There are so many unknowns. How can I risk the life I've built, slight though it may be, for just a chance at something different? Not better or happier or worthier, because I can't know it'll be any of those things. Just different. How do you risk everything for that? Right now, I have a job and an apartment and a family, and who knows? Maybe I'll finally have a career. It's what people do. Grow up, go to college, get a job, find a spouse, have children. Be content. Don't *want* all the time. Be happy with what you have. Above all, don't be selfish.

Maybe I missed my chance at having that other life, and it's too late for me now. Maybe what *could be* simply—eventually—always becomes less important than what *should be*.

I flip to the last page, where her handwriting is a hurried, messy scrawl. I wonder how much of the diary Cece read and why she didn't keep it with her, as Lola asked. We should've looked into Cecelia Craig as well. She was the closest person to Lola outside of Michael or Kate. I remember Grams talking about her aunts Kate and Goldie sometimes. They were a feisty pair. Goldie never married, and Kate made the best strawberry pie in the world.

The phone vibrates in my pocket. I ignore it, rolling over and clutching the diary to me. Searching for Lola has left me tired and sad. Finding that article changed things. It's made me uneasy with questions. Am I living the life I'm meant to lead? How much am I willing to risk to have another one? Would it be worth it? Will I ever be happy with what I have? It's that last one that bothers me most. When I think of everything I've got to be grateful for, I feel ashamed to want so much more.

***

Someone banging at the door wakes me from my nap. I scramble to my feet, my heart thumping against my chest. Franny's face looms in the peephole. I hate my neighbors. They'll clearly let anyone inside the building. I've barely turned the lock when she pushes inside.

"Hey, what's going on?" I ask.

She hands me a white envelope.

"What's this?"

"Open it." Franny takes a seat at the table. She's got this way of crossing her legs like she's creating a vacuum seal with her thighs. I'm certain her husband cringes whenever he sees it.

The school district's name and logo are printed in the top left corner. There's a jagged tear down the length of the envelope. I remove the letter and unfold it. The words float up, my eyes read them, but the message doesn't sink in. I frown at my sister.

"Congratulations!" she says in a singsong voice.

"Why do you have this?"

"Ben handled an emergency IT call at the school district yesterday, and your rep asked if he'd give it to you."

"And you opened it?"

She smiles, eager for me to share in the excitement. "Well, he tried calling, but you didn't pick up, and I was too excited to wait. You got the job!"

I read the letter again.

Dear Ms. Jeffries,

We are pleased to extend a permanent offer of employment to you for the position of social studies teacher at Downers Grove North High School.

I've waited years for this moment. Spent countless hours subbing in classrooms full of loud children who treat my lessons like spring break, kids who make ADHD look like meditation and take the phrase "higher learning" literally. I've plucked spitballs from my hair, cleaned up puke, dealt with angry parents, learned math . . . and all while slinging beer between teaching jobs. My stomach churns uncomfortably.

Franny's smile fades. "What? What's wrong? You don't look happy. Why aren't you happy?"

"I—"

"You got your dream job!"

I lift my eyes to my sister's. How can she not know anything about me? "Dream job?"

The crease between her eyebrows deepens. "Wynn, what the hell is wrong with you? You've been subbing for three years. I don't understand why you're not jumping up and down on the table right now?"

I leave the kitchen and walk toward the bed, tapping the offer against my chin. She's right. I should be excited—or at least happy I don't have to wipe down sticky tables at the bar anymore if I don't want to. I'm finally getting a return on a years-long investment. This is good news. This is a good job.

Cards are strewn across my bed. Some are crumpled from my nap. Lola's diary sticks out from beneath a pillow. I pick up the book, weighing it in one hand against the letter in the other.

"Hey." Franny's footsteps clip neatly against the floor. She stops in front of me, snapping her fingers beneath my eyes. "Snap out of it."

She takes the diary from me, turning the pages without consideration for its age or value. I watch her read it. She's starting somewhere in the middle. I see on her face the exact moment she realizes what it is and who it belonged to.

"Where did you get this?"

"We found it."

"Who? You and Mr. Rock Star?"

"Don't," I warn her. I collapse on the bed and hold my head in my hands. "It's a long story."

The pages rustle as she turns them, reading out of order. "Does Mom know about this?"

"No. I just got back a couple of hours ago."

The bed dips as she sits next to me. She drops her elbows to her knees. "This is unbelievable."

"I know."

"Have you read it all?"

"Yeah."

"What does it say?" She turns the pages slowly now, squinting to read the faded handwriting.

"It explains pretty much everything. Why she left, where she went. All that."

"Was she really a bootlegger?"

"No, not really."

"So she wasn't a showgirl either?"

"Actually"—I bite my lip, a habit I can't seem to break, and try to subdue my smile—"she was. For a little while, anyway."

We sit in silence. Franny, like Tabby, moves her lips as she reads. I let Lola tell her story in her own words, just as Oliver encouraged me to do. I have a feeling we'll interpret it differently—it's just who we are—but Franny needs to know, and she needs to understand, in her own way, why Lola did what she did. When she closes the book ten minutes later, it's with far more care.

"Wow."

"I know."

She turns the diary over in her hands, tracing the flowers with her fingers as I did. "It's insane that you found this."

I clasp my hands and nod at the wall.

The sound of her laughter startles me. I turn toward it. Her smile is incredulous. "Oh my God."

"What?"

She shakes a thought from her head. "You think she's the same as you."

I open my mouth to refute her, but she talks over me.

"That's why you're not excited about the job. You've been romanced by our dead ancestor."

"Romanced by . . . ? You're crazy."

"Oh please!" She drags the word out as she gets to her feet. "You've been wandering around for months—years—with this 'poor me' expression permanently etched onto your face—"

"Hey!"

"—And now you've found something to justify your desire not to grow up."

I jump off the bed, pointing to her. "You've got no right to—"

"To tell you the truth? To call you out on your bullshit?" Her arms cross, viselike, against her chest. "You're twenty-eight years old. You live in a one-room apartment, everything you own is secondhand. You were practically valedictorian, and you've never had a real job." Her eyes are as harsh as her words. "You love being the nobody, because then you never have to feel what it's like to fail, to go after something you really want, and lose."

I lean toward her, my skin hot with anger. "Fuck you."

"Alright, fine. But at least I try. Even she"—she gestures to the book on the bed—"tried. It cost her a daughter, but she went after what she wanted. When have you ever done that?"

Tears well up quickly behind my eyes. What hurts most is how old her anger is. It sounds as though she's been saving it up for a long time. "I do try. I've been trying. But every time I've come remotely close to doing something with my life, I've had to give it up to help one of you."

"Oh please." She shakes her head. "That's just an excuse. You're scared because you think your life has to have some big purpose, and you don't know what the hell it is. You think that makes you different from anyone else?"

I close my mouth, afraid of saying something I can't take back.

"Everyone wants to do something glamorous and exciting with their life. You don't think I want that? I've got two little kids and a needy husband. You don't think I want some grand adventure?"

Her words keep me silent. I've never thought of Franny as someone who dreams.

"Life is more than happy fun time. We all make sacrifices."

"I have made sacrifices."

"Yes, you have. And you always let those sacrifices stop you from moving forward."

"I—" I can't finish the sentence. I know she's right. "What am I supposed to do?"

Franny shoves her hands into her back pockets. The venom is gone from her voice, but she's not backing down. She never does. "It's time for you to hop off the cross, little sister. *Do something.*"

"Lola did something, and you hate her for it."

"I don't hate Lola. To be honest, I don't care much about her one way or the other. I get it. She wanted something more, and that's okay, but she's a douchebag for the way she went about it."

I aim my smile toward the floor. Franny's always had a way with words.

She steps gently on my bare feet with her sandals, tapping my toes until I raise my eyes to meet hers. "Listen, I love you."

I roll my eyes.

"I do. I know I can be a little abrasive sometimes—"

"A little?"

"—But I have your best interests at heart," she finishes loudly. "Just . . ." Her shoulders lift as she sighs toward the ceiling. "Just think about this job, okay? I know it's not a traveling circus in Mumbai, or whatever, but it's a real opportunity for you to be someone and do something with your life. And for what it's worth, you'd be really good at it."

Her arms wrap around me cautiously. When I don't raise mine immediately to hug her back, she gives me a bone-crushing hug. She can't stand for me to be mad at her. I slowly return her embrace, and she shimmies on the spot. She always has to win, and I always seem to let her. It's the nature of our relationship.

I walk her to the door. She stops in the hallway and turns to face me.

"I know being a grown-up sucks."

"God, don't say that. I hate when people say that. Why does wanting to do things that make you happy somehow mean you're not a grown-up?"

Her chin wrinkles as she frowns. "I don't know. I guess because if you're always doing things that make you happy, you're never making the hard decisions."

"What decisions are those?"

"Oh, you know, contributing to society, settling down, saving for retirement . . ."

"You make it sound so appealing."

"I never said they'd be fun."

"But why do they have to be hard?"

She smiles at me. "Because easy decisions are for pussies."

EIGHTEEN

Visions of orange pottery and poorly buttoned shirts urge caution. I ring the bell instead of stepping into my parents' home unannounced. My father's outline grows larger the closer he comes to the beveled-glass cutout in the front door. He greets me whistling.

"Hey, there. Look who it is." He smiles and pulls me in for a hug.

"Hi, Daddy."

"Hey-ya, sweet pea." He kisses, then releases, me. "How was your big trip?"

"Good. I got back last night." I follow him down the hall, happy to find the countertops and table have been cleared of the misshapen vases.

"Did you dig up any skeletons down in Kentucky?"

"Sort of. Is Mom here?"

"Your mother's out in the backyard. She took a couple of plants from your grandmother's house to put in the garden. We closed on it while you were gone, you know."

I place a hand on my stomach. I'd forgotten the sale of Grams's house was finalized this week. The realization that I missed it, that I'll never walk through her front door again, fills me with grief. "I'm so sorry, I forgot."

He pats my arm, then sits at the kitchen table. "Yeah, your mother was pretty upset about it, but she'll be alright. You're back now."

Looking through the picture window, I watch Mom, hunched over, wrestling with a glossy-leafed bush. She's on her knees. Her gardening hat is trimmed with the same red material used to make the gloves she wears.

"Why don't you go out back and say hello. Try and cheer her up?"

Unlikely. Especially considering what I've come to tell her.

Dad stands and plants another kiss on my forehead before leaving the room, whistling again. I slide the glass door open and walk through a wall of heat. I take the dozen steps to the garden and stand behind my mother. There's dirt on the back pocket of her jeans and a line of sweat down her back. I finger the hem of my blue dress and stub one poorly manicured toe into the ground, my flip-flop bending against the arch of my foot. I'm nervous about showing her the diary, about what she'll think of the story inside it.

"Mom?"

She looks over her shoulder. Her smile takes away some of my apprehension. "Hey, you. Help me with this plant for a sec'."

I try not to step on any flowers. She pushes the bush toward me and I hold it upright as she digs a deeper hole. Once she's satisfied, she drops it in place and packs dirt around the base.

I wait quietly, apprehension stirring within. Her face remains mostly smooth and lovely, but her age shows in her movements as she stands. She wipes her brow with the back of her arm, knocking the gardening hat askew.

"Thanks, babe."

"Sure." There's no ease in my smile. "Thanks for bringing me the box of Grams's stuff."

The lines around her mouth help suppress a frown. "I thought you might like to keep a few more of her things."

"I do, thank you." I fiddle with my purse. "Dad said you closed on her house?"

She can hardly meet my eyes. "Yep. All signed and delivered."

"Did you get to meet the people buying it?"

She looks around the backyard. Anywhere but at me. "No, but the realtor said they're a nice young couple with a toddler and a baby on the way."

It's strange, feeling so awkward around her. "Well, that's good."

Her eyes meet mine briefly and wrinkle at the corners, a grimace on her lips. I hate that she's mad at me and hope what Oliver and I found will somehow make her feel better. It's got to mean something that Lola regretted what she'd done and tried to make amends, doesn't it? I fumble with my purse, pulling out the diary.

"What's that?"

I hold it up. "I found it in Kentucky. It's Lola's."

My mother pulls her gloves off slowly. "I'm sorry, Wynn, but I'm just not interested." She walks past me toward the house and slides the door open, then closed, leaving me outside.

Her disinterest irritates me. I may not have the same resentment she does toward Lola, but ignoring the truth makes no sense. I yank the door open, braver now, and step into the cool house.

"Mom."

"Wynn, I don't want to hear about it." She faces away from me, toward the kitchen sink. Dad's nowhere to be found.

"It's her diary. I found it."

She turns. An argument lingers in her eyes, but instead she asks a question. "You found her diary? How?"

"We found the house she was living in when that article was written." I pause, not wanting to admit I stole it. "We sort of stumbled across it in the study there."

She walks toward me, taking the book from my hands. "Are you sure it's hers?"

"It's definitely hers. She talks a lot about Grams."

She runs her fingers across the cover. Just as I think she's going to open it, she hands it back. I watch her consciously rearrange her features into indifference.

"Well, I'm glad your trip was worth it."

"Mom, don't you want to read what it says?"

She crosses her arms and leans against the counter. "Why don't you just tell me about it?"

I open the book. The pages fan up, so I pat them down. Lola's careful cursive seems intrusive in the kitchen. Mom's eyes are focused on the diary. Her expression reveals mild indifference. There's so much I want her to believe.

I start at the beginning, reading the first couple of pages verbatim, then paraphrasing, turning the pages as I go to stay in sync with the timeline. I recount those first few weeks and her wonder over the city.

I tell my mother how afraid Lola was and how much she ached to be with her daughter. My mother rolls her eyes when I mention the Seelbach and the dance clubs. I tell her about Michael and how he rescued her, protected her, loved her. Occasionally Mom's mouth moves, usually into a frown or pursed sourness. I hear her intake of breath as I relay Lola's meeting with Michael. Once, very briefly, I see the beginning of a smile, though it fades quickly. The longer we stand in the kitchen, the faster and more animated a storyteller I become.

In some ways, it's my duty to tell Lola's story the right way, from *her* point of view. Whatever else she did or became, she began as a young woman who looked into the future and saw a life she would regret. It doesn't make what she did right or absolve her from the pain she caused, but it is understandable. It is human. I need my mother to accept that her grandmother did her best with the life she had. I need her to believe in Lola, because so much of how I feel is how she felt. She wanted passion, freedom, a full life. That's what I want, too.

When I get to the part about the blue glass necklace, Mom jumps and places a hand over her mouth. She turns toward the sink, her back straight and rigid. I knew it would be a revelation for her. It was for me. In fact I'd been waiting for it, but the shock on her face, the way she holds her hand over her heart, are more than I expected.

"Mom?"

There's true confusion in her eyes when she faces me. She walks toward the hall and I follow her into the bedroom. She stands in front of the armoire, pulling open the mirrored door, and takes a small wooden box from inside. It's old, made of pine, and there's a broach-like clasp on the front. She carries it backward until the backs of her knees touch the mattress and she sits, lowering the box to her lap.

"Mom, what is it?"

Her hands tremble as she opens the lid and pulls out a long silver chain. A piece of blue glass shaped like a tear is attached to one end.

"Oh my God." I reach out and touch the glass, letting it rest against my palm. "Where did you—"

"The movers found the box under the dresser in the guest room." She drops the chain into my hand, her eyes never leaving it. "I didn't know it was there."

The glass is small, only an inch in width, but the color is a deep cobalt blue. *The same blue as Michael's eyes . . .*

"My God." My mother's hands skim over the top of the box. Her lips turn up in a smile, but it's not happiness. It's disbelief. "Blue glass." She shakes her head and looks up at me, her stare insistent. "She never said anything. I didn't know."

I sit beside her on the bed and place the necklace in her hand. "I can't believe she kept it." Grams told her mother she gave the necklace away, but she kept it with her, all those years. And not only did she keep it, she kept the memory of that gift alive her entire life. A house filled with blue glass. "Was that the only thing in the box?" I ask.

Her head jerks in my direction. "There was . . . a picture. I didn't know who it was, but"—she cracks the box open, barely wide enough for her hand to slip inside, and pulls out a small photograph—"it must be my grandmother."

The woman in the photo isn't facing the photographer. She stands sideways, her fingers nearly touching parted lips that are laughing. A light-colored hat curves over shortly cropped dark hair. The coat she wears is thick and woolen, but I make out the softness of a dress beneath. She looks happy and young.

"You think it's her?"

Her voice shakes. "It must be."

My fingers follow the curve of the hat, as they did the outline of Lola's bowed head in the photo that accompanied the newspaper article. "She was beautiful."

My mother sighs heavily. "Yes, she was."

"Does it say when it was taken?"

She takes the picture from me and turns it over. Someone's written in pencil on the back, "1929."

I read the date several times. "That was after she left. How did Grams get this?"

"I don't know. Maybe her aunt Goldie or Kate?"

"Lola and Kate wrote to each other."

"That doesn't surprise me. I remember Aunt Goldie telling me Lola and Kate had been close."

"They were." I offer my mother the diary, which she all but forgot once she pulled the blue teardrop necklace from the wooden box. She takes the book with tentative hands. "She talks about Kate a little in here."

"Does she? What else does it say?" Much of the ire has left her voice.

I tell her about the initials carved in the oak tree near the abandoned stills and Lola's unending hope she'd one day have her daughter's forgiveness. I recount everything Eby told me about the Craig brothers, their moonshining operation, and their brush with a federal agent. Mom turns the pendant over in her hand as I talk about Michael and how much he loved Lola. About how he died, and my sadness at knowing Lola ended up alone again.

We sit on the bed for a long time. My throat feels tight and thick with emotion by the time I'm done. I wish I could finish the story, but I don't have an ending to give her.

"And you've got no idea where she might've gone?"

"No. We searched page after page of records, but we couldn't find her again."

She seems content not knowing. I wish I could feel the same.

"Did you keep in touch with any of Kate's kids? I thought they might know something."

"Her kids are all dead now. Tucker, her youngest son, died about three years ago."

"Do you think their kids might—"

"No." My mother shakes her head, sure of herself. "What happened with Lola was obviously a well-kept family secret. When my granddad was alive, we were forbidden from mentioning her name." She looks imploringly at me. "I know how it sounds to you. A woman unhappy in her marriage and her life strikes out to make it on her own. She falls in love, does exciting things. But what she did was so incredibly selfish. Can't you see that?"

"I know it seems that way, but—"

She shakes her head, quieting me. "No. She wasn't the person you've made her up to be. She ruined a lot of lives, Wynn."

My voice pleads. "She just wanted to do something with her life. It wasn't easy for her to leave, but she knew if she didn't, she'd never be happy. And it was awful for her. I understand that, can't you?"

"I know, my darling." She wraps her arm around my shoulder and hugs me to her, rocking me side to side. "I know how badly you want things, and I want you to have them. I do. But we can't hurt the people we love to get what we want. It doesn't work like that."

I lift my chin. The tightness in my throat is so complete, it's hard to swallow. "Then how is it supposed to work? I've done everything I'm supposed to do, and I'm still not happy."

Her eyes are filled with hurt I know I've put there. "That makes me so sad."

My shoulders hitch forward and all the air leaves my lungs in a sob I wasn't expecting. I rest my head against her shoulder and let years of unshed tears fall. "I'm tired, Mom. I want my life to mean something. I'm afraid I'm wasting it. I don't know what to do."

Her thumbs wipe the wetness away. "Look at me." She takes my chin in her hand. "You're not wasting your life. You think life is measured by experiences, but it's not. It's measured by your ability to give and receive love. Your Grams is a great example of that. She didn't have a fancy life. Her life was quiet, even slow, but it was full of love. Do you think she regretted it?"

The answer is no. My grandmother only ever wanted one thing: a family. And now I know why. When her mother left, pieces of Grams's life were torn away. Getting them back became her goal. *Her adventure.*

I let my mother hold me. I know there's truth in what she's saying. But I am not her. Or my Grams. Or my sisters. I want more. I can't help it. I wish I could. And whatever she says, I believe in those experiences she dismisses so easily. I crave them. Only, I can't find the words to tell her. How do you describe a need so visceral you can never remember a time when it didn't consume you? And how do you explain the shame you feel for not meeting that need, because you're a coward?

She places a series of soft kisses on the top of my head. "You already have a great life. You've got a family that loves you and a career to look forward to. I know you think going off to explore will fill some void inside you, but Wynnie, my girl, that has to come from within. You're the only one who can make *you* happy."

She hugs me, tight, and it feels comforting and safe. There've been times, so many times, when one hug from her or Grams could calm my wanderlust for weeks, months. Their embraces gave me a reason to stay. They made me feel loved and valued. As she releases me, and I stand across from her, I feel that same reassurance struggling to quiet the doubt inside.

"Here." She presses the photo of Lola into my hand.

"You should—"

"Keep it. Please."

She doesn't walk me to the front door. I let myself out, and it isn't until I'm a mile down the road that I realize I forgot the diary. Maybe it's for the best. Lola's story, the past week with Oliver? They've been diversions masquerading as answers.

The light at the intersection turns yellow, then red. I stop, the first in a growing line of cars. Lola's picture sits beside me on the passenger's seat. I look away, outside at the people who seem to be everywhere. Other drivers, women pushing strollers, men in baseball caps, couples and kids and old people. All living. All waiting for one thing or another. What makes me so special? I press a resigned laugh into my hand, then tilt my head back. Shutting everything out for a few seconds. Restless, dissatisfied, resentful . . . foolish.

I'm going to take the social studies job. I'm taking it because there's no reason not to. It'll be a good job, if I let it be. Besides, I can't go on like this. Always dreaming, always hoping things will change. It's me that needs to change. I can't live my whole life waiting for someday. If Lola's story has taught me anything, it's that life is about choices. I may get them wrong at times, as she sometimes did, but the important thing is to try. I need to start trying.

***

His back is to me when I turn into the parking lot. Hands casually stuck into jeans pockets, T-shirt half-tucked in. Maybe he has a time machine, after all. He looks almost exactly like the teenage boy I was so infatuated with.

Oliver turns toward my headlights, a big smile on his face, and I'm struck by the sameness of it. I've been waiting for him to come to me the same as I've been waiting for everything else. My life stalled when I was seventeen. I just didn't realize how much of that was my fault. Until now.

"You came." He comes to me and helps me out of the car, placing a kiss on my lips.

An ache like regret burns inside me. How much time have I wasted remembering that first kiss? How many relationships did I doom unconsciously by comparing every other kiss to that one? I pull away from him.

"What's wrong?"

"Nothing. I just went to see my mom."

"You wanna talk about it?"

"Yes. No. Maybe?"

His laugh relaxes me. "Listen, I'm sorry about yesterday."

"Me, too."

"But I haven't given up hope."

"Oh, no?"

"No." His dark stubble will turn into a beard soon if he doesn't shave.

I run my fingertips over it. "You let this grow out any longer and people are going to start calling you a hipster."

He kisses the tender spot behind my ear, then rubs his stubble against me. It tickles, and I fight to get away. "Oh, no you don't. You want a hipster boyfriend? I'll give you all the hipster boyfriend you can handle."

His words stop me. "Boyfriend?"

"Yeah." He shrugs. "I thought so. Unless you're looking to keep your options open?"

My lips always insist on making a fool of me in front of him. "No." I shake my head. "No options."

"Alright." He kisses me on the nose. "Now that's settled, I actually brought you here for a reason."

"Oh no. You're not going to try and surprise me again, are you?"

"Haha." His smile is nervous, not at all like him. He rubs the back of his neck, and his eyes shift from me to the ground and back again. "I want you to come with me."

"Come with you? Where?"

"Nashville. I've got friends there. They're making some amazing music, and I think we should go. Together."

Wait. "What?"

"I know it's sudden, but I've been thinking about it for a few days. You've inspired me, Wynn. I feel good. For the first time in a long time, I feel really, really good. Like I could write songs again. It's time for me to get back on the road, and I want you to come with me this time."

He stands tall and sure of himself now. I'd be lying if I said I hadn't dreamed of this. It's everything I thought I wanted. But I don't feel excited. I don't feel that tug against my stomach. I feel frustrated and angry and pulled in too many directions. I adore Oliver, I want to be with him, but music is his dream, not mine.

"Oliver . . ." I swallow, buying time. Trying to find honest words. "I got the job." I move my hand toward the building on my left. "They want me to start in a couple of weeks."

The confidence leaves his shoulders.

"Franny actually hand-delivered the offer."

"You're taking it?"

I need him to understand. I've been waiting to do something with my life for years. Something for myself. I'm tired of waiting. "Oliver—"

"Don't." He turns away from me, squinting into the darkness of the parking lot.

"Please understand. I would love to go with you. I want to be with you. But I need to take this job."

"Why?" His eyes flash. "What can this job possibly offer that would make missing out on this experience worth it?"

My mother's words about trading my connection to the people who love me for just the possibility of something more come back to me. I don't want to hurt him, but I can't walk out on my family. Not now. Not like this.

"You said you'd go with me."

I touch his arm, and it tenses beneath my fingers. "And I want to, but—"

"Come with me." He takes my hand in his. "I want to be with you."

"I want to be with you, too." The words hurt as they cross my lips. To lose him now feels so incredibly unfair.

"Then say you'll come."

I can't.

Oliver nods, accepting my silence as an answer. He leans back on his heels, away from me. "I thought we wanted the same things."

I'm struck by his tone and rigidity. I don't know how to fix this. I'm upside down and confused. I stutter a few times, wanting to explain myself, but he steps forward, and I lose my words altogether.

He holds me and presses his lips against my hair. His breath is warm against my skin. He turns to walk away, and I realize that the kiss was good-bye. My arm reaches out behind him, my body doing what my brain can't, trying to keep him here with me. Here in the world I know, the one that's real and safe. Not the one where people like him and Lola exist.

NINETEEN

Lucky's is full of people tonight. I'm glad it's my last shift. Working with Oliver these past two weeks has been almost impossible. Every time our fingers accidentally brush passing beer over the bar, they come back feeling bruised. He's been polite on the occasions we've had a reason to speak to one another, but otherwise he's kept his distance. It makes me feel like I did in school when all I wanted was for him to see me.

Our boss yells across the room, the *r*'s missing from the ends of his words. It sounds like, "Hey, Wynn! Grab a couple of Coo-ahs from the bah, would ya?"

I turn toward the bar and catch sight of Oliver. He's surrounded, as always, by a group of girls vying for his attention. Attention I had all to myself for a little while. I stand near the end and wait for him to notice me. It doesn't take long. I think we're each overly aware of the other's presence.

I hold up two fingers. "Coors, please."

He grabs the bottles from beneath the bar, removing the caps as he walks toward me. "Here."

I pinch them between my fingers and grab some cardboard coasters. "Thanks." He tries to smile, but I've seen him happy. He can't fool me. "How are you?"

"Alright. You?"

"Okay."

"Tonight's the night, huh? Last time you'll ever get paid to encourage public drunkenness?"

I try laughing. "I guess. I—" My voice catches in my throat. "Lucky said you're leaving, too. Are you going to Nashville?"

He lifts one shoulder. "I don't know, maybe. It's on the list, anyway. Thought I might take a month to bum around for a bit. Spend some of that hard-earned cash my accountant's been hoarding for me."

"That sounds amazing. Do you know where you'll go?"

"Not really." His eyes meet mine. "I thought I'd wing it. Maybe hit up some museums. Go and have a look at all those places you'll be teaching about come Monday."

"I'm jealous."

"Are you?" His question lacks the reservation of politeness.

My heart dips and falters. "Of course I am."

"But you still won't come with me?"

I can't go through this again. Saying good-bye once was hard enough. "I'm sorry."

"Yeah, you've said."

"Please understand. It wasn't an easy decision to make. But I need to start . . . something—something real and significant."

"And being with me isn't enough?"

"No." The word surprises us both. "I can't keep doing what everyone else wants."

"Isn't that what you're doing by staying?" He waits for my answer with parted lips. All I want to do is kiss them.

"No. This time it's my choice to stay. I need to start my life, Oliver. Mine. If I go with you now, it'll just be me taking the easy way out again."

"How?"

"Because I've been in love with you since I was a child." My voice is loud, and it draws the attention of a few customers. I flush furiously and pick at a spot on the bar. "Or infatuated, anyway. Being with you was all I thought about. Now I realize it was just another way for me to avoid something. If I was busy fawning over you, I didn't have to worry about having a date for the prom or committing to a relationship. Because those guys were never going to compare. The idea of you let me keep one foot out the door, and I've just started to realize how much that may've cost me."

"Because you could've been with someone else?"

"Because I never allowed myself to be with *anyone* else. Not fully. I've been living in a dream world. Because it's safe. It lets me feel as though everything's possible without actually taking the risk of going after what I want. And you've been doing it, too."

"What're you talking about?"

"I'm not your what-if. I never was. You were just alone and unhappy, and having something to regret gave you an excuse to come back home when things weren't working out. But you're brave. You never needed me."

He reaches out and grabs my hand over the bar. "You're wrong. I do need you."

I pull away and let my hand fall out of his grasp. Lola's words fill my mind. *I'm living for me now.* I turn away before I can't. "I'm sorry. *I* need me more."

***

"Can I have everyone's attention, please?" Lucky grins at the audience, most of whom are too drunk and rowdy to know where to look. "I've got a surprise I think you're going to like. For the first, last, and—he says—only time at Lucky's Bar, put your hands together for Oliver Reeves!"

Loud applause and cheers come from all directions. Oliver places a stool on the makeshift stage in the back of the bar, and people crowd around him. His guitar is honey colored with black wood laid beneath the strings. I watch from a corner near a blacked-out window, my eyes fixed on his face. An audience member yells something inaudible, and Oliver smiles and speaks into the microphone.

"I love you, too, man."

The room laughs. He tunes the guitar, strumming the strings until he's content with the sound they make. His eyes search the crowd until they meet mine.

"I'm leaving in a couple days."

People boo him, but he smiles.

"I'll be hitting the open road like any good musician must do. But I wanted to play one song before I go. It's about a woman I met."

Cheers now.

"She's sort of turned me inside out. So this is for her."

I will the beats inside my chest to slow down. His fingers brush the strings like a caress, and as his lips part, I try to catalog every note and word.

> *You caught me by surprise*
> *I was just a boy*
> *Lost and confused by life*
> *My future laid in your eyes . . .*

I watch his neck strain and muscles work to tell me, in his own way, that he loves me.

The audience claps and whistles for him and his story. He leaves the stage as Lucky comes to stand beside me.

"I can't believe I'm losing my two best employees in the same week."

I don't feel like small talk. I want to run to the girls bathroom and hide in the stall where Oliver's name is etched into the steel.

"In all seriousness"—his hands are gentle as they turn me to face him—"I'm going to miss you, Loyola."

I'm grateful the smile on my lips comes on its own. "I'm going to miss you, too." I let him wrap me in a bear hug that takes my breath away.

"You do us proud, now, you got it?"

"I'll try my best."

"I don't want you crawling back in on your hands and knees for your old job."

"Don't worry, I don't plan on touching another plunger for the rest of my life."

"Because," he says over me, "you're too good for this place." He punches me in the shoulder without the normal bruising zeal. "You're a classy lady, Wynn Jeffries. You deserve better than this shithole."

I look around. "I don't know. It's not so bad."

"The only good lookin' thing in here is me. And I ain't that pretty." He gives me a final pat on the arm and takes a step toward the bar before turning back. "I almost forgot. Mr. Famous asked for a word with you. He's in the kitchen."

My gut ties itself in knots. "Do you know why?"

He gives me such a knowing look, I wonder if I've underestimated how much gets past him. "My guess is he wants a review on the song he just debuted. That, or he's looking for bartending lessons. The guy's got the voice of an angel, but he can't mix a drink for shit."

My legs carry me to the door that separates the kitchen from the back of the bar. I push open the white plywood with a trembling hand. Oliver's leaning against the deep freezer.

I stop a few feet away. I can't see the color of his eyes under the fluorescent light. "Lucky said you wanted to see me?"

"I have something for you." He reaches into his back pocket, and I panic. I don't want anything from him. I don't want to drag this out any longer. My resolve is weak enough as it is. But he pulls out a folded sheet of white paper.

I take it, not understanding.

"Read it."

Swirling calligraphy takes up the top of the page. The word "death" stands out from everything else. I scan the boxes beneath. The font in them is tidy, like a typewriter. Lola Elizabeth Craig is listed as the deceased. I look up swiftly.

"I told you we'd find it."

"But how?" I look between him and the paper in my hands.

"Our favorite crazy receptionist."

I wait for him to explain, turning the name on the paper over in my mind.

"I borrowed my dad's car—for real this time—and went down to see her. She's actually pretty brilliant. After I told her about finding the diary and what it said, she went straight to her computer and searched Vital Statistics for Lola under Michael's surname. It was the third option."

The paper is dated April 27, 1951. The cause of death is automobile accident. She was forty-eight years old. I can hardly process the tragedy of it.

"Did you notice the state and county?"

I search the document. DuPage County, Illinois. "But—"

"She came back, Wynn."

***

My mother's gray-blonde hair looks white beneath the glare of my headlights. She's sitting on the concrete step in front of the door to my building. It's late, nearly midnight. The car is barely in park when I jump out and run to her, keys jingling in my hand. "Mom? Are you okay?"

"I'm fine." She stands, absorbing my hug.

"What're you doing here?"

"I needed to talk to you. Can I come up?"

I pull back, worried. As far as I know, she's never made it past the ten o'clock news. There's no way she's here for a friendly chat.

"Come on. You can make us some tea," she says, waiting for me to open the door.

I fire off a round of questions as we climb the stairs. She assures me everything's fine, but her eyes say otherwise. I unlock the door and leave her to sit at the table. I pull two mugs from the cabinet and fill them with water and tea bags. Once the microwave is set, I turn and face her.

"Mom, what's going on? You're scaring me."

She rubs a hand down her arm. "I needed to bring you something. I should have given it to you the other day, but"—she smiles and tilts one shoulder toward the ceiling—"I was worried."

The microwave dings and she stands, pushing me gently aside to collect the mugs and take them to the table. "Sit down, sweetheart."

I do as she says, watching as she steeps the tea in the water, not looking at me. She doesn't seem to know how to start.

"The diary and the blue glass. It caught me off guard."

I think of the death certificate in my purse. I need to tell her. "It's fine, Mom. I understand."

She shakes her head. "No. You don't. Your grandmother didn't tell me about what her mother had done until I was twelve. I asked her a lot of the same questions you did, but she pretended not to know anything more than a few details. I think I knew she wasn't telling me the truth, but I could see how much talking about my grandmother"—she stumbles over the word—"upset her. So I didn't press."

She blows against the tea, and I watch the water ripple. "When you told me about the necklace, I was speechless. All my life I've been surrounded by blue glass. I thought she just liked collecting it, like a hobby. If you hadn't read that to me, if the movers hadn't found that box, I don't think I could've believed it. I thought she hated her mother, and yet she surrounded herself, all of us, with a piece of her."

She swallows slowly. "My mother was a . . . complicated woman at times. She loved her family, she always put our needs before her own, but she could be very stern and unforgiving. I don't think she ever forgave her mother for what she'd done. Not even at the end."

We sit quietly, warm mugs between our hands. I know her thoughts mirror mine. She's thinking of Grams, the mother she loved and grandmother I adored, and the other woman, the one neither of us knew but who, nonetheless, impacted all of our lives.

I reach for my purse on the floor and pull out the paper Oliver gave me. "Here." I hand it to her. There's no point in trying to soften the blow. Not now.

She reads silently for less than a minute before carefully lowering the document to the table. She keeps her fingers pressed against the page, as though tethering herself to the information, the final piece of Lola's story. I told myself, and her, that I wanted only the truth. But what I really wanted was a reason to leave and do *something* for myself. Seeing the distress in the creases around her eyes makes me wish I'd never found the article to begin with.

Her mouth works to find the right words. "There was something else in the box. A letter addressed to your grandmother." She taps the paper beneath her hand. "I think her mother wrote it." She turns in her seat and removes a blue envelope from her bag.

"It's not opened?"

"No." The word is uttered quietly.

"And you didn't want to open it?"

There are tears in her eyes. "It felt like . . . a betrayal—to read something she must never have wanted read. But I couldn't throw it out." She passes the envelope to me.

I take it, feeling its weight in my hand. "Why are you giving this to me?"

Tears slide down her cheeks, and she wipes them away. It feels wrong to see my mother cry. Parents are meant to be strong, the ones who make everything better. Who makes things better for them after *their* parents are gone?

"I know I haven't been supportive of you wanting to find out about what happened to Lola. It scares me to think of you getting hurt. You're my baby. It doesn't matter how old you get. You'll always be my little girl. I wanted to protect you from whatever it was that produced the part of my mother that couldn't forgive."

"Mom—"

"I'm so proud of you, Wynn."

I reach across the table and take her hand.

"You're such a good, kind, thoughtful person. But you're restless. I was afraid if you identified with her, I'd lose you."

"You're not going to lose me."

Her fingers squeeze mine. "I know. But I also know you have this *need* inside you, and that you struggle. I want you to be happy, but I couldn't stand it if you left and something happened to you."

"Nothing's going to happen to me, Mom."

I recognize the smile she gives me. It's the same smile she showed me when I told her I could fly if only I had the right cape, the smile she gave me when I campaigned to go to Russia for a semester in high school. The smile that says, *I know you think you're invincible, but you're not.*

Her fingers touch the edge of the envelope. "I think you should be the one to read it."

She passes it to me. The seam is sealed tight by glue and time. I look at her from across the table. "Are you sure?"

She nods, holding the mug in front of her. "You know, at first I thought it was luck, you finding the article and then the diary. Now I'm starting to think it all happened for you."

"What happened?"

"Everything."

She doesn't explain further. I place my finger beneath the upper flap and carefully pull it away. A single sheet of cream paper is folded inside. It's smooth and light. Lola's familiar, loopy handwriting greets me. I begin, as I did when reading the diary to Oliver, with the date.

4th September 1950

Dear Elizabeth,

This will be my final letter to you. It seems like I've written hundreds over the years, but none have been answered. I know now you'll never forgive me. I try to understand. I know I've hurt you, but it seems cruel to make me suffer.

I wanted to tell you something about the night before I left. I was standing in the yard before supper, hanging clothes, when I made up my mind to leave. My hands were cracked and blistered from the laundry. Your father didn't see the point in buying the good soap they sold at the store, so I had to make my own from lye. It burned my skin.

I remember looking at my hands and thinking they couldn't belong to me. I had my mother's hands. Hers were soft and pale with long fingers and pretty, rounded nails. The hands I saw were red and wrinkled, an old woman's hands. My life flashed before me then. I was twenty-four years old.

I watched you through dinner. Your eyes were so bright and happy. I was jealous of you. Jealous of your light because mine had already gone out. When I tucked you in, you asked for a story, but I couldn't think of one. It had been so long since I'd held a dream of my own, I couldn't remember one to tell you. So I stroked your hair and sang a song instead.

Leaving you was the hardest thing I've ever done. But I didn't look back. I couldn't. If I had seen you at the window or heard you singing to the birds, I would have run back and grabbed you into my arms, and I knew, as much as I loved you, that if I stayed, it would kill me.

Maybe you thought then or think now that I'm weak. That I should have been content to have a home and food and some measure of security. That being your mother should have been enough to keep me from leaving. But at night what gripped my heart with terror was the certainty that every dream I had within me was dying. I wonder if you can understand how that felt. It was a hopelessness I cannot fully describe.

When you're young you think dreams are limitless, but they're not. They age with you. Your fears and burdens darken and blur them until one day you wake up and you can't dream anymore. You can only worry and grieve for yourself. If I had stayed, you would have seen that grief. It would have touched you, and no matter what you think, I wanted to spare you from that, at least. I wanted you to know hope.

I lost hope for a while, but I found it again. First in myself, which is the last place I expected, then later in a man who loved me. I know you remember his name. Michael.

He died many years ago, the victim of a jealous brother and pneumonia. He was so much more than what you think. He gave me a reason to fight. For myself. For you. I was never able to be his wife, and I admit, I made your father pay for that loss.

If he had only released me sooner, things may have turned out differently. But your father was unforgiving, and I did what I could to prevent him from finding the happiness I felt he stole from me. Not just after I left, but before as well.

It was wrong, and I believe it may have set your mind against me forever. Had I known that would be the consequence for my actions, or had I been a better person, I might have been able to tell you this face-to-face.

I floated from town to town for several years after Michael died. Without him, I lost myself to despair. It was Cecelia, a dear friend, who saved me. I went to see her and found her sick and dying from a tumor in her breast. She needed me to be strong, so I became strong. The way I should have been for you.

A week before she passed, she said something to me I have never forgotten. She said, "Death frightens only people who fear they have not lived." I knew then that it was fear that had driven me from you.

I wish things had turned out differently. I wish I had never lived a day without you, and that Michael could have known the love of a child of ours. But none of that was to be.

I saw you and your daughter boarding a bus last week. She had your blonde hair and Dutch's long gait. I walked past your apartment building as well. Please don't be angry with me. I only want to know that you're alright. I'm enclosing a key with this envelope. It's for the savings and loan down the road. I've left something for you there.

I have faltered and failed you. But I've also loved you every day and with my whole heart. I end this letter with hope that you will one day forgive me.

All my love,
Your mother, Lola

Inside the envelope is a small bronze key, the name of a local bank stamped on the rounded head. I let it fall with a soft clang to the table. The key, even more than the diary, feels private. It was Lola's last gift for her daughter. I can't bring myself to touch it.

"Is that how you feel?" She speaks so quietly, I'm not sure if she meant to ask the question aloud, but her voice grows louder. "Like your dreams are dying?"

I hold her gaze for several moments, unsure of what I should tell her: the truth, or the words I know will ease the worry she feels. In the end I say nothing at all.

She takes the letter from my hands, and after looking it over, returns it to the envelope. She lays it on the table, then pulls the diary from her bag and does the same with it.

"Don't you want to keep them?" I ask. "They belonged to Grams."

She pushes her seat back and stands, leaving the letter, key, and book in front of me. "No. You keep them." She reaches for the doorknob.

I should probably walk her out, but I'm struggling with the contents of the letter and what it could have meant to Grams, had she read it. "Mom?"

She looks back at me over her shoulder.

"I love you."

"I love you, too." She opens the door but hesitates. The closed smile she aims at me is real—not happy, exactly, but warm. Her shoulders have lost some of their heaviness. "I couldn't sleep last night," she says, half in the apartment and half out. "I was thinking about the time when you were five or six. You were mad at me for something I'd done, and you told me you were running away. Do you remember?"

I turn the mug in my hands, the tea inside getting cold. "No."

She laughs at the memory and it feels like a release for both of us. "You packed a backpack full of crayons and coloring books and a few stuffed animals. No jacket, no flashlight. I asked what you were going to do for food and where you were going to stay. You said, 'Don't worry, Mom. I'll figure it out.'" She looks at me with such fondness.

I don't want to cry, so I bite down on my lips.

"It's time to figure it out."

TWENTY

Men and women in shades of black and gray walk importantly from desk to desk. Tabby smacks her gum loudly on one side of me while Franny picks at her fingernails on the other.

"Is this going to take all day? Because Dex and I are meeting the caterer at one."

I tap the bronze key against my knees, so anxious I'm sick to my stomach. "They said it wouldn't be long. The bank manager has to escort us."

"Why do they keep safety deposit boxes in a vault, anyway? Haven't they ever seen a movie? That's the first place bank robbers go."

"You should ask to see the head of security." Franny's voice is bored and sarcastic. "I'm sure they'll be interested in your expert opinions."

Tabby's arm connects with my stomach as she reaches out to smack Franny. "Don't pick on me today."

Franny retaliates. "Don't be such an easy target."

I block each of their next attempts. "You guys. Enough. Can we just wait in silence until they come get us?"

They each turn in their seats, their backs to me. I put a hand on my knee to stop it from bouncing up and down. The silence lasts about ten seconds.

"Tell me about the showgirl stuff again," Tabby asks, the words she and Franny exchanged already forgotten. Her ability to let things go is one of my favorite things about her. I'm especially grateful for it today.

"You can read it if you want, I've got it here." I lean down to pull the diary from my bag, but she shakes her head.

"No, that's okay. I don't want to read it."

"She means she can't read it," Franny says, smiling at her own joke.

Tabby rolls her eyes and smacks her gum, not rising to the bait.

A bald man with gold wire-rimmed glasses and a tan suit marches toward us. He looks a bit sweaty, as though the exertion of walking across the lobby has taken it out of him. "Wynn Jeffries?"

"That's me." I rise and shake his hand.

"Stanley Cobix. I apologize for your wait." His voice is as rushed and hurried as his manner. "You're a very lucky woman. The person who established the account purchased the box belonging to your grandmother, and now to your mother, outright for the lifetime of the bank. Normally these things are paid monthly, but the purchase was made before the bank changed its policy, and your grandmother's contract was grandfathered in. I had to confirm that the documents your mother brought in this morning were valid and acceptable to allow you access. It's unusual for a safety deposit box to sit unopened so long."

"I understand."

He clearly doesn't think I do. "Actually, it's almost unheard of."

Franny and Tabby stand on either side of me. Franny edges forward. "Great. Can we get moving now? Since Wynn's a signer on the account, I assume there aren't any other issues."

He hesitates, seeming uncomfortable about allowing the three of us past the bank lobby. "Would you prefer to be alone with the box? Your sisters are welcome to wait out here." He eyes Franny. I can't blame him, but he also doesn't know my big sister. She's coming with me whether he thinks it's a good idea or not.

Tabby flips long, glossy blonde curls over her shoulder and smiles brilliantly at the bank manager. "We're here for moral support."

Poor Stanley. Poor bald, sweaty, manic Stanley. Between Franny's abrasiveness and Tabby's low-cut blouse, he's having a hell of an afternoon.

He leads Tabby and Franny into the small waiting room and ushers me toward the silver vault. It's round and almost three feet wide. I follow him inside to a long wall of metal boxes. He stops at number 1144 and pulls a key similar to mine from a retractable keychain connected to his belt loop. I insert my key, he inserts his, and together we turn the lock. Stanley removes the box, and I follow him back to the dimly lit room where my sisters are waiting in a square cubicle. It's furnished with a desk, lamp, and chair.

Stanley's shiny head retreats toward the lobby. The three of us stare at the box on the black table. They wait for me to open it, but I'm reluctant. Lola's letter answered most of my lingering questions, but it brought up one more. Was it worth it to her? Leaving her daughter, struggling those years, losing Michael? Did she regret it in the end?

Tabby shifts nervously beside me. "What do you think's inside?"

"I don't know."

"Do you think it's, like, jewelry, or something like that necklace Mom found?"

"Oh God." Franny leans across me to eye our baby sister. "You didn't bring your label maker, did you?"

"No," Tabby says defensively.

"Well, whatever it is, I get first crack at it."

"You?" I ask Franny.

"Tabby stole everything good from Grams's house, and you have the diary. I want something, too."

"But you don't even like Lola," Tabby says, raising a shapely eyebrow in Franny's direction.

"So what? I don't have to like her to appreciate diamonds, do I?"

I wave my hands. "Stop. Nobody's entitled to anything. The box belonged to Grams, so Mom gets to decide what happens with it. Agreed?"

My sisters nod sullenly.

"Here we go." I put my fingers beneath the lid of the box and lift. It takes effort, the box having been closed for so long. Metal grates on metal as it opens. We all move forward to look inside. Green hundred-dollar bills, stacked in thick sets and wrapped in red paper bands, fill the box. No one moves. No one breathes. We just stare at our grandmother's ignored inheritance.

Franny turns her head toward me. Her whisper is sharp and loud. "Holy shit."

Holy shit is right. There's not a doubt in my mind that the money lining this box came from the suitcase of a Chicago gangster eighty-three years ago.

"How much do you think it is?" Tabby's whisper is quieter.

I keep my voice low, too. I think we're all afraid of being overheard. "My guess? Ten thousand, give or take."

"What, did you take math lessons from Tabby?" Franny's finger taps the band on the first stack of bills. I now notice that each band is marked "$3,000" in small gold lettering. "I count six stacks just from what we can see. That's eighteen grand."

She's right. If each bundle is truly three thousand dollars, there's well over twenty thousand in this box. I begin removing the bound bills, handing them to Franny to count and stack on the table. I pull bundle after bundle until there's nothing left. Tabby and I look at our big sister, waiting to hear how much money Lola spirited away.

For the first time in her life, Franny looks almost speechless. "Just over thirty-five thousand dollars."

"Thirty-five thou—" Franny slaps her hand over Tabby's mouth. Tabby mumbles the rest of the figure through our sister's fingers.

We look down at the money. No one touches it. Maybe we're afraid it'll disappear. Tabby reaches inside the box. "What's that?"

"There isn't any more," I say in a trance.

She pulls out a small white envelope and hands it to me. "Open it."

Another envelope. *How many secrets did you have, Lola?* The glue is corroded and the envelope opens easily. Something hard is inside. I upend it over my hand and two gold rings fall out. I hand them to Tabby, who receives them with great care. The letter is short, folded once in half. I read it out loud.

> *My dearest Elizabeth,*
>
> *This won't replace our years apart, and I don't expect you to take it gladly, but you're struggling right now. No mother can stand idly by as her child suffers. You don't need to worry about seeing me again. Just accept this final gift so I'll know you'll be alright.*
>
> *I know how you feel about my past. I don't regret the choices I've made, as hard as that may be for you to hear. I've made a lot of mistakes, but knowing Michael and loving him was not one of them. He was my husband in every way that counts, and he gave me a gift far more valuable than what is inside this box. He gave me love, unconditional and eternal. The kind I have for you. Please don't let the past stand in the way of your future. Whatever else you may think of me, know that I did the best I could with my life.*
>
> *All my love, Lola*

Tabby pats the skin beneath her eyes. "Crap. This mascara isn't waterproof."

I hand her a tissue from my purse. She gives me a crooked smile and the rings in return.

I cup them in my palm. One rests on top of the other so they look intertwined.

"Why do you think she left those in the envelope?" Franny asks.

Touching something that belonged to her, to them, still feels unreal. I move the rings around with my thumb. They're light, but their significance is heavy. "I think she wanted Grams to know how much he meant to her. She probably thought it would help explain why she had to leave."

"Why's that?"

I've never seen her face, only her profile and the dip of her hat, but I know her. "She didn't feel like a whole person."

"And he made her whole?" Tabby asks, her nose buried in the tissue.

I shake my head. "She did it herself. That's why she could love him. Only, I don't think she knew that until a long time after."

"So what do we do with it?" Franny picks up a stack from the desk and runs her thumb along the edges.

"We take it to Mom."

Tabby eyes the money longingly, sighing. Franny notices and moves the bills away from her. "Don't even think about it."

"What?"

"I can read your thoughts. You're thinking about showing up at the church in Cinderella's carriage with a dozen white stallions pulling you to the altar."

Tabby crosses her arms, shoving perky breasts toward the ceiling. "Not even close."

I share Franny's skepticism.

"I'm not going to be taken to the church by something that poops in the road. I want a Bentley."

***

"Oh please, let me?" Franny grabs the cotton grocery bag Tabby talked the poor bank manager out of and dumps thirty-five thousand dollars onto Mom and Dad's kitchen table without pomp or circumstance.

Our parents drop their mouths open like a couple of synchronized swimmers. My father slowly picks up a stack of wrapped hundreds.

"Did you rob the bank while you were there?" he says, dumbstruck by the money in his hand.

"It's what was in the box." Tabby fans herself with green.

Mom looks at us, shocked. "No."

"Yes." Franny pretends to shove a bundle down the front of her shirt.

"This was in that box for the last sixty years?" She looks only at me this time.

Unlike my sisters, I'm not tempted to play with the money. I can't stop thinking about Lola, about the lengths she went to for her daughter's future, even knowing she wouldn't be a part of it.

My mother takes the bills my father hands her. "All that time, and Mom didn't even know it was there. You girls wouldn't know this, but your grandparents really struggled for a while. We were jammed in a one-bedroom apartment for a couple of years. If she'd just forgiven her mother . . . What a foolish thing." She points at the rings in my hand. "Are those—"

"Yes." I bring my hand up so she can better see them. She touches each carefully, as though it might fall apart under her fingertip. "Hers and Michael's."

"How remarkable. What're you going to do with them?"

Everyone turns to look at me.

"Me?"

Dad smiles over her head. He's always been able to read her thoughts, so I know that whatever she's about to say, he approves.

"Yes, of course you," Mom says. "You found them, Wynn. You found everything. This all belongs to you."

A single vowel escapes Tabby's lips before Franny elbows her in the stomach. My dad smiling; my mom looking at me with luminous, happy eyes; my sisters doing their best not to look too disappointed. I don't understand.

"Mom, this . . . this is yours. It belonged to Grams."

"And how much good did it do shoved beneath an old dresser?" She moves forward to hug me. "You did what your grandmother and I couldn't. You gave Lola the benefit of the doubt. You believed she was worth forgiving. Her legacy belongs to you now." She steps back and looks so proud, I'm nearly overcome.

I wave my hand toward my sisters. I don't want to leave them out. It feels wrong to take everything for myself. "But Franny and Tabs—"

"Eh, whatever." Franny tosses the cash back onto the pile as though it were Monopoly money. "Ben just got a promotion at work. If I took any of this, we'd be in a new tax bracket. Besides, I still owe you for stealing him out from under you. Now we'll be even." She shrugs, indifferent, but her smile is genuine.

Tabby looks less convinced until Franny shoves her in the back. Her money reluctantly joins the rest of the stacks on the table. "Dex's family is filthy rich, you know. I don't need any either. But"—she points a pink nail at my face—"I expect a really good wedding present."

My heart works frantically to catch up with what's happening. It's got me out of breath. "But I don't need all of this." I turn to my parents. "You guys have to take some."

Mom shakes her head. "No. These things—they don't just happen. This money is a gift you were meant to find. You inherited something from her the rest of us didn't. When you read me that letter . . . Wynn,

I don't think I realized how badly you *want* things. I knew it, in the back of my mind, but I didn't really understand. I'm still not sure I do, completely, but I know that I love you, and I want you to be happy. I don't want you to feel lost all the time. If seeing the world is what you need to do, then that's what we want for you. So take this, please."

I cover my mouth with my fingertips. "I don't know what to say."

My mother grabs the hand my dad's placed on her shoulder. "Say you'll stop letting things stand in your way. And that you'll call me once in a while and let me know how you're doing?"

I squeeze the hand holding the rings. I can't believe what they're doing for me, what they're willing to give up. My sisters embrace me from either side, and I hold them desperately. Can I do this? Can I leave them behind? I'm not even sure what I'm looking for. I'm scared I won't find it.

For the first time since Grams died, my mother's voice is strong. "Go. Figure out what you're made of. Then come back to us."

TWENTY-ONE

One night, Lisa Menopolous and I staked out Oliver Reeves's house from the front seat of her mom's gold Cutlass. We brought Oreos, Starbucks café mochas, and my dad's bird-watching binoculars. She insisted that we listen to "Every Breath You Take" at least once every half hour because, really, we were stalkers. We took turns scoping out the house for signs of him, and we were about to give up when the light went on in his room and, suddenly, he was there.

We pushed our seats back and got low so we wouldn't be seen. He opened his window and climbed onto the roof. My first reaction was to jump from the car and scream for help. After all, in my mind he was the perfect male specimen, and should anything happen to him, it was humanity that would suffer. But Lisa held me back, and we watched him come to the edge of the roof and sit down.

She passed me the binoculars, and I focused in as close as I could get. He was wearing a black T-shirt and flannel pajama bottoms. His feet were bare and he swung them off the side of the house. I thought he was looking for something, but then I realized he was staring up at the sky. If I had to choose my favorite Oliver moment, I think I'd pick that one. I watched his feet dangle in the air, and I knew he was a dreamer, like me. He captured my heart.

Now, as I watch him load a guitar case into the back of an SUV parked in his parents' driveway, I wish I could go back to that moment. I would do then what I'm going to do now. Get out of the car.

His back is to me. I tap him on the shoulder to get his attention. His face transitions quickly between surprise and confusion.

"Aren't you supposed to be shaping young minds right now?" He looks at the watch on his wrist.

"It turns out I'd make a crappy social studies teacher."

"Oh yeah? Why's that?"

"I think to teach something, you have to be good at it first. And I've never been anywhere."

He cocks his head to the side and half smiles. "What's going on?"

The past few days, the past few weeks, have felt like a lifetime. Everything I thought impossible has become possible, and everything I thought was true turned out to be, if not wrong, only one version of the truth. Everything but him.

"It's a long story."

"I've got a little time."

"Alright." I look up at the house behind him. "But I have a request."

***

My feet hang off the roof. The shingles will be unbearably hot by noon, but they're not too bad this time of morning. Oliver sits next to me, always patient and content to let me make the first move. I slide my fingers between his. His gray eyes are almost the same color as the sky around us. He sits close but doesn't try to kiss me, though I know he wants to. I shift and remove the blue envelope from my back pocket and hand it to him.

He doesn't ask whose it is or where I found it. He knew all along we'd find answers. He's the one who believed. I watch from the corner of my eye as he reads. When he's finished, he refolds the letter and places it back inside the envelope, then returns it to me. We both look ahead, at the green grass and tidy houses below us.

"That's quite a letter."

I squeeze his fingers.

"I'm guessing your grandmother never read it?"

"No."

A white cloud floats alone in the sky. It used to make me sad when I saw something all on its own, but not anymore. Now it makes me wonder things.

"She had the money in the box, didn't she?"

His cleverness delights me. He doesn't ask how much, and I don't tell him. Some of Lola's secrets I want to keep for myself. I slide the rings off my index finger and pass them to him. "These were theirs. They were in the box, too."

Oliver holds the rings up to the light before sliding them on the tips of two fingers. "It's something," he says, pensive.

"What?"

He sets the bands in my upturned hand. "Just to know they're still together in some way."

I tilt my head toward him, happy. "I like that."

"What can I say? I'm a lyricist. I like my love stories mushy." His hand rests next to mine on the roof.

"I never got to thank you for the song. It was beautiful."

"I had good inspiration."

I hold out Michael's ring. "I want you to take it."

"Why?"

"Because in a way, it feels like their story is our story." I place it in his palm.

He closes his hand around it, weighing it as I did. "Their story didn't have such a happy ending."

"True, but she never regretted a minute of it, and I bet he didn't either," I say. "When I said the other night that I loved you"—his gaze remains locked, steady, on mine—"I meant it. I do love you. And I know we really just started to get to know one another, but I just . . ." I shrug.

"I know."

The feel of his hand on the side of my face forces my eyes to close. His kiss is light but not hesitant. He knows I'm his, and I know he's mine.

"You're still not coming with me, are you?"

It's easier to answer him this time. "No."

He sighs deeply and pulls away, but the hand holding Michael's ring stays pressed to mine on the roof. "Is that what the ring is for? A memento?"

I spin Lola's ring around my finger. "It's a promise."

"To what?"

"To be together again."

He looks away. I know it hurts Oliver that I can't go with him, but I also know a part of him understands. A part of him remembers what it was like the first time he believed he could have everything he wanted. I know he doesn't want to take that from me. He raps his knuckles on the tin of the gutter. "So what are you going to do now that you've given up on gainful employment?"

This is the hard part. This is why I asked if we could sit on the roof. I need to explain everything to him in the place where he used to dream. "Funny you should mention it. You know"—I pause, thinking of the right words—"I'm starting to think I've never really dreamed. I mean, I've imagined, and I've certainly spent a few hundred hours day-dreaming about you"—I sneak a glance in his direction—"but I don't know if those qualify as dreams."

"What does then?" He cranes his neck, following a flock of black birds.

"I think a dream is something that makes you reach."

"And what are you trying to wrap your hands around?"

"A life. One that scares me a little."

His laugh is kind. He knows. "When will you be back?"

I lean on my elbows, enjoying the way the sun filters through the clouds. "I don't know. I guess I'll stay away as long as I need to." I watch him nod and feel his little finger graze my leg. It's such a small thing, but it gives me hope for what I'm about to ask. "I wondered if you'd wait for me?"

He leans back, next to me, lying down on the shingles. "Where're you going?"

I turn and wait until his eyes are on mine, and smile. "Everywhere."

***

"Do you have everything you need? Did you pack sunblock? You're going to need sunblock in Spain." My mother adjusts the backpack on my shoulder, digging through the pockets.

"Mom, I've got everything I need. It's going to be fine." Her eyes are nervous, scanning me head to toe like it's the last time she'll ever see me. I wrap my arms around her until she stills. "I love you."

"I love you, too." She buries her face in my neck.

"Jesus, Mom, she's almost thirty. You're acting like she's off to sleepaway camp in Afghanistan." Franny's hands divide me from our mother. She gives me a quick hug. "Take care, little sister. Avoid the tap water, and if someone asks you to put something up your ass and walk through customs, just say no." I don't care how brave she acts—when she steps away from me, I see a glimmer of something wet in her eyes.

Tabby's next. She bounces up, and everything bounces with her. Dex gives me two thumbs up over her shoulder. "Don't forget you promised to be home for the wedding." She's strong for such a skinny thing. She practically crushes me beneath a cloud of sweet-smelling perfume.

I assure her I'll be there, on time but tanner. My dad is all who's left, and for whatever reason it's hugging him that does me in. He pats my hair and waits until I let go first.

"You take care of yourself, sweet pea."

"I will, Daddy, thank you." Mom hands me a tissue as Franny quickly turns her back. I place my hand on her shoulder and listen as she sniffles, trying to compose herself. "Fran?"

"Yeah, what?" she says, her voice thick.

"Thank you. I don't think I would've found the courage to do any of this if you hadn't yelled at me and called me a loser."

Her eyes are bright with tears, but she smiles. Then she shoves me gently toward the security line. "Stop being such a baby. Go, already."

I wave good-bye once more after I clear security and retrieve my shoes from a white plastic bin. Whatever fear they may have over me leaving, I know they're happy for me.

I make my way to the gate and take a seat near the window. I've been on a plane only twice in my life and never out of the country. I watch them race down the tarmac and lift into the sky as though it takes no effort to fly.

I pull the necklace from beneath my shirt. Lola's gold band dangles off a new chain. I thought I'd wear it on my journey, like a talisman. Something to help keep away the doubt and keep me focused on what's ahead. I hope Oliver's wearing his, too. Wherever he is.

The plane is full of travelers. Some in sleek suits and others, like me, dressed for vacation. I pull the guidebook from the bag beneath my feet and flip open to a random page. An image of a stone path and hills sprinkled with purple heather takes up one side. I don't know what's going to happen or where I'll be in six months. I'm just excited to finally begin.

I'll be walking almost six hundred miles on foot during my pilgrimage to Santiago de Compostela. When you get there, you're supposed to fall to your knees upon entering the Cathedral of Saint James, to show gratitude for the journey. In a way I feel like I'm starting this entire experience on my knees.

A woman, a little younger than me with braided black hair, takes the open seat beside me. "Hi," she says, trying to shove her bag, which is much too big, beneath the seat in front of her.

"Hey."

"Are you walking the Camino?"

I look at her, wondering how she knows.

She reaches down to pull at the white scalloped seashell attached to my bag. It's the symbol of the pilgrim. A testament to the trials one must go through while walking the Camino. "I've got one, too."

"Oh, right."

"Are you starting in Spain, or are you taking the train to France?"

"Taking the train."

"Me, too." She settles back in her seat, excitement falling off of her in waves. "Are you with a group or are you going solo?"

I hesitate a moment before answering, not yet sure about putting my trust in strangers. "I'm on my own."

"I'm joining a group there. We met on one of the Camino chat boards. You're welcome to tag along if you like."

I smile politely and look out the window. The plane begins to move over the black pavement beneath us.

We sit in silence through the safety check, pretending to pay attention when our minds are thousands of miles away. The speed of the jet propels me back in my seat. I close my eyes and touch the gold ring hanging around my neck. The picture of Lola is tucked into the pages of my book. I've decided to take her with me everywhere I go. She didn't have an easy life, but she tried. I'll keep her close to remind myself to do the same.

The light above the "Fasten Seatbelt" sign goes off, and my seat-mate searches through a pocket of her bag, then pulls out a *Rolling Stone* magazine. She reads silently for about ten minutes, then gasps.

I turn to her. "Is something wrong?"

"My favorite band's breaking up."

Feigning interest, I lean back in my seat and watch the clouds swirl past the window. "Who are they?"

"Multitude. They're indie. You've probably never heard of them."

I touch my lips. And remember.

ONE YEAR LATER

TWENTY-TWO

The clink of glasses and scraping of chairs on the stone floor is so loud I can hardly hear my travel mate's words. "What did you say?" I call across the table, turning my ear toward her.

Amy cups her hands around her mouth and yells. "I said that guy I was telling you about is supposed to be here."

We're in a basement club in a repurposed church in Old Berlin. We arrived two days ago by train from Belgium. I've been walking around in awe of the architecture and the beauty of the city. Amy and I rented bikes this morning. The roads here twist and turn, taking you to the most interesting places. One of my favorite things about Europe in general is how varied everything is. Near-ancient relics sit next to sleek black skyscrapers. And people from all over the world blend together in a stream of culture and color. The world is so much bigger than I ever thought possible.

I stopped to check out an antique store after lunch and Amy rode on to a city park. She met some guys there, which doesn't surprise me. Amy's always meeting guys. I guess they told her about this place.

I'm exhausted. The last week has been grueling, traveling between three countries, but I've got a new rule. Whenever I feel like saying no to an unexpected opportunity, I ask myself what I could miss out on. The chance to see Amy dance on a table in the middle of Berlin definitely felt like something I wouldn't want to miss.

We splurged on an actual hotel for our stay. It was such a relief to sleep in a nice bed again. You can stay in only so many hostels before your head starts to itch just from the thought of bedbugs. I flopped down on the double bed before the door had even closed. My passport fell out of my backpack and onto the floor. The stamps, some red, some green or black, still amaze me. I pulled out the map Mom found in Grams's things and matched the stamps up with the countries printed on the back. I've been to eighteen of them in the last year. Not including a brief trip home to see Tabby become the most beautiful bride in the world. I think a lot about Grams these days. I wonder if she kept the map, like the blue glass, to remind herself of her mother.

I didn't think my own mother was going to let me leave again after the wedding. She fed me so often, I started to worry she was channeling the witch in "Hansel and Gretel" and was going to keep me prisoner. But when it was time for me to go, she didn't cry as much, and I think she was even a little excited for me. It's been hard, not seeing them. I missed Samuel's kindergarten graduation, and Lucas—my sweet seven-year-old nephew who, thank God, takes after his father—has lost two teeth since I've been away. I send them postcards and call Mom and Dad once a week. Life seems to be going on as usual. Except for me. For me it's gotten so much bigger.

In truth, the endless need to see, feel, touch, taste, and explore scares me a little. I keep expecting it to end. That I'll feel I've done enough and want to go home, but I haven't. I want more.

There's a place in Spain where the waves rolling in from the ocean are so fierce, you wonder how they don't break the earth below your feet. I sat and watched them for a long time and made a promise to myself. If one of the stones that made up the beach cracked, split open from the power of the waves, and was pulled back into the water, I'd

Wynn in Doubt

go back and be happy I'd had this experience. But they never did. They took a heavy beating, and there were times I swear I saw them sway, but they withstood the storm. They were strong, and they made me strong, too. I'm a dreamer. I want to live a life that feels honest to me.

I won't be home until Thanksgiving. That's when Amy's year abroad ends. I'm taking the opportunity to go back, see family and old friends—Lisa and I have been exchanging emails for months now—and decide my next steps. I've been frugal. Lola's money turned out to be the gift that kept on giving. Franny, my genius sister, did a little research. The bills, which were old Federal Reserve notes from 1928, had increased in value almost threefold since their original printing. In the end, I walked away with nearly a hundred thousand dollars.

Needless to say, Dex and Tabby's wedding gift was freaking awesome. And Franny's boys now have a nice start to their college funds, courtesy of their favorite aunt.

So I've got time to plan. Lately I've been thinking I might try teaching again. The Guatemala job isn't available anymore, but there's got to be an opening for an English teacher in a Mongolian village somewhere, right? I'm not tied down to any one idea. The most rewarding thing to come out of the time I've spent traveling is the ability to let go of those feelings that held me back for so long. Fear, uncertainty, doubt—they don't have a place in my life anymore. I'm excited by what's ahead of me.

Meeting Amy on the Camino was a godsend. I walked mostly on my own for a couple of weeks. At first it was liberating. Just me out there, alone, thinking and walking, walking and thinking. But thoughts get pretty loud with that much solitude. When I saw her fighting a muddy pass to win her boot back, I seized the opportunity to make a new friend. She'd been walking alone almost five weeks. I don't think she stopped talking for three days.

We shared our stories to date and our hopes for the future. She probably knows more about who I really am than almost any other

265

person on earth. With one exception. I couldn't bring myself to tell her about Oliver. You're so exposed when you travel by yourself. I wanted to keep something private, just for me.

I've sent him postcards here and there and to my utter shock, he's even sent me a few emails. We never talk about us, about the future, or what we almost were. I tell him what I've seen and he tells me what he's learned. It's hard to think about him sometimes. I know I made the right decision, but there are moments when I would give anything to hear him laugh. To feel his arms around me.

The walls of the club are carved out of natural stone. It reverberates the sound from across the room. If I move my head just right, I can hear people's conversations. I listen carefully, concentrating on their voices, and catch pieces of what they're saying.

". . . stupid tour . . ."

". . . difference between Mozart and . . ."

". . . fucking Americans . . ."

Ahh. The international call of the traveler. *Fucking Americans.*

"Want another drink?" Amy leans across the table, practically screaming into my ear.

"Yeah, okay." I hold up my beer.

She disappears and I people watch. It's one of the best things about travel. There are so many damn people in the world. It's endless. And we're all different. Or at least, we're trying to be. I like to pretend I know who they are, where they come from, and what they do. I can't tell you the hours of entertainment this little game has given me. When you're trapped in an airport in Italy for two days, you can get pretty desperate.

A man across from our table in a shiny silver shirt bops his head to the music. I'm thinking native German, possibly a Hasselhoff fan, definitely looking for some young tourists to take advantage of. The man to his left has beautiful mahogany skin and a brilliant white smile. A red scarf loops casually around his neck. Too fashionable for an

American. I'm going with French architect in town for business but out to party. I assess everyone around me, amusing myself with my answers until Amy returns.

Her grin shows all of her teeth. "Wynn, these are the guys I met in the park today!" She brushes her red hair back and turns, allowing one of them to move past her and take a seat. He's good looking with thick brown hair and an all-American quality about him. He tells me his name is Peter. Amy practically levitates off her chair when he calls her my "beautiful friend."

The man behind him has his back to me. He waves at someone out of my line of sight, but there's something very familiar about his shape. A tug low against my stomach seems to pull him around to face me. We stare at each other for a long time. And then he smiles, and I see my chip.

His eyes never leave mine. Oliver maneuvers himself between our table and the one with the Hasselhoff fan.

Peter raises his voice to yell an introduction across the table. "This is my friend Oliver!"

I offer Oliver my hand. "Nice to meet you."

"Likewise," he says, though I can barely hear him.

Our handshake continues for a considerable length of time. Amy and Peter notice.

"Oliver's a musician," Peter calls, watching us curiously.

"Oh yeah? Are you in a band?"

He bites his bottom lip, enjoying this. "I used to be," he says, loud enough for me to hear. "How about you? What do you do? Wynn, was it?"

I play along. "I don't really *do* anything."

"Come on, everybody's got to do something, right? For example, what have you been doing for the last year?"

"This year?"

"Sure. Just as an example."

Our hands remain locked across the table. He moves a finger along my palm, and it's like switching on a light in a room that's been dark for a long while. It takes me a moment to adjust. "I've been traveling."

"Where?"

I run my thumb across his knuckles and watch the heat turn up behind his eyes. "Everywhere."

He pulls me up, toward him, and I follow as he moves around the table, never letting go of me. He says something in Peter's ear and Amy waves energetically, frantic to get my attention. She mouths the question, "What's going on?" It's too difficult to explain, so I just shake my head and smile.

We weave through the other guests, emerging onto the street and the quiet summer evening. He pulls me into his arms and presses his mouth to mine. His taste, the way his mouth moves, everything is the same and yet . . . different. I'm different. I'm not scared anymore.

When he breaks away, I realize we're both out of breath.

"What're you doing here?" His voice is full of amazement.

"We came in a couple of days ago on the train. We're doing eastern Europe for the summer."

His eyes widen with amazement at my words. "You're *doing* eastern Europe? Who are you and what have you done with Wynn Jeffries from Downers Grove?"

"She's still here."

"It's so good to see you," he says, wrapping me in a hug. I hold on to him, tight.

That he's here feels like a trick. I'm so happy. I can't stop laughing into his shoulder.

He lets me go, but his smile remains. "How are you?"

"I'm good. Happy."

His hands squeeze mine and he nods. "How's everyone back home?"

"They're great. Tabby got married. My parents are taking cooking lessons, which they love, and Franny got a job as a school counselor. Can you imagine?"

That laugh—it'll never change. "Those poor kids."

I think back to my conversation with Franny after returning from Kentucky. "Her methods are unusual, but I actually think she gives pretty great advice."

People walk past us and turn their heads in our direction. I can only imagine what we must look like standing here, ridiculous smiles on our faces.

"What about you? How've you been?"

He swings a hand holding mine. "I've been busy."

"Doing what?"

"Writing songs, mostly. I've been playing in any bar that'll have me the past few months, working on a solo album."

"Wow, that's incredible. Good for you." My cheeks strain from the effort of holding my smile. "Any chance I can catch a concert while I'm in town?"

"Maybe." He pulls me to him. I place my hands high on his chest and feel something beneath his shirt. I slide my finger under the collar and tug at the strand of leather hanging around his neck. Michael's ring falls against the white cotton and gleams in the streetlight.

Relief fills every part of me.

"Do you still have yours?" he asks.

I pull the chain around my neck until the gold ring falls onto my blouse. I've worn it every day of my trip.

Oliver presses his forehead to mine, his lips curling upward.

I've often wondered if, somehow, Michael and Lola are looking down on us. I'd like them to know their story isn't over, that it continues every day we think of them. Their article woke me up. It gave me a reason to search for something missing in my life. But their story, *her* story, has given me so much more than I could've imagined. It's taught me to be strong, even when I feel afraid. To not give up on what I want for my life, even if it means risking my heart. And, most importantly, that realizing our dreams is only part of what makes us whole. We need people to root for us. We need to be able to come home again.

"I missed you," he says.

I hold him tighter.

"Have you seen enough of the world yet?" His voice is low. He's asking whether or not I'm ready to come back to him.

"No," I say, bringing my lips close to his. "But I've seen enough of it on my own."

ABOUT THE AUTHOR

Photo © 2013 Emily Hemmer

Emily Hemmer was raised in the Chicago suburbs before settling in Kansas City in 1996. As is the case with many artists, she dropped out of college to pursue a vocation in daydreaming before getting married, having kids, and starting a Roth IRA. She completed her degree in 2010 to make her mother proud.

For more information, visit www.emilyhemmer.com.